"Woul[...]
Hank said

The woman standing on his front porch was downright gorgeous. And gorgeous women did *not* routinely come calling. Not to his door, at least.

"Hank Ballantyne," she said.

He nodded. She was looking for *him*.

"I'm Natalie Lawson," she went on. "There's something I need to discuss with you. I just...where's your little boy?"

She knew he had a son. Okay, then, she'd done some homework. "My housekeeper took him shopping.... But you aren't here to talk about my son."

"Actually, I am."

"Oh?" He glanced at her briefcase, an uneasy feeling creeping up his spine. "Because...?"

Instead of replying, she opened her briefcase, pulled out a spiral-bound document and handed it to him. The title page read, "Final Report on Benjamin Lawson-Garcia."

She bit on her lower lip for a moment before saying, "I've spent days trying to think of some way to lessen the shock. There isn't one, though.... My Benjamin is your Robbie."

Hank could feel the panic growing inside him. There was only one reason Natalie Lawson had come here. *To get Robbie back!*

Dear Reader,

Hank Ballantyne first appeared in my October 2000 Superromance novel, *The Man Behind the Badge*. He was the partner and best friend of that book's hero, Travis Quinn, and long before I'd finished writing about Travis and Celeste, I'd grown to like Hank so much that I wanted to tell his story.

Initially, I had no idea what it was. All I really knew about him was that he was a single father with an adopted three-year-old son, Robbie, whom he adored. But what if…?

This is the magic phrase for writers. We take the little bit we know about our unwritten story and play "what if" in our heads.

In this case, it wasn't long before an absolutely gut-wrenching "what if" occurred to me. What if Robbie's "dead" birth mother suddenly appeared—very much alive and wanting her child back?

That's what happens at the beginning of *His Child or Hers?* And it sets up a conflict that tears at all three characters' emotions throughout the book.

I hope you enjoy reading about how they come to terms with an extremely difficult situation.

Warmest regards,

Dawn Stewardson

His Child or Hers?

Dawn Stewardson

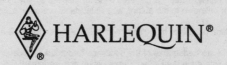

HARLEQUIN®

TORONTO • NEW YORK • LONDON
AMSTERDAM • PARIS • SYDNEY • HAMBURG
STOCKHOLM • ATHENS • TOKYO • MILAN • MADRID
PRAGUE • WARSAW • BUDAPEST • AUCKLAND

ISBN 0-373-70993-5

HIS CHILD OR HERS?

Printed in U.S.A.

To John, always

ACKNOWLEDGMENTS

With special thanks to two fellow Harlequin authors
for answering numerous questions
during the writing of this book:

Marisa Carroll provided the medical information I needed.
Illona Haus, who writes as Morgan Hayes, was (as always)
my expert on homicide detectives.

They made my research considerably easier,
and I sincerely appreciate their generosity.

I also want to thank Michele Billung-Meyer,
for being so in tune with the psychosocial development
of children—and for sharing her sense of how Robbie
and Emma would react as the story unfolded.

PROLOGUE

NOT FAR FROM Guatemala City's main plaza, the taxi turned down a narrow street, then stopped in front of a tired old colonial building.

Her hands trembling a little, Natalie paid the driver and climbed out. As he pulled away, she stood gazing at the words carved in stone above the doorway. Orfanato de las Hermanas de Socorro.

Sisters of Mercy Orphanage. Where her baby had spent the past four months. Being cared for by strangers.

She closed her eyes, not wanting to think about all the nights she'd lain awake in her hospital bed, the ache to hold Benjamin worse than any of the pains from her injuries.

But that was over. Now she was well enough to take him home, to what was left of the town of Villa Rosa, and start rebuilding their lives.

Lives without Carlos.

Blinking back the tears suddenly stinging her eyes, she told herself she was lucky she hadn't lost both her husband *and* her son in the earthquake. And lucky *she'd* survived.

If there'd been no plane to transport the critically

injured to the capital city, she wouldn't be alive to-day.

She was, though. And she was about to reclaim her son.

Brushing her hair back from her face, she started toward the front door, her excitement tinged with a trace of apprehension that she simply hadn't been able to shake.

From the first moment she'd been lucid enough to understand what people were saying, they'd assured her Benjamin was fine, that he'd escaped with only cuts and scrapes.

Even so, she wouldn't entirely believe it until she saw for herself. Until she held him and hugged him. Smelled his sweet baby smell and felt the soft smoothness of his skin.

Taking a deep breath, she opened the door and stepped into the orphanage. It reminded her of the ancient grade school she'd attended as a child—a worn slate floor at its entrance and, beyond that, a broad staircase consisting of half a dozen stone stairs.

In reality, of course, she was light-years away from her childhood in Michigan. She was a doctor practicing in a foreign country where people, for the most part, spoke only Spanish.

At first, that had caused her problems. But once her college Spanish had improved to reasonable fluency she'd been okay.

Her heart beating quickly, she headed up the stairs and across the hallway to what was obviously the administration area.

A young nun, wearing a long-sleeved brown dress that hung almost to her sturdy shoes, was working at the counter. She looked up as Natalie approached. *"¿Puedo ayudarle?"*

"Hola. Me llamo doctora Natalie Lawson. Y tengo una cita con la madre superiora."

The young woman nodded, then turned and started in the direction of an office.

Natalie nervously licked her lips. Yesterday, when she'd phoned, she'd spoken personally to the mother superior, Madre María-Teresa—who'd been thrilled at an opportunity to practice her English. And she'd assured her that all the paperwork would be ready when she arrived. So in no time at all, Benjamin would be in her arms.

She waited, trying not to watch the clock on the wall ticking away the minutes, until an older nun finally walked out of the office and approached her, her gray habit swishing quietly with each step.

"Doctora Lawson," she said, smiling. "Much pleasure to meet you."

"And I'm very glad to meet you. I can't thank you enough for everything you've done."

Acknowledging the gratitude with a slight nod, the mother superior said, "One of the sisters bring Benjamin. You will sign the forms."

"Fine." She followed along into the office, her legs feeling only a little rubbery, and wrote her name on each line indicated with an *X*.

Just as she finished, there was a tap on the open

door and another nun stepped into the office, a baby in her arms.

"Here he is," the mother superior murmured.

At first, Natalie couldn't move. She'd been waiting so long for this moment that it seemed like a dream.

It wasn't, though. Her son was mere feet from her. She took a deep breath, then pushed herself out of her chair, crossed the room and reached for him—her heart so full of love it was threatening to overwhelm her. But then...

This baby wasn't Benjamin.

The realization struck with a cold, dark sense of certainty. Aside from anything else, her son had a birthmark on the left side of his neck. This child didn't.

Telling herself not to panic, that the sister had merely brought the wrong baby from his crib, she turned to Mother María-Teresa and said, "This isn't my son."

The woman gave an understanding smile, rose from behind her desk and walked over to them.

"It has been four months, Doctora Lawson. He has grown. But he *is* your son. For now, we have only one boy child this age in our care."

Only one? Only *this* one? But he wasn't Benjamin!

Tentacles of fear had wrapped themselves around her so tightly that she could scarcely breathe. If her baby wasn't here, where was he?

"And look," the mother superior said, taking his tiny hand and fingering his identity bracelet.

Natalie stared at the name on it and numbly read, "'B. Garcia.'"

"That is his name, sí? His father was Carlos Garcia? Archaeologist from Spain? That is in the file."

"Yes," she whispered. "My husband was Carlos Garcia. But this is *not* our son."

CHAPTER ONE

HANK KNEW THE ASSAILANT was making his way toward the bedroom, sneaking down the hall as silently as possible.

Feigning sleep, he lay waiting. Coiled to move when the moment arrived. Listening to the whisper of fingers slowly turning the knob. A breathless sigh as the door opened across the carpet. Barely audible footsteps moving toward the bed.

Four...three...two... Now! He thrust his arm from beneath the covers and wrapped it around his son.

Robbie shrieked into his ear—one of the occupational hazards of fatherhood—then threw himself onto Hank's chest in a fit of giggles.

Hank caught him in a bear hug.

"I almost got you!" he hollered, struggling to get free. "I almost did!"

"Uh-huh. You had me right to the last second. Then my instincts warned me someone was there."

When Hank released his hold, Robbie scrambled around so he could sit straddling his father's chest. "Mrs. Chevy said I should come wake you up."

"By launching a kamikaze attack? Is that how she told you to do it?"

He nodded, looking so sincere that Hank would

have believed him if he didn't know Audrey Chevalier better.

But he could practically hear her saying, in her most grandmotherly voice, "Now, wake your father *very* gently, darling. You know how he likes to be a little lazy on his days off."

And he did. Working ten days at a stretch sometimes felt as if he were working forever, but he really enjoyed having four days off between shifts. Especially when the weather cooperated, which it was doing at the moment.

The next three days promised to be just as nice as yesterday—three more spring days that were going to be gorgeous, and that he intended to spend with his son.

Except for this morning, he remembered. Audrey was taking Robbie shopping for clothes.

It was a task she'd insisted on assuming more than a year ago, after Hank had arrived home with an expensive pair of jeans that Robbie put his knees through in a week, and four designer T-shirts that came out of their first wash too small for a teddy bear.

Hank lifted his son onto the floor, then rolled out of bed, aware that if he believed in guardian angels he'd be convinced his had sent Audrey to him.

She'd spent her entire life in New Jersey, most of it right in the town of Madison, and she hadn't wanted to leave the area after her husband died.

But she'd been both lonely and nervous on her own, so taking a job as a live-in housekeeper had been the perfect solution for her. And she'd been the perfect solution for a single father who worked irregular hours.

If she ever decided to leave... The mere possibility made him shudder.

"You're cold, huh, Dad? You oughta get dressed."

"Right. So why don't you go tell Mrs. Chevalier I'll be there in five."

"'Kay."

Robbie took off running, standard three-year-old speed if he was a good example.

As Hank watched him disappear, he tried to recall what life had been like without a child in the house.

He smiled to himself, thinking that it had been a whole lot quieter. And he hadn't had to worry about tripping over toys in the dark.

But he'd never once regretted adopting Robbie. Not even during those first harrowing weeks after Jane had walked out on them. Because he'd been absolutely crazy about his son from the first moment he'd laid eyes on him.

HANK'S IMMEDIATE IMPULSE was to ignore the doorbell.

He had a section of the ceiling down in his basement office, and was wrestling with a wrench and a length of old galvanized pipe he wanted to replace before Audrey and Robbie arrived back from their shopping expedition.

If he didn't make his deadline, Robbie would be down here helping. And that always resulted in jobs taking ten times longer.

As the bell rang again, he vaguely recalled Audrey saying something about a delivery. He hadn't thought she'd meant today, but he decided he'd better go check things out.

Wiping his hands on his jeans, he headed up the stairs and along to the front door. A glance through its small window almost started him rubbing his eyes in disbelief.

The woman standing on his front porch had a long tangle of dark hair, a killer figure and a face that would make any red-blooded male take a lengthy second look. A lengthy third one, too.

She was downright gorgeous. And gorgeous women did *not* routinely come calling. Not to his door, at least.

In fact, he was positive it had never happened before. It was definitely the sort of thing he'd remember.

Opening up, he gave her a warm smile. Then his gaze involuntarily flickered to her legs—and he ordered himself to keep his eyes off them.

It might be tough to do, though, because he'd always been a leg man and hers were great.

"Hank Ballantyne?" she said.

He nodded. This was getting better by the second. She hadn't just rung the bell because she was looking for directions or something. She was looking for *him*.

Of course, that briefcase she was carrying could mean trouble. She might be a lawyer or a process server—it wouldn't be the first time one had appeared out of nowhere. Or maybe she wanted to sell him something. Or she could be some sort of scam artist.

But his instincts were telling him she wasn't. And like most cops, his instincts about people were usually reliable.

"I'm Natalie Lawson," she said. "There's something I need to discuss with you."

Okay, not a process server. If that was it she'd have told him straight away.

"Would you like to come in?" he said, taking a backward step.

"I...are you alone?"

He nodded again. "I'm a pretty safe risk, though. I'm a police detective. NYPD."

"Yes. I know."

She knew. Okay then, she'd done some homework—which got him back to thinking either lawyer or a sales pitch. But if it was the latter, wouldn't she be acting friendly instead of looking so darned serious?

Glancing across his greening property to the Taurus parked in his driveway, he noted the Atlas Car Rentals sticker on its front bumper. Salespeople didn't normally drive short-term rentals.

He ushered her inside and began gathering up the toy trucks that were parked all over the couch, while she stood gazing at the pictures of Robbie on the mantel.

"There," he said. "That gives you room to sit down. Would you like coffee? Or something cold?"

"Thanks, but no. I just...where's your little boy?"

"My housekeeper took him shopping. He outgrows

his clothes awfully fast. Either that or he plays hard enough to destroy them.''

Natalie smiled. It was a great smile that made him smile back—yet he was still wondering what she was after.

As he sat down on one of the wing chairs facing the couch, she said, ''He's pretty active, then.''

The comment was almost enough to make him laugh. When he wasn't asleep, Robbie seemed to be in perpetual motion.

''That's a real understatement,'' he said. ''He gets into more...but you aren't here to talk about my son.''

''Actually, I am.''

''Oh?'' He glanced at her briefcase again, an uneasy feeling creeping up his spine.

Had she come in some sort of official capacity? If so, he had no idea what it might be. But there was a simple way to find out.

''You're here to talk about Robbie because...?''

Instead of replying, she opened the briefcase, pulled out a spiral-bound document, then leaned forward and handed it to him.

The title page read, *Final Report on Benjamin Lawson-Garcia. Prepared by Rodger Spicer, Private Investigator, Licensed by the State of Michigan.*

''Michigan?'' He looked at her uncertainly.

''That's not really relevant. I just hired him because he was recommended by a friend. One who lives in Detroit, which is where I grew up.''

She bit her lower lip for a moment before saying,

"Look, I know what a shock this is going to be, and I've spent days trying to think of some way to lessen it. There isn't one, though. Benjamin Garcia is my son, and...my Benjamin is your Robbie."

For an endless moment Hank felt as if he'd been punched in the solar plexus. He couldn't breathe and he couldn't think. He could only stare at Natalie Lawson while the meaning of her words sank in.

He finally managed to take a deep breath, which started his brain working properly again. After that, he only needed half a second to realize this picture was completely out of focus. And that maybe his instincts had been wrong. Maybe Natalie *was* a scam artist. Because she was *not* Robbie's mother.

Ordering himself to deal with this calmly, he set the report down on the coffee table and said, "Both Robbie's parents were killed in an earthquake. In Guatemala. He was just a baby at the time."

When she didn't reply, merely sat gazing at him, he decided that the more details she figured he knew the quicker she'd back off from whatever her game was.

"The quake left hundreds of children orphaned," he elaborated. "And a lot of them ended up being adopted in the U.S. Robbie only remained in Guatemala for a few weeks afterward. Then he was flown here and placed with my wife and me."

"Yes," she murmured. "It's all in the report. The adoptions were arranged by Worldwide Child Rescue and..." She shrugged. "But you know that as well as I do. What you don't know is that Rodger Spicer has spent the past three years tracking Benjamin down.''

"Three years," Hank repeated. "That's roughly how long I've had Robbie. Since he was about six months old."

"Yes, well... The Worldwide people weren't exactly cooperative. They did everything they could to prevent Rodger from accessing their records. But child by child, court order by court order, he..."

She paused, then continued. "Some of the babies they brought here came from an orphanage in Guatemala City. And Benjamin was one of them. He shouldn't have been, though. There was a mix-up, and...

"You see, my husband was killed in the quake, but I was only injured. And Benjamin was taken to the orphanage—to be cared for while I was hospitalized.

"Only, somehow the sisters mixed him up with another baby and turned him over to Worldwide."

Hank could feel panic growing inside him. What if Robbie really *was* her son? If he was, there was only one reason she'd have come here. To get him back!

But no. That report *had* to be wrong.

"Look, I'm sorry you lost your child. And your husband," he managed to say evenly. "I can only imagine what that's put you through. But this..."

His gaze flickered to the document. "Your Rodger Spicer's made a mistake."

"No, he hasn't," she said gently. "Robbie has a birthmark on the left side of his neck, doesn't he. Just above his shoulder. My baby had a birthmark there."

His heart pounding, Hank glanced over at the photos on the mantel. "You saw that three minutes ago, when you were looking at those," he said, turning back to her.

"I don't think it shows in any of them."

Did it?

He'd seen the pictures a thousand times, yet right this minute he was so upset he couldn't answer his own question.

"Then you know about it from the report," he said.

Natalie shook her head. "I've always known. It's one of the identifying features I was able to tell Rodger about way back in the beginning.

"Robbie has Benjamin's birthmark," she reiterated quietly. "And according to his medical records he has the same blood type as my son. And—"

"Fine. Your P.I.'s poked around and come up with enough coincidences to build a case. But that's a long way from proving—"

"Hank, it isn't only the birthmark and the blood type and Robbie's age. Most Guatemalans have a darker complexion than Benjamin does, and…if you read the report… There's no mistake. I'm his mother. A simple DNA test will prove that.

"In fact, I spoke to someone at a private lab in Englewood. If you'll agree to take Robbie there, we can both be tested and have a definitive answer within twenty-four hours."

He pushed himself out of his chair and paced across the room—his heart pounding harder still.

Of course he'd agree. He'd take Robbie tomorrow,

and hope to hell the test would prove Spicer *had* arrived at the wrong conclusion. But deep down his fear was telling him that wasn't going to happen.

One by one, he scrutinized the photos on the mantel and discovered Natalie was right. The birthmark didn't show in any of them. And if she'd actually told Spicer about it in the beginning, this was no scam. It was the real thing.

He turned and stood gazing at her. There were no striking similarities between her features and Robbie's, but their eyes were the identical shade of brown. And something about the way she held her head...

Dammit, if she *was* Robbie's mother, he was at risk of losing his child. The thought made his chest feel hollow.

"Maybe if you just looked at the report," she murmured.

As much to give himself some breathing space as anything else, he walked back over, picked it up and began flipping through the pages.

The document was exhaustive, even contained a brief description of his house. "A comfortable, three-bedroom bungalow in a semirural area outside Madison, New Jersey," he read before moving on to biographical information about him and Audrey.

He skimmed the summary section headed *Hank Ballantyne.* "Thirty-six years of age. NYPD homicide detective. Work involves rotating shifts and frequent overtime."

He swore under his breath. That hardly made him sound like the ideal single parent.

As for Audrey...

"Live-in housekeeper. Fifty-eight years of age. Widowed. One married daughter living in Idaho."

Hell, couldn't Spicer at least have mentioned that she was crazy about Robbie? And that she was one of the nicest people in the state of New Jersey?

Thinking that—thanks to Rodger Spicer—Natalie knew almost as much about his adult life as he did, he moved on to the next section and discovered it discussed Jane's leaving him. And their subsequent divorce.

He read through the overview, which contained details that had obviously come from the divorce pleadings.

Jane hadn't been able to have a baby and had been pressing him about adoption for quite a while. Then, when they'd seen the news coverage of the earthquake, so many children suddenly needing homes had made him agree to the idea.

Once he had, with Worldwide matching prospective parents to the orphans before they even left Guatemala, getting Robbie had been a relatively quick process.

But after he was theirs, it hadn't taken Jane long to decide that a baby wasn't actually what she'd wanted. And she'd left mere weeks after the adoption was final.

The adoption was final. Of course! There was the key fact. Why hadn't he realized that immediately?

Looking over at Natalie once more, he said, "Let's be sure we both understand something here. Even if you *are* Robbie's birth mother, my wife and I adopted him under New Jersey state law. And at this point I have sole custody. So, legally speaking, he's *my* son."

She coughed an anxious little cough, then said, "Well, the thing is, I've already consulted a lawyer. One in Trenton. And, legally speaking, it's not actually clear *whose* son he is."

ACCORDING TO RODGER SPICER'S report, Hank Ballantyne was an intelligent, rational man.

With that in mind, Natalie had told herself a million times that if they just remained reasonable, they should be able to work out a solution to their problem.

Not that she was anywhere near convinced they'd manage it, but they had to try. Aside from anything else, it would be a whole lot easier on Benjamin if they could simply come to an agreement themselves.

So even though she had the feeling Hank was tuning in and out while she went over what the lawyer had told her, she pressed on.

"Basically, his opinion is that we're looking at a legal nightmare," she said. "You believed you were adopting an orphan, but..."

She caught herself before she said "Benjamin" aloud. She had to start thinking of her son as Robbie. After all, that was the name he knew, so it was what she'd have to call him.

"But because I was actually alive," she explained,

"and didn't know what was happening, let alone agree to give up my baby...

"Well, apparently, there's almost no relevant case law in the entire country, let alone in the state of New Jersey. So if we can't agree on how to handle this, if we have to resort to the courts, it would be a precedent-setting case—which I gather could easily drag on for years. Plus cost a fortune in legal fees."

"And while it was dragging on?" Hank said. "Where would Robbie be?"

"With one of us."

"*Which* one?"

"We wouldn't be sure about that until... If we can't work things out on our own," she continued, desperately trying not to sound as though she was threatening him, "I'd have to apply for interim custody."

"You'd *have* to," he repeated, eyeing her so coldly she looked away.

Obviously, she *had* sounded threatening. But she'd just wanted him to realize what her only alternative would be.

Not that it would necessarily do her any good. Her lawyer had made that clear.

She might be the birth parent, but Hank was the one Benjamin...*Robbie* knew. The one he loved and had lived with for as long as he could remember.

That meant most judges probably wouldn't let her take him back to Guatemala until after a final decision had been reached. Far more likely, the ruling would be that he should stay right where he was for the time being. With Hank.

And if that was the end result of the first round of legal wrangling, a competent lawyer could probably manage to drag the court proceedings on until Robbie was ready for college. So resolving the problem themselves…

She said, "Hank, the most important factor in this is Robbie's well-being, right?"

"Of course."

"And I realize that my walking in here and trying to take him away from you would *not* be in his best interest, so it isn't what I'm trying to do.

"It really isn't," she added when he looked as if he wasn't buying that for a second. "But I've been working on finding him since the day I went to that orphanage and learned…

"If we just come up with a compromise that we can both live with…Hank, I know how awful this must be for you, but he *is* my son."

"And he's been *my* son since he was six months old. Do you think I don't love him?"

"I know you do," she whispered, her throat tight. "Now that I'm here…now that we've met, I can tell—"

"Let's get back to what your lawyer said," he interrupted. "What did he figure would happen if you *did* apply for interim custody?"

She thought about what to say for a few seconds, deciding there was no point in trying to make her case sound stronger than it actually was. Not when Hank would undoubtedly talk to a lawyer of his own.

"He basically told me," she finally said, "that how the hearing went would depend on the legal arguments and the particular judge."

She watched Hank shake his head when she finished speaking, trying not to feel sorry for him but finding it impossible.

There was no trick at all to putting herself in his shoes when they were pretty much identical to her own. They loved the same child, but he couldn't be with both of them at once. And the problem was no more Hank's fault than hers.

"All right," he finally said. "You've had a lot more time to consider this than me. How do *you* see us resolving it?"

Nervously she licked her lips. In her dreams, she simply whisked her son back to Guatemala with her. But she knew she couldn't do that in reality. Aside from anything else, it would be too horribly traumatic for him.

As far as he was concerned, Hank was his father. While she was…it hurt to even think about. At this point, she was nothing to him.

"You *have* come up with some ideas, haven't you?" Hank said.

"Not specifically detailed ones. But I thought we could consider some sort of shared custody arrangement."

Hank eyed her, his expression unreadable.

"I realize we'd have to take this slowly. That Robbie would have to get to know me, feel comfortable with me, before we could even consider anything more long term.

"So, for the moment, I was just hoping you'd let me spend some time with him. I'm staying at the Whispering Winds Motel, only a few miles from here."

He nodded that he knew where it was.

"We could take things step by step, give ourselves the chance to really consider our options—"

Before she completed the sentence she heard a door open. Seconds later, a whirlwind of a little boy charged into the living room.

"We had ice cream," he said, throwing himself at Hank. "'Cuz I was good."

Natalie's heart flooded with emotion. After all this time, her son was right here before her—alive and well and the most beautiful child she'd ever seen.

She desperately wanted to gather him up in her arms and never let him go. But he was already in Hank's arms.

And to his mind that's where he belongs, an imaginary voice whispered.

Taking a long, deep breath, she told herself she was *not* going to cry.

Yet even though she'd realized that when she found him he'd have no idea who she was, contemplating that in the abstract and coming face-to-face with the reality were two completely different things.

Watching him hug Hank, without even glancing

her way, tore at her far more than she'd ever have imagined.

"Oh, you've got company," a woman said from the hallway.

Looking over, Natalie forced a smile as Hank said, "Audrey, this is Natalie Lawson. Audrey Chevalier, my housekeeper.

"Of course, you've already guessed that," he added quietly to Natalie, nodding toward the report lying on the coffee table between them.

"Yes," she murmured, thinking that both Hank and Audrey were far different from what she'd been expecting.

Learning he was a homicide detective had made her leap to some conclusions she'd already realized weren't accurate.

Oh, not *all* of them were wrong. Being a big-city police officer was far from the safest job in the world. That was an undeniable fact. And to her mind, at least, it hardly made cops ideal father material.

But she'd been imagining Hank as a man who was much too involved in his work to really have time for a child—especially since he'd only adopted at his ex-wife's insistence. Yet that wasn't the impression she was getting now.

She gazed at him cuddling her son for another moment, a dull ache around her heart, then glanced toward the hallway once more.

She'd pictured Audrey as a stern woman too old to be caring for an active little boy. In reality, she seemed like a very pleasant, very young fifty-eight-year-old.

When Natalie focused on Robbie once more, he was watching her, his big brown eyes full of curiosity and a dried smudge of chocolate ice cream on his cheek.

He looked like Carlos.

She hadn't been certain, just from seeing those photographs, but he did. And that sent a fresh rush of emotion through her. Getting him back would be getting back a part of her husband, as well.

She continued to gaze at the little boy snuggled in Hank's lap, and realized that anyone who didn't know better would never suspect the man wasn't his natural father.

Hank didn't actually resemble Carlos very much, but there were similarities. Regular yet rugged features. Hair that was almost ebony and eyes the color of black coffee. The sort of dark good looks that had always appealed to her.

Not that Hank Ballantyne appealed to her. Lord, no. He was the man standing between her and her son.

Focusing on Benjamin...*Robbie,* once more, she softly said, "Hi."

The instant she spoke, he hid his face against Hank's chest.

"We're in a playing-shy-with-strangers phase," he said.

Strangers. Nodding again, she tried not to let the remark sting. It did, though. Hard.

"Would you like me to make lemonade or anything?" Audrey asked.

"No, thanks," Hank said quickly. "In fact, we're going out for a while. We've got some things to discuss."

CHAPTER TWO

HANK HAD DRIVEN Robbie to the lab in Englewood first thing, and Natalie had said she'd go as well. That meant, come tomorrow, they'd know *for sure* whether she was his mother.

However, the chance she wasn't seemed so tiny that Hank hadn't waited to consult a lawyer of his own.

By calling in a favor, he'd gotten a last-minute appointment with Doris Wagner—whom he'd known only by reputation until he'd walked into her office half an hour ago.

He eyed her as she sat gazing at her computer screen. A small, middle-aged woman, she looked as timid as a sparrow. However, she had a reputation as a veritable tigress in the courtroom, and was acknowledged to be one of the best lawyers around when it came to custody battles.

Not that he wanted to find himself in the midst of one. But he loved his son more than anything else on earth and there was no way he was letting Natalie Lawson take Robbie out of his life.

For the thousandth time, he recollected her words. "I realize that my walking in here and trying to take him away from you would *not* be in his best interest, so it isn't what I'm trying to do.''

He mentally shook his head. How could she have said that in one breath and raised the idea of shared custody in the next?

Shared custody. Did she *honestly* believe that was even a possibility?

He suspected she didn't. Because by the time they'd finished talking, he'd realized that the prospect of coming to *any* mutually acceptable compromise was virtually unimaginable.

Maybe, if there wasn't such a major geographic obstacle, some sort of sharing would be feasible. But saying she didn't live nearby was the understatement of the year.

He'd been surprised when she'd told him she was a doctor, and a quantum leap beyond surprised when she'd said she still lived in Guatemala.

She ran a clinic in Villa Rosa, a little town there, she'd explained. And…

He turned his thoughts back to the moment as Doris Wagner swiveled the computer screen away from herself and looked across the desk at him.

''Whoever Dr. Lawson consulted was right,'' she said. ''There's virtually no relevant case law. Which means that even if a judge found in your favor an appeals court could easily find in hers. So I suggest you explore her proposal of a joint custody agreement very thoroughly before you reject it.''

''But I just can't see any way one could work. Not with her in a different country.''

"Did you ask if she'd be willing to move back to the U.S.?"

"I didn't come right out and ask, but I got the distinct impression it's not an option. She told me how important the clinic and the people down there are to her. And if that's where she sees her future, it makes her suggestion…"

The word on the tip of his tongue was *ludicrous,* but instead of saying it, he merely shrugged.

"She didn't get any more specific about what she has in mind?" Doris asked. "Nothing more than you've already told me? Didn't say how *much* time she wants?"

"No."

"Then maybe things aren't as bad as you think. She's a single woman with a demanding career. And she knows as well as you do that nothing like Robbie alternating a week with her, a week with you, is possible. So she *could* be thinking more along the lines of a month or two a year."

"I doubt it, although I could live with *that.* I wouldn't like it, but…"

He paused, shaking his head. With Doris basically suggesting that he was probably looking at *some* sort of joint custody, what he'd like or wouldn't like didn't really matter.

"I have the sense that she wants him *at least* half the time," he continued. "And once he starts school he'll have to be in one place or the other for that, which throws even half-and-half out the window. School's *ten* months a year, not six."

After pausing again, he added, "I doubt there's a hope in hell that she'd settle for only summer vacations. Not even summer vacations *and* Christmas."

And he wouldn't voluntarily agree to so little, either, which made it seem obvious that they had an insurmountable stumbling block.

"Guatemala's a poor country," Doris said. "She'll be aware the education system here is far superior, and she undoubtedly wants the best for her child."

"I've thought about that, and I'll certainly use it as an argument. Even if I convince her, though... maybe she'd agree to only a little time at first. But what if that turned out to just be the proverbial thin edge of the wedge? What if she pushed for more and more until I eventually lost him entirely?"

"It could happen," Doris said gently. "The problem is, you haven't really got a choice.

"She's already warned you that if you don't work something out with her, she'll apply for interim custody. And if she was awarded it—"

"Wait!" he interrupted, feeling a sudden pounding in his chest.

When Natalie had raised that possibility, he'd assumed it was highly unlikely. But if Doris thought...

"Do you figure she *would* be?" he made himself ask.

"I doubt the odds are high, but she certainly might be. Regardless of that, though, consider the final result if you go to court.

"Instead of an agreement the two of you arrive at,

a third party will impose the rules. And keep in mind that, under the circumstances, there's absolutely no doubt a judge would grant her *some* amount of access to Robbie. The only question is how much.''

''How much would you guess?''

Doris shook her head. ''Since there aren't any real precedents, it would be pretty well up to the particular judge. Worst-case scenario, she'd be named the permanent primary guardian.''

''You can't be serious.''

''I'm afraid I am. I don't believe in deluding my clients, Hank. If this ends up in a courtroom, there'll be the risk of your losing custody. But we're getting ahead of ourselves. Until you have the results of the DNA testing...''

''They're only going to confirm what I already know,'' he said, the pounding in his chest even harder now. ''I went through that report very carefully last night, and Rodger Spicer did a thorough job. I'd say the chance that Robbie isn't Natalie's son is about one in a million.''

''Then let's consider how this might play out in a courtroom. Even assuming she *is* his mother, you have several things going for you. You've been the single constant in the boy's life since he was six months old. And despite your divorce and shift work, you've managed to provide a stable home environment.

''Judges are reluctant to order custody changes when things are going smoothly. So, assuming your relationship with Robbie is as good as you claim—''

"It is," he assured her. "And he adores Audrey Chevalier."

"Then, if this was an ordinary instance of a birth mother trying to reclaim her child, Natalie Lawson wouldn't have a prayer."

"But it's not ordinary at all."

"Exactly. You only have him because those nuns made a mistake. And as soon as Natalie learned about it she hired a private detective to locate him. Plus she's a professional woman who can support him and provide a loving home."

"In a village in Guatemala," Hank muttered.

Doris nodded again. "That's something else you have on your side. If she was awarded custody, she'd take him to a foreign country. He'd be totally uprooted, living in Spanish-speaking surroundings, and you'd rarely be able to see him.

"Yet if she *is* his birth mother, and never even considered giving him up for adoption... Some judges would find that awfully hard to get past."

Hank stared at the floor, thinking that if this ended up in court it sure wouldn't be the sort of legal proceeding he was used to.

As a detective, he dealt with facts that added up to either guilty or innocent. But this case wasn't merely a question of facts.

Considerable weight would be given to extenuating circumstances. And one particular judge's mind-set would be critical.

The subjectiveness of that made him very, very anxious.

Focusing on Doris again, he said, "So what do I do?"

"Absolutely nothing until you get those lab results. But if they do prove she's his mother, here's what I'd suggest."

IT WAS THE HEIGHT of the afternoon rush hour when Hank's meeting with Doris Wagner ended, and heading through the parking garage, he decided there wasn't much point in starting for New Jersey just yet. The commute to his place took a minimum of forty-five minutes when the traffic was light.

Besides, he could do with a little extra time to think—and someone to bounce things around with—before he got home and had to face Audrey's questions. She was so worried about the possibility of losing Robbie that she'd have a million of them.

He reached his Blazer and climbed in, then took his phone from his pocket and pressed the speed dial for Travis Quinn's cellular.

Travis and he were the best of buddies, as well as partners, and Travis had a knack for seeing situations clearly. Unless the situation involved Celeste, of course.

Last fall, Celeste had been the prime suspect in a homicide they'd investigated. Yet the moment Travis had laid eyes on her something had short-circuited in his brain, making him absolutely refuse to even consider the possibility she could be guilty.

Fortunately, it had turned out she wasn't. Because they were getting married in June and the C.O. would have a heart attack if one of his detectives married a murderer.

"Quinn," he answered on the fourth ring.

"It's Hank. Where are you?"

"At Celeste's. What's up?"

"I've got a problem."

"A serious one?"

"Yeah. And I'm only a few blocks away, so I thought if you weren't in the middle of anything..."

"No, come on over."

"Thanks, I'll be there in five."

The city was practically in gridlock, making his trip to the West 74th brownstone actually take a lot longer—but he finally got there.

Once he'd buzzed Celeste's apartment and she released the lock, he headed up the stairs to the third floor. He'd barely started down the hall before Travis opened the door.

Celeste's cat, Snoops, peered warily out from behind his ankles, making Hank think about how badly his son wanted a pet.

It was something he'd been holding off on until Robbie was older. But the way things stood now, he might be living in Guatemala before he was much older.

As Travis gestured him inside, he told himself not to be a pessimist. One way or another, he'd insure that things turned out okay. But telling himself that and feeling confident of it were two different things.

When they reached the living room, Celeste took one look at him and disappeared into the kitchen—to emerge a minute later with a couple of beers. She handed one to him and one to Travis, saying, "Is this problem just a guy thing? I've got some work I can go do if—"

"No, I'd like your thoughts, too."

She smiled and he managed to smile back. He'd grown to like her after he'd realized the idea of her being a killer was ridiculous. And it was easy to understand why Travis had fallen so hard for her. Aside from being a terrific person, she was great-looking— even though she wasn't Hank's type.

He'd never gone for blondes. Dark-haired women were the ones who always caught his eye.

Women like Natalie, he thought, an unexpected image of her taking him by surprise.

Women *like* Natalie, maybe, he silently repeated. But not *her,* specifically.

Oh, he might initially have figured she was good-looking, but he sure didn't think so at this stage of the game.

Well, that wasn't entirely true. He was objective enough to realize she hadn't suddenly turned from a beautiful woman into a toad. His *attraction* to her, though, had done an instantaneous fizzle when he'd learned what she wanted.

He focused on Celeste once more, as she perched on the end of the couch next to Travis and automatically reached for his hand.

Seeing that made him feel a little…envious? Was that it?

Probably, he admitted.

If any woman had ever been as crazy about him as Celeste was about Travis, it had been a long, long time ago. And facing the risk of losing his son had made him very aware of how alone he'd be if that happened.

"So?" Travis said. "What's wrong?"

"It's about Robbie," he began.

Neither Travis nor Celeste interrupted as he told them how Natalie Lawson had shown up and dropped her little bombshell.

When he was finished, Travis slowly shook his head, saying, "Talk about a shocker. But something doesn't ring quite true. Why would her baby have ended up in an orphanage? Wasn't there anyone who could have looked after him? No relatives or—"

"Uh-uh. She mentioned she has virtually no relatives *here,* let alone in Guatemala."

"Here?" Celeste said.

"In the U.S., I mean. She's originally from Detroit. Did her medical degree at the University of Michigan."

"Then how did she end up in Guatemala?"

"She got involved with…I think she said it's called American Physicians Abroad—one of those organizations that provides health care in foreign countries.

"At any rate, neither she nor her husband had any relatives down there. He was from Spain, an archaeologist working on a site near the town where her clinic is.

"But getting back to how Robbie ended up in an orphanage, the quake literally devastated the area.

Half the population was either killed or injured, so a lot of people were left without anyone to care for them. And with Natalie in the hospital...I guess it made sense, given the situation.''

"Oh, Hank," Celeste said, "this is really awful. What are you going to do?"

"Well, I've just been to see a lawyer. That's why I'm in the city. Natalie had already gotten legal advice, so I figured I'd better do the same."

"And?" Travis prompted.

Briefly he filled them in on what Doris had told him. "Her final advice," he concluded, "was to play things cool, to wait until Natalie comes right out and tells me *exactly* what she wants—then use that as the starting position to negotiate her down."

"I don't believe this," Celeste said, shaking her head. "You're being forced to negotiate because a judge might rule in her favor? Even though you've had Robbie since he was a baby?"

He shrugged, doubting the casual gesture would fool either of them for a second. They were like family; Robbie even called them Uncle Travis and Aunt Celeste. So they certainly knew how much his son meant to him.

"Oh, man," Travis muttered. "And we complain about the *criminal* justice system."

"Yeah, well, that's how things stand. So I have to let Natalie get to know Robbie while we try to work out an agreement."

Travis eyed him for a moment, then said, "You'll be careful, huh?"

Hank nodded, knowing exactly what his partner meant. He didn't intend to give Natalie the slightest opportunity to take off with Robbie.

"I'll be with them every minute they're together," he said. "I'd trust Audrey to supervise, but since she'll be leaving any day now—"

"Where's she going?" Celeste interrupted.

"Oh, I thought I told you," Travis said. "Her daughter's having a baby, so she's heading out west for a couple of weeks. Idaho, isn't it?" he added to Hank.

"Right. She's just waiting until Valerie goes into labor, then she'll be on a plane."

"And what about Robbie?" Celeste asked.

"We've got that covered. One of her friends is going to fill in. A woman he knows."

Travis nodded, then turned their conversation back to the problem, saying, "So Natalie is here for how long? I mean, if her clinic is so important to her... "

"I asked about a time frame," Hank said, "but she hedged on answering. This American Physicians Abroad sent a doctor to fill in for her, though, and I have a feeling she intends to stay here until the situation is completely resolved."

They were all silent for a minute, then Celeste slowly said, "Do you think the two of you *will* be able to work something out? Does she seem like a reasonable woman?"

"She seems..." He raked his fingers through his hair, not entirely sure how to answer that.

His life would never again be the way it was before

Natalie Lawson came knocking on his door. And part of him hated her for that—the same part that was itching to tell her she could see how happy Robbie was, so she should just go home and leave them alone. Yet he couldn't stop himself from considering things from her point of view.

If *his* son had gone missing, he'd have done exactly what she had. Turned the earth upside down if that was what it took to find him. But why did *her* child have to be *his* child?

"Hank?" Celeste murmured.

He tried to recall what she'd just asked.

"She doesn't seem *unreasonable*," he said, once he had. "She just wants her son.

"*Just*," he repeated, wearily shaking his head. All she wanted was what had been stolen from her, yet if she got him back...

"Take it easy," Travis said.

"Yeah, I know. I'm not in the greatest shape. I lay awake all last night, thinking, and the more I thought the less I could see how any sort of sharing arrangement would be even remotely feasible."

He paused and took a long, slow breath, then continued. "In any event, Doris said that if Natalie and I can't work things out on our own she'll recommend someone for us to meet with. Some sort of counselor or mediator. But there'd still be no guarantee we could agree on a plan."

"And in the meantime?" Celeste said. "While Natalie's getting to know Robbie? Are you going to tell him she's his mother?"

Hank looked at her, only then realizing he and Natalie hadn't discussed that. But since she was intent on being part of his life, they'd have to tell him sooner or later. And after they did...

He ran his fingers through his hair once more, the sense that his son was already beginning to slip away from him gnawing at his insides.

"HANK?" AUDREY SAID GENTLY. "You might as well get it over with."

He glanced across the kitchen table at her and nodded. But then, instead of making the call, he pushed back his chair and headed for the living room—where Robbie was playing with his friend Gary, whose mother routinely left him here while she did her grocery shopping.

When he walked into the room, Robbie shot him a grin and said, "We're playin' trucks."

"Yeah, I can see that."

As if Robbie didn't have enough trucks for half a dozen kids, Gary had brought his own backpackful. The floor was wall-to-wall with them.

"Wanna play with us, Dad?"

"Thanks, but not right now."

"You can have my fire engine," Gary offered.

He was almost a year older than Robbie, and had gotten much more into the idea of sharing.

"Hey, that's really tempting," Hank told him, "but I just wanted to make sure you guys were having fun."

He watched them for a minute or two. Well, actually, he watched Robbie. Then he backtracked to the kitchen, where the number of that lab in Englewood was sitting next to the phone.

"It's past ten," Audrey said.

"Uh-huh." And the lab people had told him he could call any time after nine-thirty.

Fleetingly he wondered if Natalie had phoned them yet. Then he told himself she didn't really need to. She was *positive* that Robbie was her child.

Glancing at Audrey again, he thought she looked as if she'd aged overnight. Her hair seemed to have more gray mixed with the brown than it had only yesterday, and she was clearly tired. Of course, she probably hadn't slept any better than he had the past couple of nights.

After procrastinating for a few more seconds, he forced himself to pick up the phone and punch in the number.

"This is Hank Ballantyne," he told the woman who answered. "My son, Robbie, was tested there yesterday. As was a Dr. Natalie Lawson. I'm calling for the results."

"Just a minute, sir."

Audrey eyed him while he waited, her expression anxious.

The woman at the lab finally picked up again. "Mr. Ballantyne?"

"Yes."

"There's a positive match."

She said more, something about his getting written documentation in the mail, but he only half heard the rest of her words because "there's a positive match" kept repeating in his ear.

"Thank you," he said when she stopped speaking. Then he clicked the phone off and numbly told Audrey the news.

Her eyes filled with tears. "Oh, Hank, I'm so, so, sorry," she murmured.

"Yeah," he managed. "Me, too."

NATALIE HAD BARELY LEFT her motel room since she'd driven back from the lab in Englewood yesterday. She'd been sitting by the phone, waiting for Hank Ballantyne to call. And worrying about what he'd say when he did.

Or should that be *if* he did?

He'd promised he would, as soon as he'd done some thinking about letting her spend time with Robbie. But maybe he'd changed his mind.

Maybe, instead of phoning, he'd have a lawyer get in touch, because he'd decided that he wouldn't let her see any more of her son unless a judge forced him to.

Or he might simply vanish with Robbie. Then she'd have to start searching all over again.

Closing her eyes, she reminded herself that Rodger Spicer's report hadn't painted Hank as the sort of man who'd run. He was the type who'd stand and fight.

She only hoped he wasn't going to fight *her*.

It would be so much better for Robbie if they didn't end up battling over him. Yet, if that was the route Hank decided to take...

Well, if her alternatives were to start legal proceedings or forget about ever seeing her child again, there'd be only one real choice—no option at all. She was just afraid she might not have enough emotional reserve left to carry her much further.

She'd been running on empty ever since that day in the orphanage. And now that she'd finally found her son, now that she'd seen him...

She told herself to calm down. Whatever happened, she'd cope. The way she'd been doing for what seemed like forever.

As she glanced at the silent phone once more it suddenly rang. Her heart slammed against her ribs, then began to race.

Her throat dry, she answered.

"It's Hank," he said.

"Yes. Hi."

"I called the lab a while ago."

"Me, too."

Barely breathing, she waited for him to say something more, each second like an hour.

"We'd better talk again," he said at last.

"Yes. Fine."

"Is it okay if I come there?"

She desperately wanted to ask how he'd decided to play things, but all she said was, "Of course."

"Good. I'll see you in ten."

CHAPTER THREE

TELLING HERSELF THAT HANK would be here any second now, Natalie wandered into the bathroom and halfheartedly brushed her hair. It wasn't even a little less wild after she finished than before she'd started.

Wash-and-wear hair, her mother always used to call it, a kind way of saying it had a will of its own. An iron will. Over the years, she must have tried to tame it a hundred different ways—none of them successful.

Eventually she'd given up, and now just left it long so she could at least tie it back out of the way when she was working.

Hearing the crunch of tires on the gravel, she hurried to the window, in time to see Hank getting out of his Blazer.

He did *not* look pleased, but she could scarcely expect him to. Until she'd suddenly appeared, he'd been under the impression she was dead. And she'd bet he wished, with all his heart, she actually was.

She headed over and opened the door, the thought that homicide detectives undoubtedly knew how to commit perfect murders sending a shiver down her spine.

As he stepped inside and glanced around the room, her gaze followed his.

The Whispering Winds wasn't a dump, but it wasn't luxurious, either. She didn't know how long she'd be away from home, and her funds were nowhere near unlimited.

Finding her son had taken almost all the money she'd inherited from her parents. And while working with American Physicians Abroad was emotionally rewarding, she didn't earn anything like what doctors in the U.S. made.

If she and Hank *did* end up fighting each other in court, she'd be hard-pressed to pay her legal fees.

"It's nice out," he said at last. "Do you want to take a walk?"

"Sure."

She grabbed a sweater from the closet, doing her best to appear nonchalant when she was feeling anything but. His expression hadn't given her an inkling about what he was thinking, which left her still totally up in the air.

The motel backed onto a stretch of green space that lent the air an earthy scent of spring, and the path they followed ran alongside a gurgling stream.

Under most circumstances she'd find it a relaxing setting, but the longer they walked the more anxious she grew.

"Spring's my favorite season," she finally said to break the silence.

"Yeah?" Hank said, barely glancing at her.

"I guess that's one of the reasons I fell in love

with Guatemala. It's known as the land of eternal spring.''

All that got her was a second "Yeah?" so she lapsed back into silence.

They walked a little farther, then he said, "I saw a lawyer yesterday."

Her pulse skipped a beat. She wasn't surprised that he had, but what advice had he gotten?

"And?" she prompted when he didn't continue.

"She basically said what yours did—that we should try to work things out ourselves."

"Ah…good. I mean, I'm glad they agreed."

"Right. So…I guess we'd better talk about your seeing Robbie."

"Fine," she murmured, afraid that if she said even one more word he'd start having second thoughts.

"There'll have to be some ground rules."

She nodded.

"First off, I'll be there whenever you're with him."

"That's fine," she said, not hesitating for a second. She'd agree to just about anything when he was going along with this.

"Good. Then…well, I guess we could start with your coming back to the house once we finish talking. If you'd like, I mean."

"That would be great," she said, still trying for nonchalance although she felt like doing cartwheels in the grass.

"But this is my last day off," he continued. "I'm back at work tomorrow, and I'll be on the midnight-to-eight shift for the next ten days, which means I don't get home till after nine—later if we're in the middle of something at the end of the shift. So, by the time I've slept...well, the earliest you'll be able to see Robbie will be around four or five."

"Hank, I'll fit in with whatever works for you. I realize how difficult you must find this. And I knew that even if you decided to let me see Robbie, you wouldn't want me constantly hanging around. So I was thinking I'd see if the hospital in Madison wants a volunteer.

"I wouldn't be able to do hands-on work with patients. I'm not licensed to practice in New Jersey. But if there's anything else they could use me for..."

"I'm sure there'll be something. I keep hearing how short staffed they are."

"Good. I'd hate to just sit around in the motel."

She hesitated then, not really wanting to mention the present, in case he thought she was resorting to bribery, yet knowing she'd better.

Finally she said, "When I was in Englewood I got something for Robbie. A fire engine. Is it okay if I bring it along today?"

"Sure," he said, almost making her smile with relief. "He'll love it. Anything with wheels."

"Right. I kind of figured that after seeing all his cars and trucks."

She told herself to stop there. Being nervous often made her talk too much. And, sure enough, the next instant she heard herself saying, "I guess it was silly, but once I'd bought it I started thinking I shouldn't have. That it might jinx things and you'd tell me I

couldn't see him. So the fact that you're letting me...
Well, it really does mean a lot.''

He eyed her for a moment, before saying, ''Look,
Natalie, don't read too much into it, okay. If my lawyer hadn't advised me to try compromising with you,
I'm not sure I would be. Because regardless of what
arrangement we work out, assuming we can even do
that, every day Robbie spends with you will be a day
he isn't spending with me. And I'm not happy about
that.''

''I don't blame you,'' she murmured. ''I wouldn't
be, either.''

''Right...well...we should probably turn back.''

They walked in silence again until he said,
''There's something else we have to decide. Whether
we should tell Robbie you're his mother.''

Her automatic response was, of course they should,
but she caught herself before the words came out. It
hadn't occurred to her there'd be any question about
that. There obviously was, though.

''What do *you* think?'' she asked.

''Well, I talked it over with Audrey and we both
feel that for the time being I should say you're a
friend. And he should call you Natalie.''

''Oh,'' she said, trying to pretend that didn't hurt.

''After all, he's only three. Three and a half.''

Hank stopped and looked at her then. ''I've never
known his real birth date. We chose one based on the
pediatrician's guess because the records weren't complete and... Hell, as it's turned out, the records
weren't even Robbie's, were they.''

"He was born on October 11," she said quietly.
"And the earthquake struck on February 15. Those
four months were all I had with him."

While Hank had had three years. She tried to force
that thought away.

"October 11. The doctor's guess was pretty close.
But the point I wanted to make is that Robbie isn't
old enough to really understand the concept of a
mother. Not the fact that a mother's the woman who
gives birth to a person, I mean.

"Sometimes," Hank added after a moment, "it's
hard to know exactly what he *does* understand."

"Well, as you said, he's only three and a half."

"Yeah."

A few beats passed, then Hank said, "I guess I
should tell you that he knows he's adopted—sort of,
at least. I talked to him about it a few months ago,
but I don't think my explanation really made much
sense to him.

"And getting back to his concept of a mother...as
far as he's concerned, I think she's just someone who
lives with a child and looks after him. Something his
friends have but he doesn't."

"Has he ever asked *why* he doesn't?"

"Uh-huh. And I told him his mother was dead."

"Oh," she murmured again. Even though she realized it shouldn't, that hurt, too.

"Looking at things now," Hank continued, "I
guess it wasn't the best answer. But it seemed to be
at the time. My ex-wife doesn't keep in touch, which
meant there was no point in even mentioning her to

him. And as far as I knew, you actually *were* dead, so...

"Well, he doesn't really understand the concept of death, either. And he seems quite content that he has only me and Audrey. At any rate, I think we'd just confuse him if we got into how you can be his mother."

She merely nodded, aware her voice would give her away if she spoke.

She'd studied child development in med school, and half the patients she treated in Villa Rosa were children. She *knew* the stages of growth their minds went through, was perfectly aware what a child Robbie's age could comprehend and what he couldn't.

Even so, when it came to her son, she'd been deluding herself—imagining that they'd tell him she was his mother, he'd wrap his little arms around her neck and the three missing years would simply melt away. But that wasn't going to happen.

Hank had those years and they could never be hers.

HANK CUT THE IGNITION, then stared into the rearview mirror as Natalie's rental pulled up behind his Blazer.

She'd suggested coming over in her own car so he wouldn't have to take her back to the motel, and it had struck him as a good idea.

He'd figured that driving home alone would give him a chance to sort through something he was having trouble with—the fact that the more time he spent with her the nicer she seemed.

Oh, not that he'd rather she was evil incarnate. After all, she *was* Robbie's mother.

Still, he'd find their situation easier to cope with if he was obviously the guy wearing the white hat and she was Cruella De Vil.

But it was clear that *nothing* about this mess was going to be black and white. And unfortunately, like most cops, he wasn't as good at dealing with shades of gray.

Opening the door of the truck, he told himself that—as far as their negotiations were concerned—whether Natalie was nice or not was immaterial. Even if she was a reincarnation of Mother Teresa, he didn't want her ending up with the lion's share of time with Robbie.

He watched her get out of the Taurus, thinking she looked nervous. Maybe even frightened. But that was hardly surprising after Robbie had basically ignored her the first time around.

She had to be concerned about what kind of reception she'd get today. And worried that he'd *never* decide he liked her.

Audrey had raised that possibility last night. And after she had, they'd discussed it. They'd even flirted with the idea of trying to insure Robbie *wouldn't* warm to Natalie.

They'd both been a little ashamed of themselves, but they *had* considered it—although ultimately they'd rejected it because he had a right to know his mother.

Like it or not, he did. A moral right and a legal

one, as well. Doris Wagner had left no doubt on that
score. Still, Hank couldn't help wondering how long
Natalie would persist if Robbie didn't take to her.

Maybe she'd get discouraged pretty fast. Discouraged enough to pack up and head back to Guatemala.
Alone.

He fantasized about that for a few seconds, then
told himself it was nothing but wishful thinking. After
spending three years and heaven only knows how
much money to find her son, she wouldn't quit now
that she had.

Besides, her quiet manner probably made most kids
feel at ease with her. And Robbie was basically a
pretty friendly little guy, so he'd come around.

Glancing at the shopping bag she was holding, he
thought about how many points she'd score with that
fire engine—likely enough that she'd have Robbie on
side in no time. And once he decided he liked her…

Hank gestured that they should head for the house,
not wanting to let his thoughts wander any farther
down that road right now.

Sooner or later they'd have to start talking about
how much sharing each of them was prepared to do.
But he was in no rush. Discussing the idea would only
make it seem more real.

When Hank started forward Natalie followed
along, telling herself there was no reason to feel even
half as uncomfortable as she did. That wasn't actually
true, though.

The man wished she was *anywhere* else. She could

read that in his body language—in his walk and the stiff set of his broad shoulders.

Telling herself not to go there, she turned her attention to the house. In contrast to him, it seemed positively welcoming.

The first time around, she'd been so nervous that she'd barely noticed what the exterior was like. Today, she was a little more observant. And the Cape Cod styling, the gray board-and-batten construction, the long front porch with its white railing... everything about it added up to a "friendly" sort of place.

The setting was appealing, too. On either side of the house, the lawn gave way to shrubs and trees that seemed to stretch forever—although she could make out a weathered split-rail fence that said he didn't own anywhere near as far as she could see.

They'd almost reached the porch steps when the door flew open and her son came racing out. Just as it had the other day, her breath caught at the sight of him.

"Hey," Hank said, swinging him up into his arms. "I haven't been gone for a month, you know."

"Yeah, but Mrs. Chevy made cookies. For the company. So I hadda wait for you. And her," he added in a loud whisper, looking over at the "company."

Natalie shot him the warmest smile she could manage.

"This is Natalie," Hank said. "Do you remember her?"

As Robbie gave an exaggerated shrug, Audrey appeared in the doorway. Her expression said she was determined to be pleasant if it killed her—and that she was convinced it might.

"Hi," Natalie said, managing another smile, also.

"Hi. I heard Robbie telling you I baked some cookies. So come in and we'll see how they turned out."

GLAD SHE'D HAD the foresight to wear jeans, Natalie scuttled across the living room, trying her hardest to stay ahead of Robbie.

The fire engine had proved a major hit. And while he raced it around the floor, making loud siren wails, she was in charge of moving cars out of its path.

Unfortunately, there were so many of them that she kept hearing impatient honking noises among the wailing.

Every so often, when she'd managed to clear a stretch of "road," she glanced over to where Hank was sitting on the couch. He was pretending to read the paper. But since he hadn't turned a page in half an hour, she knew he was actually keeping a close eye on them. And she couldn't stop imagining what he must be thinking—not to mention feeling.

Looking away, she reminded herself that she had every right to spend some time with her own son. She shouldn't have a sense of guilt about it.

But she knew why she did. She was getting what she wanted at Hank's expense, and she'd really prefer that wasn't the way things had to be.

"Robbie?" he said.

They both turned toward him.

"You're going to wear Natalie out. Maybe you should do something a little quieter for a while."

"What?"

"Play with one of your puzzles? Or see if she'll read you a story?"

"Wanna do a puzzle?" he asked her.

"Sure."

She watched him hurry over to the bookcase, the bottom two shelves of which were obviously his. Then, as he knelt poking through his things, she glanced at Hank once more.

Because her anxiety level had been sky-high the other day, her memory of the entire visit was a bit of a blur. But she recalled realizing that he wasn't what she'd expected. And that those conclusions she'd jumped to, after reading Rodger Spicer's report, hadn't all been accurate.

Oh, she still had trouble with his being a police detective. Aside from anything else, she couldn't understand what would make someone want to work in homicide.

But setting that aside, he'd obviously been doing a great job with Robbie—which gave her strangely mixed feelings.

She'd always hoped and prayed that, wherever her son was, he'd been adopted by good people. But somehow, at the same time, she'd imagined that when she finally found him she'd be rescuing him from a family that hadn't given him nearly as much love as he deserved.

Now, however, she'd come face-to-face with reality. And the reality was that Robbie was a happy, secure child—whom Hank loved very much.

It was almost enough to start her wondering if she was making a mistake. If she should back away and content herself with being far less a part of his life than she wanted to be.

But how could she?

She'd felt him growing inside her, and had given birth to him. Held him when he was barely a minute old. Nursed him. And she'd never stopped loving him with all her heart.

He was part of her. Part of Carlos. How could she back away from that?

The sound of a phone ringing interrupted her thoughts, and a second later Robbie trotted over to her with a painted wooden puzzle. They'd just spread all the pieces right side up on the floor, when Audrey hurried into the room.

"That was Mark," she told Hank. "He and Valerie just got to the hospital."

"Do you want me to call about a flight?" Hank asked her. "Get you on the earliest one I can?"

"Oh, yes, please. I'm so excited I can hardly think straight, let alone deal with the airlines."

"Oh, and Hank," she added as he was heading off, "don't book a return one that comes in too late.

"My daughter's having her first baby," she explained to Natalie as Hank disappeared. "They live in Idaho, so I'm not likely to arrive before she delivers.

"But we decided it made more sense to have most of my time there afterward, with her and the baby, than sit around just waiting, beforehand.

"You know how it is with firstborns. Well, of course you do—you're a doctor. They can be weeks late."

"Yes, they certainly can."

She glanced at *her* firstborn. Her *only* born. He'd been a mere eight days late, but she'd thought she'd never go into labor.

"Oh, now I'm wondering if I should have said I'd stay longer than two weeks and gone earlier," Audrey murmured. "Then I could be in the delivery room with her. But I just didn't want to take *too* much time away from Robbie."

"Who'll be looking after him while you're away?"

For a fleeting second, the hope that they might have no one lined up and that she could do it flitted through her mind.

But she told herself they'd have something arranged, even before Audrey said, "One of my friends. She's a widow, too, so she can move in on a moment's notice."

Audrey turned toward Robbie, saying, "You're going to be good as gold for Mrs. Harmand, aren't you."

He nodded.

"And will you miss me?"

"Uh-huh."

"How much?"

Grinning, he stretched his arms apart as widely as they'd go.

"Well, good, because I'm going to miss you, too. A whole bunch. But I'll be back soon."

Focusing on Natalie again, she said, "Will you be all right here until Hank's off the phone? I'm basically packed, but I've got some last-minute things to gather up."

"Sure, we'll be fine. We're just getting started on the puzzle. Right, Robbie?"

"Uh-huh." He turned his attention back to it as Audrey hurried from the room.

Natalie sat on the floor beside him, very aware this was her first time alone with him in over three years.

Her throat tight with emotion, she desperately wanted to wrap her arms around him and hug him half to death. She didn't make a move, though.

She knew better than to try to force herself on a child—even if he was her own—so she merely watched him, her eyes drinking in the way his dark hair curled onto his neck, the smoothness of his skin, the perfection of his little hands hovering over the pieces of the puzzle.

The last time she'd seen him...

But there was no sense thinking about how many milestones she'd missed in his life. The past was past, and the important thing was that she'd finally found him. Now all she had left to do was work things out with Hank.

All? she silently repeated. What was she trying to

do? Fool herself into believing that arriving at an agreement with him would be easy?

There was no point in that, especially not when something he'd said earlier was still lingering in her memory.

"Every day Robbie spends with you will be a day he isn't spending with me," he'd pointed out. "And I'm not happy about that."

Of course, she could say the same thing. So arriving at a plan they could both live with was going to be tough.

"There," Robbie said.

Focusing on the puzzle, she saw he'd put a couple of the pieces together.

"Good," she said.

As she was reaching for the one that would fit next to them, Hank reappeared.

"I have Audrey on a flight that leaves in two hours," he told her. "So I'm afraid we'll have to cut this short. If the traffic around Newark's bad, we could be tight for time.

"Let's get some shoes on you," he added to Robbie. "You can't walk around an airport in just socks."

Without even thinking before speaking, she said, "If it would be easier to leave him here, I'd be glad to stay with him."

"No," Hank said so sharply that Robbie's gaze darted to him.

"I mean…thanks," he added more gently. "But I like taking him places. Especially ones we don't often go to."

She nodded, telling herself not to let his initial reaction bother her. But it was hard to do when he so obviously didn't trust her. He was afraid that if he left Robbie with her, he'd come back to discover they'd vanished.

"Crazy thinking," she whispered under her breath.

Even if kidnapping was something she'd consider, which she wouldn't, the man was a police detective. If she tried to make a run for it with Robbie, Hank would have their descriptions all over the country in no time flat.

Yet he figured she might try. And that made her wonder if he actually intended to *ever* let her be alone with her son.

Maybe he was only putting on an act, only pretending he'd be willing to agree to some sort of compromise. Maybe, right this minute, his lawyer was working on a way to simply get her out of the picture.

If that was it, if Hank Ballantyne was playing her for a fool, the sooner she talked to *her* lawyer again the better.

But how could she possibly know whether that was it or not?

CHAPTER FOUR

BEFORE NATALIE HAD LEFT Hank's he'd apologized a second time for having to cut short her visit with Robbie. Then he'd suggested she come again tomorrow—and promised to call after he got back from taking Audrey to the airport, so they could decide on a time.

But darkness had closed in around the Whispering Winds and she hadn't heard from him, which was doing absolutely nothing for her peace of mind. The longer she waited, the more worried she was growing that her suspicions were right. That he was merely stringing her along with no real intention of trying to work out a compromise.

Restlessly she wandered across the room and opened the door to the cool night air, thinking again that maybe she'd better phone her lawyer first thing in the morning.

On the other hand, she might be wiser to hold off until she felt absolutely *certain* that Hank was playing games.

Gazing into the moonlit night, she reminded herself one more time that working things out with him would be a thousand times preferable to starting a legal battle.

When even their lawyers agreed on that, didn't it make sense not to push too hard? To give him the benefit of the doubt? At least for the moment?

While she was trying to decide if that was actually how she should proceed, the phone finally rang.

"It's Hank," he said when she answered. "I'm sorry I didn't call earlier, but it took me a while to get hold of Betty Harmand. The woman who'll be looking after Robbie."

"Yes, Audrey mentioned her name."

"Well, I figured it made sense to talk to her before I set anything up with you. And she wants to spend most of tomorrow at the house—not just come over when I'm leaving for work. She said she'd feel more comfortable if I was here with Robbie for a while.

"But getting to the point, she's bringing her things over in the morning, so would you mind waiting until later to come?"

Telling herself that was a reasonable request, not an attempt to keep her away from her son every minute he possibly could, she said, "When did you have in mind?"

"Oh...sometime after lunch? She won't be arriving very early, because the days I start on midnights I sleep in as late as I can. Or as late as Robbie lets me, to be more accurate."

"Then why don't I call around one and see how things are going."

"Great. Talk to you then. Bye."

"Bye."

The moment she hung up, her mind returned to the

question of whether the man was playing straight or playing games. It made her realize she was well on the way to driving herself crazy. She simply couldn't spend much more time in this motel room, alone with her thoughts.

Yet Hank started midnights tomorrow. And he'd said that meant she wouldn't be able to see Robbie until late in the afternoons. Which meant she definitely had to start *doing* something.

At home, she'd be able to immerse herself in her work, the way she had when she'd first returned to Villa Rosa after the earthquake—her husband dead and her son missing.

She'd thrown all her energy into her practice and into supervising the rebuilding of the clinic, working such long hours that she was always far too exhausted to think.

That was what she needed now. A way of keeping herself occupied. And if she could be useful at the same time, she would. So, come morning, she was going to call that hospital in Madison and offer to volunteer.

THE MADISON PLAINS HOSPITAL, although not imposingly large, was a modern three-story building. Natalie parked in the visitors' lot, then headed inside and across the front lobby to the elevators.

She had a 10:15 a.m. appointment with the chief of staff, a Dr. Brian Eisenberg, and she was hoping he'd give her suggestion an immediate thumbs-up.

When she'd spoken with his secretary, first thing,

she'd both explained why she wanted to see Eisenberg and asked the woman to call and verify her credentials with the AMA.

Hospitals had to check out people they took on as volunteers, but if the medical association had already confirmed she was legit, there shouldn't be any delay about her getting the go-ahead—assuming Eisenberg was as receptive to the idea as his secretary had implied was likely.

He proved to be a pleasant, chubby man in his midfifties who listened without interrupting while she briefly explained her circumstances.

When she'd finished he shook his head, saying, "What an awful thing for both you *and* Mr. Ballantyne."

She nodded. "It is, but hopefully we'll manage to work something out. In the meantime... Well, as I told your secretary, I'm only licensed to practice in Michigan—and Guatemala, of course. But if I can help *somehow*..."

"Oh, there's no doubt about that. The only question is where we can make the best use of you. Is there anything in particular you see yourself doing?"

"Not really. Since I don't know how long I'll be here, I wouldn't expect—or want—any responsibility. So, just whatever you think."

"Well, you seem like a people person."

She smiled. "I'll take that as a compliment."

"That's how I meant it. And do you enjoy working with children?"

"Absolutely."

"And you're fluent in Spanish," he said, glancing once more at the brief C.V. she'd written out and brought along.

"You know, I think we've got a place you'd fit perfectly. The psychologist on Pediatrics left recently, and we haven't managed to replace her yet. So if you basically filled in for her…

"I'm not talking about the paperwork or anything like that, but we need someone who's accessible to the patients and their families.

"Our staff members often can't make time to spend with children who are upset about being here. Or sit down and talk to parents who've got questions. Does that sound like something you'd be comfortable doing?"

"Sure. There'd be questions I couldn't answer, though. Hopefully not medical ones, but when it comes to hospital regulations and such…"

"You'll be able to check things like that. And we'll put Visiting Consultant on your ID badge, so that when you don't know something about the system, nobody will find it strange."

His gaze flickered to her C.V. again before he said, "Your Spanish is going to be a real bonus. We've got a situation at the moment that…

"But it makes more sense to have you meet Dr. Koehler, the chief of Pediatrics, and have her tell you the details. I only know the general story."

Minutes later the two of them were on the second floor, in Cynthia Koehler's office. She was forty-something, with a warm smile, and seemed pleased at the prospect of having Natalie on her unit.

"And I thought that since Dr. Lawson speaks Spanish," Eisenberg continued his explanation, "she'd be a particular help with Señora Perez."

"A help?" Koehler said. "She'll be more like a godsend."

"Good. Then why don't I leave her with you. She's here for another hour or two today, and... Well, you can discuss what sort of schedule will work."

He turned to Natalie, adding, "I'm sure you'll be just fine. But if you have any problems, feel free to bring them to me."

As he left the office, Cynthia said, "How about we're Natalie and Cynthia when we're alone, doctors Lawson and Koehler on the ward?"

"Sounds fine."

"And you can use the psychologist's office whenever you need privacy. A lot of parents have concerns that they don't want to raise in front of their children.

"I'll have someone get you an office key later, but first let me tell you about Señora Perez. Because she's *always* on the unit, and as soon as she discovers you speak her language..."

Cynthia paused and smiled. "I'm getting ahead of myself. I have a bad habit of doing that."

"So do I."

"Ah, good, then we should have an easy time understanding each other. But as for Señora Perez, she's the grandmother of Emma Perez, who's a patient here. And I think it'll be easier if I fill you in on the grandmother first, Emma second.''

Natalie nodded.

''Señora Perez spent most of her life on a farm in Puerto Rico, never learned English. And although we have enough Spanish-speaking staff that it wasn't hard to get her basic background story, we can't make a habit of dragging people away from their regular jobs to translate.

''Fortunately, Emma's bilingual, so that's a big help. But she's only seven. And...''

Cynthia paused again, as if organizing her thoughts.

''A couple of years ago,'' she said after a moment, ''Señora Perez came to live with her daughter, Emma's mother, who's been in New Jersey for... I'm not sure *exactly* how long, but she met Emma's father after she moved here, so it must be at least eight years.

''The father's immaterial, though. They never married and he took off before Emma was born.

''At any rate, getting to why Emma is here...there was a fire in the Perezes' building. The grandmother wasn't home at the time, but Emma and her mother were trapped in their third-floor apartment. And the mother threw Emma off the balcony to save her.''

Natalie grimaced. Injuries from falling that far could be life-threatening.

''She's basically okay,'' Cynthia continued. ''She's in traction, with multiple fractures to her right leg, but her prognosis is good. The X-rays don't indicate any complications, so she'll mend just fine.

"However, her mother's a different story. Rather than jumping, she went back into the apartment.

"We don't know why," she added before Natalie could ask. "All we know is that she was overcome by smoke, and by the time the firefighters got to her..."

Cynthia gave an unhappy little shrug. "She was taken to St. Aidan's, which is the nearest level-one trauma hospital, and the word we have is that they doubt she'll make it."

"Oh, Lord," Natalie whispered.

She'd been taught in med school that remaining emotionally detached from patients was critical to a doctor's mental health. Still, every now and then she heard or saw something that managed to sneak right past her defenses. And the thought of a seven-year-old hospital patient with no father and a dying mother was one of those things.

"Since her daughter can't have visitors," Cynthia was saying, "Señora Perez is spending all her time with Emma. Well, no, I'm exaggerating. It isn't actually *all* her time.

"She's temporarily staying with a neighbor and goes there in the evenings. But we've got her every day and...Natalie, she's in really rough shape.

"She's been told that her daughter will probably die, but my read is that she's in complete denial."

"That's hardly surprising, is it. I mean, the prospect of not only losing your daughter but being left with a seven-year-old to look after..."

"Actually, there's no question of her ending up with Emma. I'm not sure if she's aware of that, but Child Welfare will step in before Emma's released from the hospital. Señora Perez just isn't in a position—financially or otherwise—to care for a child alone."

"Aren't there any other relatives?"

"We had someone ask her about that, and there don't seem to be. There are none in New Jersey, and she said she moved here to be with her daughter because she had no one in Puerto Rico.

"But figuring out exactly what will become of Emma isn't urgent at this point. She's nowhere near ready for discharge, and we can't be *certain* about the mother's outcome. So, for the moment, we're pretty much in a holding pattern.

"Given that, maybe you could just spend some time with her. She's a sweet little girl and trying hard to be brave. But seven-year-olds are worriers at the best of times."

Natalie nodded.

"And, of course, Señora Perez needs help with working her way through all of this. Someone has to explain to her that even if her daughter lives, the long-term ramifications..."

"I understand."

"And you'll do it?"

She nodded slowly. She'd never dreamed that her volunteering would involve crisis intervention or grief counseling. But she'd wanted to make herself useful, and she was certainly being given the opportunity.

Looking decidedly relieved, Cynthia said, "I realize how much I'm asking, and I'd sit down and talk to Señora Perez myself if I could. But since my Spanish pretty much consists of *por favor* and *gracias*...

"The thing is, if she doesn't at least start coming to terms with the big picture... Well, as sorry as I feel for her, Emma is my prime concern. And if Señora Perez completely falls apart when her daughter dies, there'll be no one for the child to turn to. No one except for the staff here, and we're not much of a substitute for family."

"Does Emma know about her mother?"

"I don't think so. *We've* only said she isn't able to come visit because she was taken to a different hospital. Of course, I'm not sure what Señora Perez has told Emma, but I suspect she's assuring her that her mother's going to be okay. Which means that, assuming she does die..."

"It'll be just awful," Natalie murmured.

"SHE'S HERE," Robbie shouted, jumping off the couch and racing for the door.

Hank followed along, his son's excitement about Betty Harmand's arrival making him feel a lot better.

He'd met the woman in passing several times but didn't know her well. So even though Audrey had assured him that Betty was someone Robbie liked, and that she paid him a lot of attention whenever she dropped by, it was good to see that he really was okay with her.

They started down from the porch as she got out of her ancient Volvo. She was older than Audrey—somewhere in her midsixties, Hank figured. But since she had young grandchildren...well, hopefully, she wouldn't find Robbie too much of a handful.

"Hi," she said, giving them a smile as they started toward the drive. "Has Audrey called you yet?"

"Uh-huh, about an hour ago. She sounded as if she was smiling ear to ear."

"Well, the birth of your first grandchild is awfully exciting."

"She said the baby's the most beautiful she's ever seen. You don't think she could be biased, do you?"

When Betty laughed, Robbie suddenly turned shy and wrapped his arms around Hank's knee.

"Hey, I can't walk if you do that," he said as Betty opened the trunk.

She eyed her two large suitcases for a moment, before saying, "I probably brought too much. But this time of year the temperature always seems to bounce up and down like crazy."

While Hank took the cases from the trunk and closed it, she stood gazing out across his property. Then, as they started for the house, she said, "You know, it's strange. In all the times I've been here I never thought of your house as being isolated. It kind of is, though, isn't it."

He felt a ripple of uneasiness and hoped to hell her remark didn't mean she was nervous about his working midnights. Robbie would pick up on that sort of vibe like a hound scenting a fox.

"The lot's only a little over three acres," he told her.

"I guess that woodland's what makes it seem bigger." She gestured toward the nature preserve he backed onto. "That and the fact your next-door neighbor isn't very close," she added, nodding in the direction of the Kubiceks' place—the only house within shouting distance of his.

"Close enough," he said, deciding this was *not* the time to mention that the Kubiceks were off vacationing in California.

"And if you run into any problems while I'm at work, which I'm *sure* won't happen, you'll have my cellular number. I could get the Madison police out here faster than you'd believe."

Betty nodded, looking somewhat reassured.

Inside, he took her cases to Audrey's room, set them on the bed and said, "Do you want to unpack right away?"

"That's probably a good idea. It won't take me long, and it will mean fewer wrinkles."

"I can help," Robbie told her.

Hank grinned, imagining how long the job would take if he did.

"How about helping me instead," he suggested. "It's a little early to start lunch, but we'll make some coffee."

"Juice, too."

"Right. And you can be in charge of putting out the plates for the cookies."

Robbie gave the suitcases a lingering look, but the lure of cookies was irresistible.

As the two of them headed for the kitchen, Hank's thoughts turned to Natalie. He'd promised she could come over this afternoon, and before she did, he had to explain things to Betty.

He'd hoped that Audrey would do that before she left, but when she'd called Betty from the airport there'd been no answer. So he was stuck.

And even though Audrey claimed that her friend was both understanding and circumspect, which meant he shouldn't have to worry about her saying the wrong thing in front of Robbie, he didn't relish the prospect of telling the story to someone he barely knew.

After starting the coffee, he opened the cupboard to get what was left of the cookies Audrey had made the other day.

No—it had been yesterday, he corrected himself, setting out a stack of three small plates for his son to distribute around the table. She'd made them because Natalie was coming for her first "getting to know Robbie" session.

But how could it possibly have been only yesterday?

For that matter, how could it be a mere three days since she'd first appeared? He felt as if he'd been in emotional turmoil for weeks.

Telling himself to forget about Natalie for the time

being, he strode over to take the juice from the fridge—and the note he'd stuck on its door caught his gaze.

Natalie, he'd written, along with the number of the Whispering Winds Motel.

So much for forgetting about her. Now her image was forming in his mind's eye, while the recollection of his initial impression of her began creeping around in his brain.

He'd been attracted to her. And if they'd met under different circumstances...

But they hadn't. And under the existing circumstances, she was the enemy. The woman trying to take Robbie from him.

Natalie. As hard as he tried, he couldn't stop himself from staring at her name.

He wished he'd never so much as heard it. And wished, even harder, that there was no reason on earth he'd ever have to see her again.

"Daddy?"

He looked at his son. *Her* son.

"Natalie's comin' after lunch, huh?"

"Uh-huh."

"Good."

Robbie smiled happily.

It almost broke Hank's heart.

CYNTHIA HAD SENT NATALIE to the audiovisual department to have a picture taken for her photo-ID, and they'd produced the laminated badge on the spot—

complete with the promised Visiting Consultant designation.

When she returned to the second floor, Cynthia introduced her to the staff in the nursing station and gave her a key to the psychologist's office.

"I'll show you where it is so you can leave your purse there," she said. "Then we'll do a quick tour."

Natalie hadn't been in a small American hospital for years, but there was nothing strange or startling about the Madison Plains pediatric unit.

The walls were painted in cheery colors, rather than the standard institutional green or beige of adult wards, and were adorned with framed posters of cartoon characters. Some of the patient rooms they glanced into on passing were singles, some doubles and a few contained four beds.

Cynthia stopped just before they reached the last room on the right and quietly said, "This is where Emma Perez is, so I'll take you in to meet her. And her grandmother."

But when they walked into the room, they found only four little girls there.

"Hi, Dr. Koehler," they chorused from their beds.

As she greeted them, Natalie focused on the one who had to be Emma, the one with the angelic face, straight, glossy black hair and her left leg in traction. Instantly, something inside her reached out to the child.

After the earthquake, she'd spent weeks in traction with a broken leg. So she knew firsthand how bad the postsurgical pain was. Yet there was more to the affinity she felt with Emma than that.

She hadn't realized when she'd been lying in her hospital bed in Guatemala City that the worst was yet to come. Hadn't known, until she went to the Sisters of Mercy Orphanage, that her son was gone.

And Emma didn't know her mother was going to die.

Natalie swallowed over the sudden lump in her throat as Cynthia said, "This is Dr. Lawson, girls. She's come to visit all of you, but especially you, Emma, because she speaks English *and* Spanish, just like you."

Natalie smiled; Emma gave her a shy smile in return.

"So she'll be able to talk to your grandmother," Cynthia added. "I thought we'd find her here."

"She went for a walk," Emma said. "Her ankles puff up if she sits too long."

"Well, I'd like to meet her," Natalie said. "So maybe I'll wait here until she gets back. Would it be okay if I visit with you until she does?"

"Sure. I don't get any visitors. 'Cept for my grandma, I mean."

"A couple of your friends came to see you," Cynthia reminded her.

"Oh, yeah. Carol and Annie. Annie's mom brought them."

"That was nice of her, huh?" Natalie said.

Emma nodded. "And my teacher came, too. I

guess she counts. She brought some books from school.''

''We have volunteer tutors for the children who'll be out of school for a while,'' Cynthia explained.

''So we won't get behind,'' Emma added. '''Cuz if I got behind they might not let me go to grade three.

''My mom can't come see me, though. 'Cuz she's in a hospital. But not this one.''

''I know. Dr. Koehler told me about the fire. It must have been awfully scary.''

''It was. And now I have bad dreams. Every night.''

''I'm not surprised. And it's terrible when you wake up from them, isn't it.''

Emma nodded.

''Sometimes when she wakes up, she cries,'' one of the other girls said. ''And that wakes *us* up.''

''She doesn't mean it to,'' Cynthia told her.

''I know. But it does.''

''The dreams will gradually go away,'' Natalie said, her gaze still on Emma. ''It just takes time.''

''That's what Dr. Koehler said, too.''

Natalie smiled. ''Then it must be true, right?''

''I guess,'' Emma murmured doubtfully.

''Ah, Señora Perez,'' Cynthia said.

When Natalie turned toward the doorway, a frail, tired-looking woman was standing in it—one of those people whose age is impossible to guess. She could be in her fifties or her seventies.

''Señora Perez?'' Natalie said to her. ''*Me llamo doctora Lawson.*''

The woman seemed startled for an instant, then said, *"Habla español?"*

"Sí." Briefly she explained that she was here, temporarily, from Guatemala.

"Dr. Koehler," she continued in Spanish, "thought that you might like to talk to me about Emma's treatment. And about your daughter's."

Her eyes filled with tears—bringing a fresh lump to Natalie's throat. *"Sí,"* she murmured. *"A mi me lo gustaria mucho. Gracias."*

Natalie swallowed hard. Señora Perez might be saying she'd very much like to talk about where things stood, but they both knew it would be a difficult conversation.

CHAPTER FIVE

AS PROMISED, Natalie had phoned—and Hank had reluctantly told her to come over. Now she was here, her Taurus swinging into the driveway.

He switched off the lawn mower and brushed some bits of grass from the legs of his jeans as the car tires crunched along the gravel.

Then he glanced over at the porch, where Betty Harmand and Robbie were playing with an educational toy consisting of a large magnet, magnetized marbles and brightly colored paper clips that disappeared at such an alarming rate he'd already bought three boxes of replacements.

The porch, with cracks between its floorboards, was hardly an ideal place for that particular game. But Robbie and Betty were getting along well, so he wasn't going to worry about a few dozen more lost paper clips.

He focused on the driveway again, in time to watch Natalie climb out of her car.

The white dress she was wearing made her hair seem almost coal-black in contrast. And when she pushed her sunglasses up onto her head, her eyes looked even bigger and darker than he'd recalled. She really was an incredibly attractive woman.

For the thousandth time, he told himself to stop noticing that. And while he was at it, to stop thinking she was so damned nice—nice enough that if circumstances were different...

But they weren't. The bottom line hadn't changed in the slightest. She wanted his son, and the last thing he intended to do was let himself start liking her.

If he had no positive feelings for her, it would be a whole lot easier to negotiate firmly. Or to dig in his heels and be downright ornery, if that was what it came to.

"Hi," he said when she started across the lawn.

"Hi."

She glanced toward the porch, then back at him. "You know, I was halfway here before I realized I hadn't asked about Audrey's daughter. Has she had her baby yet?"

He nodded. "A little girl they're calling Beth. And Audrey made it to the hospital just before the delivery, so she's floating."

Natalie smiled; the thought that she had a great smile sneaked into his mind.

Mentally shoving it back out, he said, "Come meet Betty."

As they neared the porch, Betty caught his eye. She clearly felt uneasy, which was hardly surprising.

When she'd agreed to fill in for Audrey she hadn't expected to find herself in the midst of a disconcerting situation like this one. And even though she'd uttered the right phrases when he'd explained it to her—saying "How awful," and "What a terrible thing to happen''—he could tell she'd rather not have to deal with a complication she hadn't anticipated.

"Robbie, look who's here," he said as they headed up the steps.

Maybe Robbie picked up on the lack of enthusiasm in his voice. But whatever the reason, despite his earlier excitement about Natalie's visit, he barely glanced at her.

After Hank had introduced her to Betty and they'd exchanged a few pleasantries, she crouched down next to Robbie and asked what he was playing.

Hank *almost* managed not to watch the way her dress hiked up on her thighs; Robbie merely gave her a disinterested shrug.

"Well, now that you've arrived, Natalie," Betty said, "I think I'll go inside for a while."

"You promised to read me a story," Robbie reminded her.

She shot Hank an uncertain glance, then said, "Maybe Natalie would like to do that."

"But I want *you* to."

The whining tone that was becoming more common every day had crept into his voice.

According to the current bible—*Your Three-Year-Old's Behavior*—that was perfectly normal. But it was something Hank could do happily without.

"Robbie, I think you've worn Mrs. Harmand out," he said. "She deserves a rest."

"But she *promised.*"

While he was still trying to decide how to deal with his son's behavior, Natalie stood up, saying, "You know, I need to stretch my legs. Is it okay if I wander around for a few minutes?''

''Sure,'' he said, ordering himself to ignore her hurt expression.

As she started down off the porch, Betty murmured, ''Hank? What do you want me to do?''

He looked at his son. ''Robbie?''

Robbie ignored him.

Dropping to one knee, he said, ''Robbie, listen to me.''

''What?'' he muttered, still not making eye contact.

''Mrs. Harmand is going to read you a story because she promised she would. But after that I want you to be nice to Natalie. When someone talks to you and you don't talk back, you make the person feel bad. Understand?''

He silently nodded.

''Okay. Then go inside and pick a book.''

''Sorry about this,'' he said as Robbie disappeared into the house.

''That's all right. It's not your fault.''

''No, but you shouldn't be getting dragged into it.''

He gazed across the lawn, now trying to decide what to do about Natalie.

She'd vanished from sight, was probably walking down toward the nature preserve. And while half of him hoped she'd keep right on walking forever, the other half felt sorry for her—which he *knew* was ridiculous.

Wasn't his fantasy that Robbie would decide he

didn't like her? That she'd eventually give up and go away?

But even though her doing so would solve his problem, something was making him feel guilty as hell about how badly she must be feeling. So did he act on that? Or did he listen to the voice of reason telling him it would be far smarter to simply leave her be?

He swore under his breath, then said to Betty, "I guess I'd better see if she's okay."

Once he reached the side of the house, he spotted her. He'd been right; she was heading toward the bottom of the yard. By walking rapidly, he caught up with her as she reached the fence.

She must have heard him coming, but she simply stood gazing straight ahead, her hands on the top rail.

"Robbie's just overexcited," he said. "With first Betty arriving today, then you…"

"Look, I read a fair bit of child psychology. If I didn't, I wouldn't have a clue how to handle him half the time. But my point is that I gather three-and-a-half can be a really difficult age."

"I know," she said softly. "Thanks for reminding me, though. This isn't exactly the way I expected it to be."

He hesitated, telling himself to just let that pass, then found he was saying, "How *did* you expect it to be?"

Slowly shaking her head, she said, "Oh, I imagined a whole lot of different scenarios—none of them very realistic. For someone who's normally logical…"

She paused, gave him a wan smile, then continued. "In one version you were a veritable ogre who slammed the door in my face. In another, totally the far end of the spectrum, you were *relieved* to see me. You found being a single parent way too much, and were happy to let me take Robbie home with me.

"In another—but it's silly to even tell you about them when, as I said, none of them is realistic.

"So let's talk about something else," she added before he could say a word. "When I phoned you I was calling from the Madison Plains Hospital. I'm now officially a Visiting Consultant there."

"Hey, that's great. I told you they'd be glad to have you. What will you be doing?"

"Actually, a lot more than I bargained for. They're missing a psychologist in the pediatric unit, so I'll sort of be filling in for her. Which would be fine, except..."

Natalie hesitated. She'd only mentioned the hospital as a way of changing the subject, and she wasn't at all sure she should confide in him.

The more impersonal their relationship remained the better. Particularly since she was already having trouble dealing with the fact that he was a good man, doing a good job as a parent—and that Robbie was perfectly happy with his life the way it was. Plus, there was still the problem of not knowing whether Hank was honestly prepared to compromise.

Her fear that he had his lawyer busily at work in

the background, trying to pull a fast one on her, certainly hadn't vanished during the night.

Yet even though she knew his "reasonable" approach might merely be an act, she couldn't help feeling terrible about what she was putting him through. Because regardless of whether he was being straight with her or not, he loved Robbie. That was painfully obvious. And—

"Except what?" he said.

It took her a moment to backtrack to what she'd been saying. When she did, she looked at him.

His dark eyes caught her gaze. Held it. And she suddenly *wanted* to tell him what had happened this morning.

She didn't know why. He'd only been making conversation, certainly wouldn't have been asking out of friendly interest. Not when he had to hate her.

Even so, the next thing she knew, she was saying, "It wasn't only Robbie who got me upset. When I arrived here I was already feeling…

"There's a little girl named Emma Perez in the hospital, and she and her grandmother have been assigned to me—sort of my special project."

She briefly explained about the fire and Emma's mother and what Cynthia had asked her to do.

"And when we went to Emma's room," she continued, "the moment I saw her I felt something connect between us. You know what I mean? Does that sort of thing ever happen to you?"

"Now and then."

"Well, just after I'd met Emma the grandmother

appeared, so since Cynthia wanted me to talk with her, I took her down to the office they gave me to use. And..." She shook her head, feeling awful about that conversation all over again.

"It was really sad. She kept insisting her daughter would get better. But since all the staff believe she'll die, nobody had bothered to explain that even if she does survive she'll never be a healthy woman again. That the damage from the smoke inhalation will leave her an invalid, and the burns she sustained...

"I tried to get into that, but when I did Señora Perez started crying. And I thought she'd never stop."

She turned away from Hank and stared unseeingly at the forest beyond his property, not wanting him to suspect her "assignment" had gotten to her more than she should have let it.

"Natalie?" he said.

When she didn't reply, he tentatively rested his hand on her arm and said, "Look, this mess with Robbie already has you under a lot of emotional stress. So maybe Emma and Señora Perez aren't the best special project for you."

"I know they aren't," she admitted. "I realized that as soon as I sat down and started talking with her. But I went to the hospital wanting to help, and I agreed to take this on, and they need someone who speaks Spanish and...

"I'll cope with it. I just...they took me by surprise, that's all."

Hank nodded, his chest strangely tight. He could tell how upset she was, and like it or not—and he definitely *didn't* like it—he had an almost irresistible urge to fold her into his arms and simply hold her until she got her emotions under control.

He wasn't going to, though. He knew it would be a terrible mistake. He just *couldn't* let himself start feeling... But, dammit, he was already feeling things for her, wasn't he.

He could try pretending otherwise from now till next year, yet the truth was that he'd been aware of one of those instantaneous connections she'd mentioned the first moment he'd seen her on his porch. Oh, maybe he hadn't been *fully* conscious of it at the time, but it had existed. And as often as he told himself there really wasn't any pull between them, every time he looked at her...

He silently swore again. Pull or no pull, he was simply *not* going to do anything foolish when it came to this woman.

Regardless of *anything* else, she was the enemy. Period. End of story.

WHEN HANK ARRIVED at the Manhattan North Precinct a little before twelve, Homicide was quieter than usual. A few detectives on the four-to-midnight shift were getting ready to head home, but not many of the guys just coming on had arrived yet.

His partner had already gotten down to work, though. Travis was sitting at his desk with an open file in front of him.

"So?" he said, looking up as Hank neared him. "How's it going?"

Hank shrugged.

He didn't especially want to talk about the "it" he knew Travis was referring to. However, after he'd unloaded on Travis and Celeste the other day he felt obliged to provide an update, so he said, "Audrey got her call and flew to Idaho yesterday. And Natalie's been spending a little time with Robbie."

"How much?"

"A couple of hours yesterday," he said, trying to sound casual. "Then today she came by this afternoon and, well, she actually didn't leave until he went to bed."

He stopped there, not volunteering that she'd read Robbie his bedtime story.

Travis's expression was already saying he figured Hank was misplaying things.

Leaning back in his chair, he said, "And you were okay with her being there that long?"

"It wasn't what I originally had in mind, but..."

"But what?"

"Well, she'd had a rough morning."

Travis simply eyed him, until he told himself to just get it over with.

After he'd finished explaining, Travis said, "So you felt sorry for her and let her stay all that time. Fed her dinner, too, I bet."

"The rest of us could hardly eat in front of her, could we. Besides, she helped make it."

"Oh, man, don't you see what she's doing?"

Hank knew he wouldn't enjoy hearing Travis's the-

ory on that subject so he merely shrugged again—
hoping his partner would let it go.

He didn't.

"What does she look like?" he demanded.

"She's okay."

"Okay. On a scale of one to ten?"

"A seven," he lied.

"Maybe an eight," he said when Travis shot him
a skeptical glance.

"Or maybe a nine? Oh, jeez, Hank, she's a ten,
isn't she? It's written all over your face."

"Is there a point you want to make?"

"I'm getting to it. Has she told you exactly what
sort of sharing arrangement she has in mind yet?"

"No."

"Don't you think she should have by now?"

"I guess that isn't how she wants to play it."

"Apparently not."

Travis was silent for a few beats, long enough to
start Hank hoping he was done before he said, "You
know how *I* think she's playing it? I think she's hoping to soften you up before she says another word
about it. That she's trying to make you like her. Then,
whatever she asks for won't seem as bad as if she'd
just hit you with it cold.

"And not only that. She's figuring that she'll spend
enough time with Robbie to ensure *he* likes her, too.
So if you can't reach a compromise and some judge
ends up asking Robbie how he feels about her..."

That possibility had already occurred to Hank, of
course, which was why he had no intention of letting

himself feel anything for Natalie. Or, rather, why he'd *started out* with that intention.

The saying about the road to hell being paved with good intentions drifted through his mind.

Before it had completely drifted on out, Len Espizito strode into the squad room. Most C.O.s never worked the graveyard shift, but Espizito made a point of taking one every so often.

"I just got a call from St. Luke's—Roosevelt," he told them. "There was a shooting at 82nd and First half an hour ago. The vic was DOA when the ambulance reached the hospital, so the case is ours now. You two take it.

"Oh, and the vic's brother is a reporter with the *Times*. So get back to me as soon as you size things up. We can do without any negative press on this one."

NATALIE CHECKED the bedside clock once more. It was past one o'clock and she still hadn't managed to fall asleep. Her brain hadn't let her.

She simply couldn't stop herself from thinking. About Robbie. And Hank.

Each time she saw her son, she loved him more. And wanted him back in her life even more desperately. She wouldn't have believed that was possible, but it was happening.

And each time she saw Hank, Lord, that was a *real* problem. The more she saw of him, the less she wanted to do anything that would hurt him. Still, no matter how reasonable she tried to be...

Tightly closing her eyes, she had another shot at ordering her mind to shut down. But she might as well have told the earth to stop turning. Mere seconds later she was thinking about Hank and Robbie again.

She'd been surprised when Hank had trailed after her this afternoon—as if he'd actually cared that she was upset. And when he'd rested his hand on her arm, quietly trying to make her feel better...

He'd succeeded. But his touch had done something else—something alarming. It had suddenly made her aware she was attracted to him.

Until that moment, she hadn't recognized the chemistry between them for what it was. It had been so long since she'd met a man who...

She hadn't felt even a twinge of sexual desire in all the time since Carlos had died. But there was something about Hank...

Those dark good looks, for one thing: his rock-solid jaw, the straight line of his eyebrows, his broad shoulders and the appealing way his hair didn't *quite* behave.

Over the past few days she must have been absently aware of all those things. Yet it was only today, after he'd touched her, that she'd become conscious of how often she was sneaking glances at him. Realized she felt a rush of heat whenever her gaze met his. Noticed that his smile made her heartbeat accelerate.

But after years of feeling nothing toward *any* man,

why him? And why here and now, when a complication like that was the last thing she needed?

She had to remain focused on her goal—unless she wanted her son growing up as little more than a stranger to her. And that meant she simply couldn't let herself start feeling all liquid and brainless when it came to Hank.

Because compromising with him was one thing. Giving away more than she had to was something else entirely.

Rolling over, she scrunched her head into the pillow, almost wishing Hank wasn't the way he was. Almost wishing he hadn't invited her to stay for dinner tonight or let her help put Robbie to bed.

Lord, nothing her imagination had conjured up after she'd read Rodger Spicer's report had prepared her for the real-life Hank Ballantyne.

Oh, she still hadn't *entirely* ruled out the possibility he wasn't exactly what he seemed, that he might be trying to orchestrate something behind her back.

But it struck her as a lot less likely than it had only yesterday. Than it had only this morning, for that matter. Yet even if he *was* sincerely prepared to compromise, how were they going to work out a sharing arrangement when both of them really wanted to have Robbie full-time? And how was Robbie going to handle whatever—

The jarring ring of the phone started her pulse racing.

She fumbled for the receiver in the darkness, thinking it had to be a wrong number. Almost no one knew she was here?

Then she picked up and a woman said, "Natalie?"

"Yes?" The voice was somewhat familiar, but she couldn't—

"Natalie, it's Betty Harmand."

Something was wrong with Robbie!

"Natalie, I…I'm afraid I'm having a heart attack."

CHAPTER SIX

NATALIE WRIGGLED into her jeans and a sweater while she spoke with the 911 operator. Once he'd promised to dispatch an ambulance to Hank's, she hurried out to her car.

Betty had assumed her early symptoms were merely indigestion. As they'd grown worse, she'd explained, she'd tried to reach Hank. And when she'd only gotten his voice mail, she'd phoned the motel.

Thank heavens Hank had put the number on the fridge. And thank heavens she was a doctor, although Betty really should have called 911 herself. In the very beginning. But people often spent far longer than they should trying to convince themselves nothing was *seriously* wrong.

With the full moon making the visibility better than it would normally be, Natalie sped through the night well above the posted limit—only too aware that time was a critical factor. When it came to heart attacks, minutes could mean the difference between life and death.

As she turned off the highway and onto the road that would take her to Hank's, she fleetingly wished she had her medical bag along. But it was back in Guatemala.

If worse came to worst, though, she could do CPR until the paramedics got there. Assuming *she* didn't arrive too late.

That thought in mind, she pressed down even harder on the accelerator.

When she wheeled into Hank's driveway, the car was still traveling so fast that it sprayed gravel in every direction.

She pulled to a stop, scrambled out and ran for the house. The porch light was on and the front door was unlocked.

"Betty?" she called, yanking it open.

"Here," came a faint reply.

Thank heavens.

Betty was lying on the living room couch, her face white, her lips bluish, her expression one of raw terror. The almost-empty glass of water on the coffee table undoubtedly meant she'd taken the aspirins Natalie had told her to.

"How are you doing?" she said, perching beside the woman and checking her pulse.

It was racing.

"My chest feels as if something's crushing it," Betty whispered. "And those pains in my arm have been getting worse."

"Well, just try to take it easy. The ambulance will be here in no time and you're going to be fine.

"Really," she added for emphasis. "Now, what about your family? Is there someone I should call?"

"My son. And daughter. Numbers in my wallet."

"Good. I'll…" She paused, listened for a few seconds and breathed a sigh of relief.

"There's the ambulance," she said. "Can you hear the siren?"

Its wail grew rapidly louder, then she could see the lights flashing down the road. The shrill sound died as the vehicle turned into the driveway.

"I'll go let them in."

She gave Betty's hand a reassuring squeeze before starting toward the door. Just as she reached it, Robbie appeared from his bedroom.

He looked confused and half-asleep, but when he said, "Where's Daddy?" he seemed wide-awake—frightened.

"Your daddy's at work, darling. And everything's okay. Don't worry."

She scooped him up into her arms, then opened the door to the paramedics with their gurney and gestured them in the direction of the living room.

"Mrs. Harmand isn't feeling well," she explained to Robbie. "So these men are taking her to the hospital. But she'll be all right.

"And so will you," she added as he wrapped his arms around her neck and buried his face against her shoulder.

She carried him into the living room, where the paramedics were already strapping their patient onto the gurney.

"Betty, do you want us to ride in the ambulance with you? Or follow in my car?"

"Thanks, but just phone my kids."

"Sure. And you *are* going to be fine." She gave the woman's hand another squeeze, then the two men began wheeling her toward the door.

THERE WAS A CORRELATION between a full moon and the city being even crazier than usual.

Scientific types sometimes claimed statistics didn't back that up, but Hank knew it was fact. All cops did. All emergency room staff, as well. And tonight was no exception.

The woman who'd called in the shooting at 82nd and First had heard the shots from her apartment. According to her, when she'd looked out to see what was happening, there'd been at least a dozen people in the vicinity. But the first-response officers hadn't turned up a soul who admitted actually seeing the shooting. Or the shooter.

Hank and Travis assigned some uniforms to do a door-to-door of all the apartments with windows overlooking the street. Then they made a few more notes. After that, Hank called Espizito, as requested, and brought him up to speed.

"So we've done as much as we can for the time being," he concluded. "The crime-scene techs won't be finished until morning, and we'll see what they get. But now we're heading for Little Italy. We haven't been able to catch up with our prime suspect in the Lowenstein case, and we hear he sometimes hangs out in a bar down there."

"Save it for later," the C.O. said. "Right now we've got a mutilated body outside a renovation site on West 95th—just east of Amsterdam. A bag lady discovered it in a Dumpster. I need you to handle that.''

''Right.''

Hank clicked off, stuck his cellular away and told his partner they weren't going to Little Italy after all.

They walked down the block to where Travis had parked his Mustang, which he always drove in preference to one of the cars from the detectives' pool, and climbed in. As Travis pulled away from the curb, Hank dug his cell phone back out of his pocket and checked his voice mail.

There was a message from a detective in the two-five precinct, wanting information on a perp Hank had arrested a few months ago. Apparently, he might be linked to an unsolved homicide the dets down there had on their hands.

After that there was a hang-up. His breath caught as he listened to the third message.

''Hank, this is Natalie. Robbie's fine, but there's been a problem. Call me at your place.''

''Something's happened at home,'' he said, hitting the speed dial for the house number. ''Natalie's there. She said Robbie's okay,'' he added, as much to reassure himself as inform Travis.

The call connected; she answered so quickly that she must have had the cordless right beside her.

''It's me. What's wrong?'' he demanded.

''Hank, Betty's had a heart attack.''

He had an instantaneous, panic-laden flashback to

last October—when he'd rushed to Chicago because his father had suffered a heart attack.

But he'd pulled through, and when Hank tuned back into what Natalie was saying, she was telling him that Betty should make it, too.

"You're sure?"

"As sure as anyone can be."

Okay. Natalie was a doctor. She knew what she was talking about. So Betty would be okay, and that was the important thing.

Still trying to force away the image of his father lying in a hospital bed with a dozen tubes attached to him, he made a mental note to phone Audrey in the morning, then said, "How did you end up at the house?"

"Betty called me. She only got your voice mail, so she tried me."

Got his voice mail. Then she'd been the hang-up.

"I'll be home as soon as I can," he said.

"Don't feel you've got to come right away. I've talked to her children and they both said they'd go straight to the hospital. And she'll be in ICU, so only family will be allowed to see her anyway."

"But Robbie—"

"Don't worry about him. I can stay here until morning. In fact, I'd prefer that to driving back to the motel in the middle of the night."

"Well...is he okay? Not upset or anything?"

"No. He was, but I got him calmed down. He's fallen asleep again."

"Then I guess..."

"It's fine, Hank. Really."

"You're sure?"

"Yes."

"Well...all right. And thanks. I'll see you in a few hours."

As he stuck the phone away, Travis said, "What happened?"

Briefly, Hank filled him in.

When he was done, Travis said, "Betty's lucky. If she hadn't gotten hold of Natalie, she might be a goner."

He nodded, not wanting to even think about Robbie having woken up in the morning to find her dead.

"But...look," Travis continued slowly, "if you want to head home, I can finish the shift on my own."

"No, I'll hang in. There's really no need for me to be there."

"So you figure that Natalie being alone with Robbie is okay?"

"Yeah. It's not a problem."

He wouldn't have said that a few days ago. But by this point he knew she wasn't the type to try anything crazy. Hell, he wouldn't be surprised if she was one of the most responsible women he'd ever met.

Travis turned onto East 96th, which would let them cut through Central Park, then said, "Now what do you do for a sitter?"

"I don't know. Maybe talk to Espizito about taking some time off."

Travis shot him a glance that said the C.O. would be far from thrilled with that idea. They were chronically overworked, and being unexpectedly short-staffed never helped.

"Or maybe I can arrange something with one of the neighbors," he said. "Or find someone through an agency."

Travis was silent for a minute. "You know who's going to offer to look after him," he said at last.

Hank stared out into the darkness, not a doubt in his mind that his partner was right.

"What will you say when she does?"

"I don't know," he answered truthfully.

HANK AND TRAVIS SPENT an hour or so at the crime scene on West 95th—Hank unable to keep his mind on the job for more than ten seconds at a stretch.

Rationally, he *knew* Robbie was just fine, but all kinds of irrational fears kept sneaking into his head.

Glancing at his watch once more, he saw it wasn't even four-thirty yet. How could the night be dragging by so slowly?

"You know how often you've been checking the time?" Travis said.

He shrugged.

"About every five minutes. And, look, we're done here and it's too late to try Little Italy now. So why don't we just head back to Manhattan North. You can pick up your truck and take off. I'll go in and play catch-up with some paperwork."

"No, I'm okay."

"You're not okay. You're useless. So go home and make *sure* everything's all right."

He hesitated but finally said, "Yeah, I guess that makes sense."

They walked over to the Mustang and climbed in, then drove north to East 119th.

"I'm parked by the stairs," Hank said as they neared the entrance to the precinct's parking garage. "So I'll just get out when you pull in."

Travis turned into the garage, then stopped, saying, "Take it easy, huh?"

"Yeah, thanks. See you tomorrow."

Hank headed up to the second level where he'd left the Blazer, and barely fifteen minutes later was driving through the Lincoln Tunnel toward Jersey.

With only the sparse, middle-of-the-night traffic, it was just another half hour until he pulled into his driveway and parked behind Natalie's rental.

The sight of her car sent a ripple of relief through him, which forced him to silently admit that one of his irrational fears had been that he'd come to the wrong conclusion about her—and would arrive home to discover she actually *had* taken off with Robbie.

Jeez, no wonder he'd been so damned distracted after her call.

Getting out of the truck, he took a deep breath of the cool air. Above, the sky was still dark. But the faint pink of morning had begun creeping up from the horizon.

His eyes lingered on that for a moment, then he started across the lawn. The porch light cast a welcoming glow; the interior of the house was in darkness.

He half expected to find Natalie stretched out on the couch, but didn't. Assuming she'd decided to use Audrey's bed, he quietly made his way to Robbie's room, the way he always did when he got home late.

The door was only partially closed and pale illumination from the night-light was spilling into the hall.

He pushed the door fully open, took half a step forward, then stopped.

Natalie was curled up on Robbie's narrow bed with him. They were lying on top of the blanket, he in pajamas, she in jeans and a sweater—both fast asleep, his body snuggled spoonlike against hers and her arm wrapped protectively around him.

Hank's throat was suddenly tight. He didn't want her to be lying there with his son. As if they belonged together.

Yet she was his mother. How could he honestly say they *didn't?*

If they did, though, where did that leave him?

His throat tighter still, he stood watching the gentle rise and fall of her shoulder.

For all her strength and determination, when she was sleeping she seemed incredibly fragile. Her features were delicate, and her hair looked like a mass of rich black silk against the white of the pillowcase.

He let his gaze drift down her body, detailing her narrow waist, the enticing curve of her hips, the way her jeans clung to her perfect little behind.

Then he closed his eyes, because watching her ly-

ing there was making him fantasize about all sorts of
things that weren't even remotely related to reality.

Reality was that Natalie Lawson had lost her son.
And due to a stupid error, Hank Ballantyne had
adopted him. Now they had to deal with the fallout,
which was the sole reason she was here.

Once they'd hammered out a plan, she'd be gone.
And so would Robbie. At least part of the time.

That fact made him feel so empty inside he ordered
himself to think about *anything* else.

The next thing he knew he was gazing at her again
and thinking that in an ideal world the two of them
would fall in love. Then she'd stay here with him and
Robbie forever.

But that wasn't going to happen.

Oh, he didn't have much trouble imagining himself
falling in love with her. She was beautiful, smart
and…well, even though it had been a long time, he
recognized the signs.

The way his heart began hammering when she
walked into the room. His inability to take his eyes
off her and his constant desire to touch her—which
he was continuously reminding himself would *not* be
smart.

Hell, if he let down his reserves he'd probably be
downright crazy about her within hours.

But he was only one side of the equation. And he'd
be deluding himself if he figured there was a chance
she'd fall in love with him and decide to stay.

Yesterday, Betty had asked about her life in Guatemala. And her reaction had firmly reinforced his

sense that she intended to spend the rest of her days
there. The way her face had lit up when she began
talking about her clinic and her friends...

Well, if he'd had any hopes that she'd even consider moving someplace a whole lot nearer, they'd
have been dashed right there and then.

HE SIMPLY COULDN'T keep his hands to himself any
longer. He rested them on the soft warmth of Natalie's bare arms, praying he wasn't making a terrible
mistake.

"Oh, Hank," she whispered.

He drew her to him, breathing her seductive scent
and lowering his mouth to hers.

The kiss was an explosion of desire. He—

"You awake, Daddy?"

The loud whisper sliced through his dream like an
oar through water.

Almost groaning with disappointment, he blinked
against the bright sunlight sneaking into the room via
a crack between the curtains. Even the aroma of fresh
coffee, wafting past the now-open door, didn't make
him glad that Robbie had woken him.

"You know who's here, Daddy?"

"Who?" he said instead of "Yes." Robbie loved
being the bearer of news.

"Natalie." His son gave him a huge grin. "She
made me breakfast and we played outside and she
read me a story and stuff."

Hank checked the bedside clock, thinking if they'd

done all that it must be lunchtime. It was actually only a little past ten.

"Mrs. Harmand's in the hospital. That's how come Natalie's here."

He sat up and swung his legs over the edge of the bed.

"But she's gonna be okay. Natalie phoned. And talked to a doctor."

"This morning, you mean?"

"Uh-huh. After we played."

"Good. It's really good that she's not too sick."

Rubbing his jaw, he wondered if he should shave before he did anything else. But he normally showered and shaved shortly before he left for work—regardless of what shift he was on. So why would he change his routine just because Natalie was here?

Ignoring the imaginary voice that began telling him, he grabbed his jeans from the chair and pulled them on. Then he tugged a clean T-shirt over his head and fished his loafers out from under the bed.

"Is Mrs. Chevy comin' home today?"

"No. She'll be away for a couple of weeks. You know that."

"Then is Natalie stayin'? To look after me?"

Hank stared across the room, Travis's words from last night echoing in his memory.

You know who's going to offer to look after him, he'd said.

"Daddy? Is she?"

"Would you like her to?"

Robbie nodded vigorously.

"Well, I'll tell you what. You can watch one of your videos and I'll talk to her about it. Okay?"

"'Kay."

He took Robbie's hand as they started down the hall, wondering what on earth he should do.

She *was* going to offer. And it would be a logical solution to his problem. But the prospect of her and Robbie together for so much of the time...

Mentally shaking his head, he told himself he wasn't thinking straight. Whatever agreement they eventually reached would have Robbie spending far more than a couple of weeks with her.

After they'd chosen a video and he turned on the TV, he headed for the kitchen. When he got there, Natalie was standing with her back to him, rinsing off some dishes in the sink.

For a few seconds he merely watched her, trying not to let himself start contemplating the impossible. Then he cleared his throat and she turned toward him—giving him such a warm smile that he felt his heart skip a beat.

"I was surprised to see your Blazer when I got up," she said. "I didn't think you'd be home until at least nine."

"I cut out early. Got here around five-thirty."

She glanced at her watch. "And you've had enough sleep already?"

"Not really, but Robbie figured I had."

She smiled again, then said, "I phoned the hospital and checked on Betty."

"He told me. She's definitely all right?"

"There's *some* damage, but not nearly as much as there might have been. They'll keep her in Intensive Care for a few days, just in case there are unexpected complications, but she should be fine."

"Good. I'll call Audrey in a while. Let her know what's happened."

"She'll be worried about Robbie."

Hank nodded.

"About who's going to take care of him until she gets back, I mean."

"Yeah."

He'd known exactly what she meant, of course. Just as he knew exactly what she was thinking right this second. Her expression told him that she was dying to volunteer but didn't want to seem too eager.

He poured himself a mugful of coffee, delaying the inevitable. Her looking after Robbie made perfect sense. Yet he felt as if letting her do it would be driving another nail into the proverbial coffin.

His coffin.

"I spoke to Cynthia Koehler, too," she said.

"Dr. Koehler. At the hospital," she added when he eyed her blankly.

"Oh, right."

"She was expecting me this morning, so I wanted to explain why I'd be late. And that we might have to adjust the schedule we decided on. Because I thought…"

Hank met her gaze, waiting for her to get to where she was heading.

"I don't know if you have a backup plan for Robbie, but if you don't...

"Well, I was thinking...especially since you're working nights... It wouldn't make any difference to me whether I slept at the motel or here. And I could go to the hospital later in the day. After you get up. I mean, as I said, if you don't have a backup plan."

"I don't," he made himself admit.

"Oh...well, then if you think that would work..."

"You're sure you wouldn't mind?" he asked, even though he realized it was a ridiculous question.

She shrugged, still trying for not too eager. "I'd enjoy spending the time with him."

Again, Hank had to *force* himself to speak.

"Then I guess that solves the problem," he said. "But there's no point in paying for a motel room if you'll be either here or at the hospital. So after I've had something to eat, why don't we go pick up your things."

For a long moment she was silent. Then she said, "Are you sure that would be okay?"

"Sure," he said, telling himself he couldn't *actually* hear the sound of another nail being driven home.

CHAPTER SEVEN

AFTER HANK AND ROBBIE HELPED move her things, Natalie left for the hospital—unable to shake the worry that she should have done a little more thinking before checking out of the motel. Or, possibly, a *lot* more.

When Hank had suggested she come stay at the house, her first reaction had been that it made perfect sense. And that she could certainly do with the money she'd save.

Once she'd really begun contemplating the idea of being right there under his roof with him, though...

She made the turn toward Madison, wondering how she could conceivably be growing more attracted to the man with each passing day. Especially when there was no way in the world he'd ever be attracted to her.

Of course, even if he was, getting involved with him would still be the last thing she wanted to do. All she'd need, when she got home, was to discover she missed a man who lived thousands of miles away.

However, that was *not* going to happen. As long as she just ignored the way she felt when he was near...

But she was already aware that wouldn't be the easiest thing to do. The emotions she'd been convinced had died with Carlos had come alive once more—those crazy, primitive feelings of desire for a man...

No, not *a* man. They were focused on one *specific* man. And they were so strong that every time she looked at Hank she felt...

She ordered herself to stop right there. Dwelling on how he made her feel was distinctly counterproductive.

Instead, she should be reminding herself that all she had to do was act like a rational adult rather than a teenager with out-of-control hormones. And it shouldn't *really* be too tough a task. Especially considering she'd hardly be seeing Hank.

He'd said that when he worked midnights he usually slept until about three in the afternoon. If she headed for the hospital then, by the time she got back he'd be almost ready to leave for work again.

Of course, she reflected, pulling into the Madison Plains parking lot, she was assuming Cynthia would agree to those hours. Which might not happen.

Once inside the hospital, she made a quick stop by the ICU. After introducing herself to the head nurse, who had no problem with a visiting consultant being on the unit, she slipped in to see Betty Harmand.

She looked pale and felt weak, and wasn't up to much of a conversation. But both her chart and the monitors indicated she was doing well.

Feeling better after assuring herself of that, Natalie headed for Pediatrics—where she found Cynthia working in her office.

"Sorry I'm so late," she said by way of a greeting.

Cynthia gestured toward one of the visitors' chairs, saying, "After you called, I started wondering if you'd actually come in at all."

"You know, I might not have. But I promised Emma I'd be here." And while she *always* tried to keep her promises, something had made her feel it was particularly important to keep that one.

"She'll be really glad you came," Cynthia said. "The neighbor her grandmother's staying with phoned not long after you did this morning—to tell us that Señora Perez won't be in today. She has some sort of chronic breathing problem, and I guess all the spring stuff in the air…"

"Or the stress," Natalie suggested.

"I'm sure that's part of it, too. But, whatever, if it wasn't for you…

"Well, the parents of the other patients in Emma's room are here a lot, which means she's got to be feeling kind of… "

When Cynthia ended the sentence with a shrug, Natalie merely nodded. She wondered, though, whether Cynthia had been going to complete it with *lonely, neglected, depressed,* or another word entirely. There were certainly plenty she could have chosen from.

Forcing her thoughts from Emma, she said, "It's turned out we *will* have to reschedule my hours. I'll have to start later in the day."

Cynthia shot her a curious glance. "Does that mean Mr. Ballantyne agreed to let you look after Robbie?"

"Yes."

"Oh, that's really good, isn't it. Being able to spend more time with him while you're sorting things out."

"It's wonderful," Natalie murmured. For her, at any rate. But she knew Hank had very mixed feelings about it.

"So what hours are you thinking of now?"

"Well, how about if I start around four and stay till eight or nine."

Cynthia hesitated for a second, then nodded. "That shouldn't be a problem. In fact, it might even be better. If you're here into the evening, you'll be accessible to people who can't make it during the day.

"And there's a little boy we've been running tests on whose parents never arrive until after I leave. So if you could stop by his room later on, I'm sure they have a ton of questions.

"Let me go over his records with you," she continued, rummaging through the stack of folders on her desk.

Once Cynthia had briefed her on little Tod Baxter and they'd discussed a few other things, Natalie headed to Emma's room. Her three roommates all had company—two mothers and one father, she guessed.

After saying brief hellos, she sat down on the chair beside Emma's bed.

This time, there was nothing shy about the girl's smile. She was obviously thrilled to have a visitor.

"I heard your grandmother can't come today,"

Natalie said. "So I was thinking you must be awfully bored."

"Uh-huh. I am."

"Then why don't you tell me a story."

Emma looked at her uncertainly. "No...*you're* supposed to tell *me* a story."

"Oh? Really?" she teased. "Are you *sure* that's the way it works?"

The little girl grinned. "Uh-huh. Positive."

"Oh, well, then... *Once upon a time,*" she began in Spanish.

When Emma looked uncertain again, she said, "Since I've been in New Jersey, I've had to speak English all the time. And I miss Spanish, because that's what I usually speak at home."

"How come you can't talk Spanish in New Jersey? My grandma does. And my mom, too. Just not *all* the time, like Grandma."

"Well, until I met you, I didn't have anyone who'd understand what I was saying. But now I do."

"Me."

"Exactly."

Emma's glance swept over the other three girls, then she refocused on Natalie.

"If we talk in Spanish," she said quietly, "nobody else will understand what we're saying."

She was clearly pleased by that prospect, so Natalie gave her a conspiratorial smile and went back to Spanish. "That means we can have all the secrets we want, doesn't it."

Emma shot her another grin. "Tell me one."

"Well…it's not exactly a secret, but it's something none of them know. I live in a country called Guatemala. Have you heard of it?"

"Nope. But I've heard of Puerto Rico. It's *like* a country only…" Emma paused, clearly thinking hard.

"It's called a commonwealth," she said, finally coming up with the word. "And it's where my grandma's from.

"My mom used ta live there, too. A long, long time ago. Before I was born."

"I've been to Puerto Rico."

"Really?"

"Uh-huh. My parents took me there on a vacation, when I was a teenager."

"I'm gonna go someday. My mom's gonna take me. She promised."

Natalie swallowed over the lump forming in her throat.

"But now it can't be till my leg's better," Emma added, making a face at her cast.

"That won't be too long."

"And it'll be *all* better?" she asked, her expression suddenly one of concern.

"Yes. Completely. Oh, after the cast comes off, your leg will be weak for a while. But there'll be people to help you with exercises that'll make it strong again."

"So I can walk on it just the same as the other one?"

"Absolutely."

Emma gazed at her for a moment, then nodded toward one of the other patients. "*She* said I'll have a limp. Forever."

Natalie quickly thought back to what Cynthia had said. *No complications. She'll mend just fine.*

"Dr. Koehler told me you'll be as good as new."

"Really?"

"Uh-huh. And I'll bet she knows a million times more about broken legs than that girl. But why don't I have a look at your chart, then we'll be sure."

She rose and walked over to the door, took the chart out of its holder and glanced through it, Emma watching her.

"Just as I thought," she said when she returned to the bed. "Dr. Koehler's right. No limp. Not even a tiny one."

Looking relieved, Emma said, "Good. 'Cuz if I had one I might not be able to jump rope. Or play hopscotch."

"Are those your favorite things?"

"Sometimes. But not in the apartment. My mom doesn't let me play outside games in the apartment."

After eyeing Natalie for another moment, she said, "When we had the fire?"

"Uh-huh?"

"All our stuff got burned. My grandma has to stay with Señora Barreda, down the hall, 'cuz *everything* got burned. Our furniture and clothes and my stuffed animals and books and everything."

"Oh, Emma, that must make you awfully sad."

She nodded. "Even my favorite bear. His name was Teddy."

"What color was he?"

"Brown."

"And how big?"

Emma held her hands about a foot apart, then gestured toward the pink bear peering over at her from the bedside table. "One of the nurses gave me *him* to sleep with. She got him from the playroom, 'cuz I told her I missed Teddy. But he's not the same."

"No, he's not Teddy. He looks like a nice bear, though."

Emma shrugged. "He's okay, but he's not the same."

She stared at her cast for a minute, then looked at Natalie once more. "Are they fixin' our apartment?"

"I guess so. Yes, I'm sure they must be."

"So when I'm better? And my mom's better? It'll be fixed by then?"

A fresh lump in her throat, Natalie reached for the little girl's hand. "Emma, even if it isn't fixed by then, there'll be a place for you to live."

"You promise."

"Yes, I promise."

"So SPARKY CURLED UP at the bottom of Billy's bed and they both fell fast asleep. Which is exactly what I want you to do now," Hank added, closing the book.

He kissed his son good-night, but before he could push himself off the bed, Robbie said, "Daddy?"

"What."

"We need a dog. And he could sleep with me."

"Maybe when you're older."

He tried to stop the *if you're still here enough of the time* thought from forming, but failed.

"How old?"

"We'll have to see."

"See what?"

"Well, see what Mrs. Chevalier thinks about the idea, for one thing."

"She likes dogs."

"Oh? Did she tell you that?"

Robbie nodded emphatically, although Hank seriously doubted the subject had ever come up. It was the sort of thing Audrey would have mentioned.

Glancing at his watch, he told himself he had to phone her as soon as he got Robbie tucked in.

He should have done it hours ago, but he'd been procrastinating—knowing that once he told her about Betty she'd ask who was going to look after Robbie the rest of the time she was away. And he had a pretty good idea what her reaction would be when she heard.

"Daddy?"

"Uh-huh?"

"Are you *sure* Natalie's comin' back?"

"Positive."

"When?"

"Soon."

"Then I should stay awake. So she can kiss me good-night, too."

The horrible feeling that he'd end up losing his son entirely began creeping around in his chest once more.

"She can kiss you good-night even if you're asleep."

"But...Daddy?"

"Last question, Robbie."

"Did she tell you I waked up last night?"

"Yes. When the ambulance came, right?"

"Uh-huh. But after, too. And I was scared. So she laid down with me till I went back to sleep."

"Ah." That explained why he'd found them here together.

"What if I get scared tonight?"

He knew he'd said no more questions, but this wasn't a good place to end the conversation.

Robbie's fear of the dark seemed to have been diminishing lately. Now, though, with Audrey away, then Betty...

"Robbie, we've talked about this a lot of times. There isn't any real reason to be frightened. Someone's *always* in the house with you. And you've got your night-light, so you can see that everything's okay."

"But there's the monsters that hide under beds," he whispered—as if afraid one of the monsters might hear him.

Hank got down on the floor and peered under the bed. "Nothing here except some dust bunnies."

"There's the ones that hide in the closet."

He crossed the room, opened the closet door and rummaged around inside. "None in here, either. Is there anywhere else they hide?"

"They can come in the window."

"Nothing can come in if it's locked," he said, walking over to it and checking.

"Locked tight. So how about this? You snuggle down and try to go to sleep, and I'll leave the hall light on."

"Well...'kay."

Hank gave him another kiss, then rapidly made his escape before his son could think of any more delaying tactics.

His son. The words echoed in his mind as he walked toward the kitchen, making him reflect on just how much this situation was getting to him.

Of course, it *had* been from day one. But by this point, the uncertainty about how things were going to play out was a constant gnawing in his gut. If Doris Wagner hadn't told him to wait for *Natalie* to initiate the negotiating, he'd have started it long before now.

He checked the list beside the phone for Audrey's daughter's number and punched it in. The son-in-law answered, accepted his congratulations on their baby's safe arrival, then called Audrey.

"Hank?" she said, picking up. "Is everything okay?"

"Well...no." Quickly he filled her in about Betty.

"Oh, that's just awful," she murmured. "But she *is* going to be all right?"

"That's what everybody's saying."

"Thank heavens. Can I phone her, or...?"

"I don't think they'd put you through just yet."

"Then I'll call her daughter first thing in the morning. I want Betty to know I'm thinking about her. But

where does this leave you? Have you found someone
else to look after Robbie?''

"Ah, yeah. Natalie's going to take care of him.''

There was a lengthy pause before Audrey said,
"Do you think that's a good idea?''

"Frankly, I'm not entirely thrilled with it. But she
offered and I didn't have many options.''

"Oh, Hank, I don't like that at all. It'll give her so
much time with him.''

"Yeah…well, that's where we're at.''

"And where are you at with…the rest of it?''

By "the rest of it,'' he knew she meant Natalie's
sharing proposal.

"The same place we were when you left,'' he said.
"I've been doing what Doris Wagner suggested.
Waiting for her to make the first move—and she
hasn't.''

Ordering himself to tell Audrey the rest, he added,
"Speaking of moving, Natalie's going to be staying
here at the house. I hope you don't mind that I said
she could use your room, but it made a lot more sense
than her driving back and forth to the motel.''

"No, I don't mind. Betty would have been using
it anyway. But…Hank, maybe I'd better come home
sooner than I was planning. I could change my return
booking and—''

"No, don't do that. You stay right there with Valerie. Everything will be okay here.''

"But…Hank…''

"What?''

"Oh, I know I shouldn't ask about this right now,

with all the rest of what's going on. But ever since Natalie came into the picture and said she wanted...

"Well, I just can't stop wondering. If Robbie's not going to be living with you all the time... "

Would he still want *her* living there? she was asking.

He'd realized, days ago, this was going to come up, so he didn't have to think about it before saying, "Audrey, you and I get along so well that if you want to stay, that'll be just fine.

"No, wait, that didn't come out quite right. What I meant was I'd *want* you to stay. Otherwise, what would I do when Robbie *was* here?

"So don't worry, huh? We'll see where this ends up, what agreement Natalie and I reach. Then you and I can talk about the rest of it."

"Yes, you're right," she murmured. "We'll just have to play it by ear."

After a brief silence, she added, "Will you phone me again tomorrow night? Let me know how Betty's doing? As I said, I'll call her daughter in the morning. But I don't want to keep bothering her after that."

"Sure, I'll give you a shout before I leave for work."

"Thanks. And, Hank, if having Natalie there turns out to be a problem, you *will* tell me. Immediately."

"It won't be a problem, so don't worry. Just enjoy your granddaughter."

"Oh, I already am. She's wonderful."

"And you're completely unbiased."

Audrey laughed, then said, "I'll talk to you tomorrow."

"And everything will be just fine here when you do."

"I certainly hope so. Bye."

Thinking that he certainly hoped so, too, he said goodbye. Then he wandered into the living room, sank onto the couch and switched on the TV.

He flicked through a dozen channels without seeing anything that looked even marginally interesting. Finally he clicked to CNN. Maybe something major had happened in the world.

The film that appeared on the screen showed rescuers digging through rubble from some disaster. The voice-over was saying, "Authorities are estimating the death toll at three hundred but state that it would have been much higher if the epicenter had been closer to Guatemala City."

The woman suddenly had Hank's complete attention.

"The country has a long history of destructive earthquakes," she continued. "In the past five hundred years, more than four thousand significant seismic occurrences have been recorded.

"Guatemala City, the largest capital city in Central America, was virtually destroyed by quakes that struck in 1917 and 1918. More recently, in 1976, one measuring 7.5 on the Richter Scale claimed over 23,000 lives and caused more than two billion dollars' worth of damage.

"In other news..."

Hank switched off the set, his heart hammering.

Obviously, he'd known Guatemala had earthquakes. But he hadn't realized they were anywhere near as frequent or as bad.

And *that* was where Natalie intended to spend the rest of her life? Where she wanted to take Robbie?

He raked his fingers through his hair, telling himself to calm down.

It didn't help. Despite Doris Wagner's advice, he and Natalie *had* to start discussing the future.

HANK HAD GIVEN NATALIE a house key, but when she reached the front door she felt funny about just walking in.

She knocked as she stuck the key into the lock, then called "Hi" from the doorway.

"Hi," Hank called back.

He was sitting in one of the two wing chairs in the living room. The Robert Crais novel that, earlier, had been lying on the coffee table was open on his lap—and his expression was so serious it sent a ripple of uneasiness through her.

"Is Robbie okay?" she said.

"Fine. He's already asleep."

"But there's *something* wrong."

Hank nodded. "There was an earthquake in Guatemala. I caught part of the coverage on CNN."

"Oh, Lord. How bad?"

She no longer relived her own earthquake nightmare in vivid detail every time she heard about one, but she still got shaky inside. Especially when the quake was in Guatemala.

"They're estimating three hundred dead. Said the number would be a lot higher if the epicenter had been nearer Guatemala City."

"Then it must have been somewhere in that vicinity, which means it was nowhere close to Villa Rosa."

That meant her clinic and the people in the town were all safe. Still, she needed to know more than Hank was telling her.

"I...would you mind if I phone someone back home?" she said. "To get the details. I'll put the call on my card."

"Sure. Go ahead."

A minute or so later, Hank could faintly hear her in the kitchen, talking. He closed his book and sat gazing at nothing, thinking that as soon as she was finished he'd...

Hell, he didn't know whether this was a good or bad time to start in about Robbie with her. But he knew he had to do it. He just couldn't wait any longer.

It was at least ten minutes before she reappeared.

"So?" he said, putting the book aside as she sat down on the couch.

"The epicenter was about forty miles west of the capital, and the quake itself wasn't *too* strong."

"It was strong enough to kill three hundred people," he reminded her.

"I know," she murmured. "And even if it had only been three that would be three too many."

"The news coverage said serious earthquakes are pretty common down there."

"Well...I guess that depends on how you define *serious*. And common."

Hank could feel annoyance verging on anger building inside him.

"I think the figure they mentioned was four thousand *significant* ones in the past five hundred years," he said.

Natalie simply gazed at him. "That's only an average of eight a year," she said after a few seconds. "Spread out over the entire country."

"*Only* an average of eight a year?"

"Hank," she said slowly, "how many are there in California each year?"

"I have no idea, but we're not talking about California."

For the second time in barely an hour, he ordered himself to calm down. Then he said, "Look, seeing that news segment really threw me. The idea of Robbie being in an earthquake-prone country for any length of...

"Natalie, let's cut to the chase. Just how much time do you want with him? Are you thinking he should spend part of each summer there?"

He knew she had way longer than that in mind, but the lower he started the better.

She gave him a sad little shrug. "Before I came here, I was hoping *you'd* be willing to settle for part of each summer. Now, though…I've seen how much you and Robbie love each other. But…''

"Natalie, there's an obvious solution to the problem."

"Which is?"

"Well, it would be a million times easier to work out some sort of sharing agreement if you didn't live in a different country."

"But I do. And—"

"Wait," he said, holding up his hand. "Just listen for a minute. Please."

"All right. I'm listening," she murmured.

"Okay. I know you're happy where you are, doing what you're doing," he began in his most reasonable tone. "But getting licensed to practice in New Jersey or New York wouldn't be a major deal, would it?"

"No, it wouldn't."

"And if you lived somewhere near here, we could—"

"Hank, Guatemala is my *home*."

"It's your *adopted* home."

Even as the words came out, he couldn't believe he'd said them. He'd just implied that an adoptive home wasn't the same as a where-you-were-born one.

Meeting Natalie's gaze, he waited to see what she'd say in response. She had the good grace to say nothing.

He sat quietly, giving her a few more seconds.

When she remained silent, he said, "I just don't understand why you won't even *consider* leaving. I hadn't realized earthquakes were as serious a problem down there as they are, but you did.

"And you were almost killed in one. Your husband *was* killed. Why didn't that make you want to leave and never return?"

She slowly shook her head. "That's like asking why everybody doesn't leave San Francisco or Los Angeles. I guess, when you live in a place that's prone to natural disasters you just come to accept them as part of life. Whether it's earthquakes or hurricanes or tornadoes or whatever.

"Maybe...I think we sort of convince ourselves that nothing awful will ever happen to *us*. Or, in my case, won't happen again."

Giving him another little shrug, she added, "Lightning never strikes the same place twice."

"That's not true. Of either lightning or earthquakes."

"No...you're right. But...do you want me to try to explain exactly why I still live there?"

He nodded.

"Okay," she said slowly. "But I have to start way back."

She paused, then continued. "When I was halfway through med school, my parents died. Friends of theirs had a small plane, and the four of them were flying to South Carolina for a long weekend. The plane crashed and they were all killed."

"I'm sorry."

She nodded. "It was very difficult to cope with. Med students are *always* under a lot of stress and that…well, I think I told you before that I don't have any close relatives, and I just felt completely alone in the world.

"At any rate, I managed to graduate—although hardly at the top of my class. Then I took a position with a hospital in Detroit. Working in Emergency, which turned out to be like working in hell.

"Every night we'd see kids totally wasted on drugs, drunks beaten half to death in brawls, mugging victims sliced up or shot because they hadn't handed over their wallets quickly enough. There was even the occasional street person someone had set on fire for kicks.

"I started to think that half the population of the city didn't put the slightest value on human life—either their own or anyone else's.

"And…I'd gone into medicine because I wanted to help people. But all I was doing was patching them up and sending them back out into the night. That really got to me, made me more and more depressed.

"Then a friend suggested I try something completely different—working in a foreign country, a different culture, and…

"It was the best advice I've ever gotten. Going to Villa Rosa literally gave me a new life. The people there needed me. And they really appreciated what I did for them.

"Then I met Carlos, and… Do you believe in fate, Hank?"

"Maybe sometimes," he said slowly. Things happened and you dealt with them. But he'd never been

much of a philosopher, never spent a lot of time pon-
dering *why* they happened.

"Well, with Carlos and me it seemed as if fate had
brought us together. He was from Spain. I was from
Michigan. The odds on us ever meeting had to be a
zillion to one. Yet there we were, in the same place
at the same time.

"At any rate, once we were married and had Robbie, my life was better than I'd ever imagined it being.
I…naturally, it hasn't been that way since the earthquake. Suddenly I was alone again.

"Only, I wasn't, really. Once I recovered and went
back to Villa Rosa…

"Hank, the people there were so kind to me. Not
only the clinic staff but the entire community. And
they still are. It's…they make me feel as if I'm part
of a big extended family. Make me feel that I *belong*.

"And it's where Robbie was born. Where he'd still
be if that mistake hadn't been made.

"So I want him to get to know the country. To see
there are ways of living that are completely different
from this one. To learn about wildlife and breathe
fresh air and swim in the streams and… "

She slowly shook her head. "I want him to expe-
rience a place where people need me. Where I feel
good about myself. And even though I can see how
my moving to somewhere near here makes perfect
sense to you, I don't ever want to be part of a rat race
again.

"I'm happy where I am, and leaving just isn't
something I could do."

CHAPTER EIGHT

HANK AND TRAVIS TOUCHED base with a few of the other detectives in Manhattan North Homicide, then headed for the parking garage. Tonight, their first order of business was a drive down to Little Italy so they could drop into the bar their suspect in the Lowenstein homicide frequented.

"Vests?" Travis said as they reached his car.

"If you think so."

Hank took off his jacket, trying not to grin as his partner popped the trunk.

While uniformed officers routinely wore Kevlar vests, detectives rarely did. It was just part of the dets' culture—even though they had special-issue ones designed for wearing under sport jackets.

Possibly, they were a little *too* cavalier about not using them. That thought crossed Hank's mind every time he heard about a detective being shot or knifed on the job.

But the prevailing attitude was that vests were a pain, only worth bothering with if you were raiding a place. Or serving a search-and-seizure warrant on a suspect you figured was armed and dangerous.

Travis's attitude had been no different until he'd gotten engaged to Celeste. Now, though, he was much more cautious. And Hank had no doubt who was behind that.

But what the hell, he told himself as he put on his vest, then shrugged back into his jacket. He had Robbie to think about. And Joey Noguchi, known on the street as Joey Nogood, probably *would* be carrying when they caught up with him.

As for dangerous, he'd been in and out of trouble for years. Most recently, until three months ago, he'd been a guest of the state, serving a stretch in Sing Sing for armed robbery.

And it wasn't likely he'd done an about-face while out of circulation. Especially not when a couple of witnesses had put a man matching his description in the vicinity of Lowenstein's liquor store two weeks back, the night someone had walked in and shot the man point-blank.

Hank had a gut feeling Joey was their shooter. If he was, arresting him would mean case closed, and it always felt good to put another slimeball away.

However, step one was finding him, then interrogating him about his activities on the night in question.

After Travis had driven out of the parking garage, he glanced over and said, "So? Who's looking after Robbie? Natalie?"

"Uh-huh."

"You're going to let her do it until Audrey's back?"

"I guess," Hank said, hoping his partner would leave it at that.

Otherwise, he might end up having to admit that he'd invited Natalie to stay at the house, which he didn't particularly want to do. Travis would figure he was nuts.

But he wasn't, he told himself firmly. Nuts would have been her driving back and forth to the motel all the time.

Still, he'd already realized that having her right there in the house was far from ideal.

His physical attraction to her was part of the problem, of course, although he was handling that— mostly by doing his damnedest to ignore it. But the other part was even trickier to deal with.

The more time he spent with her, the better he got to know her. And the better he got to know her, the—''

"Has she elaborated on her sharing idea yet?" Travis asked.

"Well, we sort of started discussing it before I left tonight, but we really just talked around it."

"Oh?"

He shrugged, then filled Travis in on the earthquake and what Natalie had said about not leaving Guatemala.

After he'd finished, Travis said, "A country prone to earthquakes. As if things weren't bad enough already. But why didn't you come right out and ask how much time she's after?"

"Actually, I did."

"And?"

"She didn't give me an answer. In fact, I got the sense she isn't really sure."

When Travis shot him a curious glance, he added, "I think she originally came here hoping she'd be able to just take Robbie home with her—that I wouldn't really care."

"In other words, she's delusional."

"I said, *hoping*," Hank repeated. "I doubt she actually figured it was likely. But now...now we *both* seem to have accepted that there's just no easy resolution to this."

Travis glanced at him again. "Don't forget what I said last night, huh? Because it still sounds as if she's trying to soften you up. *And* as if she's succeeding. But if you agree to too much..."

"Yeah. I know."

Unfortunately, though, what he knew in his head and was beginning to feel in his heart didn't correlate.

He had to play hardball with Natalie. Otherwise he might end up losing Robbie entirely. Yet every time he saw the way she looked at the boy, something inside began whispering about how much she'd been through. And how much effort she'd put into finding her son.

But he *couldn't* let that get to him. Because Travis was right. If he agreed to too much he'd regret it forever.

They turned onto Mulberry, parked down the block from the Blue Cat Club, then walked back to it and flashed their shields for the gorilla guarding the door.

He grudgingly gestured them in—much to the annoyance of the people waiting on line for admittance.

The air inside was smoky, the room dark and crowded, but they found two empty stools at the bar and ordered a couple of beers.

If they were going by the book, they'd have coffee. In a place like this, though, that would be a dead giveaway they were heat. And if Joey Nogood was here and made them for cops, he'd be out the back door before their eyes had time to adjust to the darkness.

Hank took a swig of beer, then let his gaze begin drifting casually from table to table.

They'd never seen their suspect in person, but his lengthy rap sheet meant there'd been no shortage of mug shots. Unfortunately, none of the customers bore much resemblance to them.

"He's not here," Travis finally said.

"No, but he might show, so how about giving him a few more minutes."

They gave him ten, then Hank said, "Okay, let's head out and try to drop by again later."

"Or there's always tomorrow," Travis said. "It's not as if we have nothing else to do tonight."

"DADDY'S HOME!" Robbie called from the living room.

His announcement sent a rush of relief through Natalie. It was almost ten o'clock and she'd been worrying about why Hank hadn't appeared yet. Worrying that something had happened to him.

She didn't like the fact that she had been. No more than she liked the little buzz of excitement she was feeling. She simply could *not* let herself get caught up by the mere prospect of seeing him again.

Peering into the mirror above the dresser, she ran her brush through her hair one more time—then gave up. It was futile even trying to make herself look as if she hadn't just come in out of a strong wind.

She could hear Hank's footsteps on the porch as she headed from Audrey's bedroom.

By the time she came in sight of the front door, he was opening it and Robbie was bouncing excitedly in the hallway. He was so obviously happy to see Hank that she cringed a little inside.

"Hi, Daddy!"

"Hi, big guy." He swung Robbie up and tucked him under his arm like a human football.

"Everything go all right?" he asked her, while Robbie squealed and struggled for freedom.

"Fine. How about with you?"

"Oh, just another night in the city that never sleeps," he said, setting Robbie back down.

"I'm not usually this late," he added. "We try to avoid being smack in the middle of something at the end of a shift, but it doesn't always work out that way."

She nodded, thinking he looked tired. The little laugh lines at the sides of his eyes were more noticeable than usual.

"We're goin' to the mall," Robbie said. "Me and Natalie."

"If that's all right with you," she quickly added. "I was waiting for you to get home before we left."

"Sure. It's fine. I'll be in bed anyway."

In bed. She tried to force away the picture that conjured up.

Lord, since she'd never seen the man except when he was fully dressed, her imagination must have slipped into high gear. Because she had a clear-as-a-Guatemalan-sky vision of him lying in bed, his broad shoulders naked above the sheet, his dark hair tousled against the pillow and his face sporting the sexiest four-o'clock shadow she'd ever seen.

Sexiest. Sexy. She'd better work on purging those words from her mind. At least in reference to this particular man.

"Natalie has ta buy a bear," Robbie said.

"A bear?" Hank repeated, giving her a weary smile.

"At the toy store," Robbie told him. "But it's not for me. I'd want a truck."

When Hank continued to eye her, clearly curious, she shrugged and said, "It's for Emma Perez. She lost everything in the fire, including her favorite bear."

"Ah." Hank glanced at Robbie's feet. "You'll need your shoes in the mall, so why don't you go find them."

"'Kay."

As he started for his bedroom, Hank focused on Natalie again, saying, "I know it's none of my business, but didn't we agree that Emma and her grandmother weren't the best special project for you?''

"Well...yes. The problem is, I'd already told Cynthia I'd help with them."

"Ah," he said again, his dark gaze holding hers. "On the job, it's sometimes hard to stay emotionally detached. But we make a point of it. I'd assumed doctors operated under the same principle."

"And you're saying I'm not? That I'm getting emotionally involved with Emma? By buying her a stuffed animal?

"Hank, we're talking about a seven-year-old child who's in traction, lying in a bed twenty-four hours a day. With virtually no visitors except for me.

"Yesterday, her grandmother wasn't even there because she was sick. So if I can make her a little happier by giving her a bear, I'm going to. And I hardly think that constitutes getting emotionally involved."

He slowly shrugged. "As I said, it's none of my business."

"Got 'em," Robbie called, scurrying back down the hall with his shoes in his hands.

"Then we'd better get them *on* you," Natalie said.

She knelt down beside him, thankful the shoes hadn't been hard to find. Because if she wanted to buy Emma a bear it *wasn't* any of Hank's business. And she didn't want to discuss it with him.

Especially not when she knew he was right. That she *was* at risk of becoming emotionally involved.

No, it was worse than "at risk," she silently admitted. She'd already become involved. Now she was merely letting herself get more so. Even though she realized she was only asking for heartache.

Hank stood towering over them for a few more seconds, then said, "Well, I'm going to hit the hay. I'll see you two later."

"And have fun," Robbie said.

"Pardon?"

"That's what you say. When Mrs. Chevy takes me to the mall. You say, have fun."

"Do I?"

"Uh-huh."

"Then...have fun."

Natalie fiddled with the second shoe until Hank turned away. Once he had, she grabbed Robbie's little jacket off its peg and helped him into it. Fifteen minutes later, she was taking his hand to walk across the mall's parking lot.

"Know what?" he said as they made their way between a couple of rows of cars.

"What?"

"When Mrs. Chevy brings me here, I have ice cream. If I'm good."

She smiled, recalling the first moment she'd seen him last week. He'd come flying into the house after a trip to the mall, a dried smudge of ice cream on his cheek—and her heart had suddenly been so full she'd thought it would burst.

"Well, we wouldn't want to break with tradition," she said. "So we'll buy the bear, then we'll get some ice cream."

"If I'm good."

"Right. If you're good."

Natalie spotted a chocolate shop as soon as they entered the mall. When she started toward it, Robbie excitedly said, "We're goin' there?"

"Uh-huh. Just for a minute."

Inside the store, she selected three colorfully wrapped chocolate novelties for the other girls in Emma's room and told Robbie he could choose one of the little foil-covered chocolate trucks.

"It's for later, though," she warned. "If you ate it now, you might not have room for the ice cream."

Once she'd paid for the items, they made their way to the toy store and checked out the bears.

"It has to be brown," she explained. "And not really big, yet not really small, either."

There were almost too many to choose from, but she finally decided on a chubby one wearing a cheery red sweater. She had no idea whether "Teddy" had been the kind of bear that wore clothes. However, if Emma didn't like the sweater she could simply take it off.

Robbie carried the bear to the sales desk, where Natalie asked to have it gift-wrapped.

Rocking from one foot to the other, he watched the clerk tape up the paper and tie some ribbon around the box she'd found.

"Was I good?" he asked as the woman finally put the box into a shopping bag.

"You were perfect," Natalie assured him.

When he rewarded her words with a huge grin, the clerk said, "Your son is gorgeous. You should see about getting him into commercials. My daughter did that with my grandson and they're building up quite a college fund.''

''That's something to think about,'' Natalie said, taking the bag and reaching for Robbie's hand once more.

''She thought you were my *mom!*'' he whispered loudly enough that everyone in the store probably heard him.

Natalie's throat suddenly felt tight. She wanted Robbie to know she *was* his mom. So badly it hurt. But she couldn't tell him until Hank agreed the time was right.

HANK HAD SLEPT well past three, which made Natalie late getting to the hospital. And briefly popping in to see Betty again made her even later arriving on Pediatrics.

There was no sign of Cynthia, so she simply stuck her purse into the office she was using and continued along to Emma's room—armed with her shopping bag full of goodies.

Once again, the other three girls had visitors, but Emma didn't. When she saw Natalie in the doorway, her face lit up like sunshine.

Telling herself she hadn't *really* felt a tug on her heartstrings, she gave Emma a wave, then said to the room in general, ''I was shopping this morning, and I started thinking about all of you, so...''

She produced the three chocolate novelties and handed them out—to a chorus of oohs and aahs, followed by thank-yous after parental prompting. Then she stepped over to Emma's bed and switched into Spanish, saying, "Your grandma's still sick?"

Emma nodded, but her gaze didn't leave the shopping bag.

"I got you something special. Something I'm hoping you'll like even more than chocolate."

"More than chocolate?" she repeated.

Her dubious tone started Natalie hoping she hadn't made a mistake. But it was too late if she had, so she took the box from the shopping bag and handed it over.

"Mine's way bigger than theirs," Emma said, eyeing it.

"Uh-huh. Go ahead, open it."

Carefully she slid off the ribbon and undid the paper. When she lifted the lid off the box and saw the bear, her smile told Natalie she definitely *hadn't* made a mistake.

"Oh, he's beautiful," she said, taking him out and gazing at him. "What's his name?"

"I don't know. I asked him, but he wouldn't tell me."

Emma giggled.

"Maybe he'll tell you."

"You think so?"

"I'm not sure. He seems pretty shy. But he might whisper it in your ear."

Emma solemnly put the bear's mouth to her ear. A moment later, she smiled at Natalie. "He *did* tell me. And guess what?"

"What?"

"His name's Teddy."

"Really?"

"Uh-huh. And you know what else he said?"

"No. What?"

"That he thinks he should sleep with me."

"Did he? And is that okay with you?"

"Uh-huh. It's fine."

"Then should we put *him* back in the playroom?" she said, pointing at the pink bear.

"I think we better. 'Cuz I don't think Teddy likes him."

"Okay, I'll take him with me when I go."

"But you're not going yet, are you?" Emma said quickly.

"No, I'd rather stay and talk to you for a while."

"About what?"

"Anything you'd like."

Emma hesitated, then said, "About my mom?"

Natalie's heart skipped an uneasy beat. "Sure," she said, hoping she didn't sound as anxious as she felt. What about her?

"Well, I know why she can't come see me. But I was wondering, why can't she phone me?"

Oh, Lord. Before she could decide what to say, Emma added, "I asked my grandma why not."

"And what did she tell you?"

"She said it was 'cuz there's no phone in her room. But why can't she use a cordless one?"

Natalie could feel her heart hammering now. She

didn't want to lie, but she didn't want to upset Emma, either.

"Emma, I don't know why," she said at last. "Maybe they don't have any cordless phones in her hospital."

"Could you find out?"

"Yes, I probably could."

"And if they do? Then you could get her to phone me?"

"Emma, let me check into it, okay?"

"And by tomorrow you'll know?"

She nodded unhappily. "I'll try to."

TONIGHT, WHEN NATALIE GOT BACK to Hank's, he was engrossed in a baseball game on TV.

She said hello, then wandered down the hall to Robbie's room and just stood watching him sleep—thinking how ironic life could be. Ironic and unfair.

He had two parents who wanted him. And regardless of how she and Hank worked things out, he'd always know they both loved him.

Whereas Emma had a dying mother and a grandmother in no position to care for her. According to Cynthia, Emma would become a ward of the state. Then what?

Cynthia hadn't gone into the specifics of that, but Natalie doubted it was easy to find adoptive parents for a seven-year-old. Which meant Emma could well end up living in a series of foster homes.

Knowing she'd be wise not to dwell on that thought, she kissed Robbie and went to change from her dress into a pair of jeans. Then she headed for the kitchen.

Her insides felt cold. Clammy, almost. But a cup of herbal tea should help.

There was none in the cupboard. There *was* hot chocolate, though.

Chocolate. Comfort food. All right, that might work.

Once she'd taken the container of powder down from the shelf, she went to see if Hank was a hot-chocolate person.

When she asked, he looked a little taken aback.

"I haven't had any for years," he said. "But sure. Why not?"

Instead of continuing to watch his game, as she'd expected, he followed her to the kitchen, leaned against a counter and watched *her* while she measured milk into the saucepan and added the powder.

His presence made her anxious, although she wasn't quite sure why.

Maybe it was because she couldn't stop noticing that his broad shoulders seemed even broader within the confines of the kitchen. And because no matter which way she moved he was always almost within touching distance.

Not that she had any intention of touching him. But it was very disconcerting that his being near had her nerve endings tingling.

The problem, she decided, was that the scene seemed very domestic. And the last thing she wanted to do was to start feeling as if she were playing house with Hank Ballantyne.

After searching for something to say, she settled on, "I stopped by to see Betty again today. She's doing really well."

He nodded. "I phoned the hospital earlier. I'd promised Audrey I'd call her with an update."

"Ah."

As she stirred the hot chocolate, he said, "So how did the bear go over?"

She looked at him again, surprised he'd thought to ask. "Emma really liked it."

He smiled. "Robbie told me it was a very nice bear."

"It is."

"But not as nice as a truck. Not to his way of thinking, at least."

That made her laugh—which, in turn, made her feel a little less anxious.

"Well, I'm sure Emma would rather have it than a truck. She named it Teddy, after the one she lost."

Hank hesitated, as if there was a subject he wasn't entirely sure he should raise. Then he said, "Robbie also told me someone in the mall called you his mother."

Her heart stopped for an instant while she studied his expression, trying to decipher how he felt about that.

"It made me think," he went on at last, "that we're going to have to fill him in sooner or later."

She licked her suddenly dry lips.

"But...Natalie, he'll find it very confusing."

"Yes, I know," she murmured.

"And I want us to be able to explain exactly how it will affect him. So I'd like to sit down with you, right now, and try to figure out just how we're going to divide up our time with him."

CHAPTER NINE

HAD FORCING THE ISSUE been a good idea or not?

Hank didn't know, although he was positive that Doris Wagner wouldn't approve. However, she wasn't the one being driven crazy by the uncertainty.

At any rate, he'd done it, unsettling Natalie so badly in the process that her hands had been trembling when she'd poured the hot chocolate from the saucepan.

She set one of the mugs in front of him, then sat down on the opposite side of the table. In Audrey's place.

That reminded him of the question Audrey had asked him last night. If Robbie wasn't living here all the time…

As he'd told her, he'd be happy to have her stay, regardless. But she might decide she'd prefer to work for a family with full-time children. And if that happened, then when Robbie *was* here…

He wrapped his hands around the mug and told himself to take things one step at a time.

"So," he said, gazing over at Natalie. "The question that didn't get answered last night is just how much time do you want with him?"

He watched her lick her lips, amazed when he realized he was thinking how kissable they looked. He didn't *want* to be thinking that. And how could he be thinking about *anything* except what her answer would be?

She picked up her mug and took a sip, then carefully put it back down. But she couldn't delay answering forever.

"What I would *like*," she said at last, "is to have Robbie living with me full-time. To have him come and visit you when you're on vacation. Or have you come and visit him."

His pulse pounding in his ears, he simply shook his head, afraid that if he opened his mouth he'd yell at her.

"Wait, Hank," she said. "That's what I'd *like*. That's not what I'm suggesting. I know it wouldn't be fair to either of you. He loves you. And you love him. So do I, though, and..."

"This isn't *at all* what I imagined I'd be saying— in the beginning, I mean. But now that I've seen you together..."

She paused for what seemed like an eternity, then said, "How would you feel about six months each?"

For a moment he had trouble believing he'd heard right. She was prepared to settle for half of the time, which was the best he could have realistically hoped for. And that was without *any* negotiating on his part.

But what if she was playing the sort of game Doris had told *him* to play? Starting at what she considered high, because she assumed he'd do his utmost to talk her down.

If that was it, she must not figure most judges would award her as much as six months. So would she actually settle for less?

Looking across the table at her again, he knew he couldn't make himself even try to find out. Not when his instincts were telling him that she really did want to be fair.

And fifty-fifty was probably as good as it got—for them. Yet would it be best for Robbie?

He took a few seconds to consider what he should say and decided on, "Six and six would work short-term. But what about when it's time for Robbie to start school? Then we're talking *ten* months in one place or the other.

"I can't claim to know much about the education system in Guatemala," he added, launching into the argument he'd rehearsed a thousand times in his head. "But I don't imagine it's anywhere near as good as the one here. Plus the teachers would speak Spanish, which he'd still only be learning."

Amazingly, instead of disagreeing, she nodded. "I was thinking that he could live with you from September through February, and with me from March through August. That way, he'd be here for most of the school year. Then I could get his books and an outline of the rest of what he's got to cover. Make sure he learns everything he should.

"It would be home schooling," she added. "And as long as he ended up knowing what the school board says he has to... "

"Yeah, I guess," Hank made himself say.

When she was being so damned reasonable, how could he not? But every time he thought about why she'd lost Robbie in the first place...

"And I guess it's the most logical plan," he finally continued. "Only...Natalie, the thought of his spending six months a year in a country prone to earthquakes scares the hell out of me."

For a long minute she was silent.

He watched her staring at the table, her tangle of silky hair hiding her face. He was aware his heart was beating fast—and aware it wasn't only the discussion that had it racing. Sitting here with her, just the two of them...

As improbable as the timing might be, he was acutely conscious of the chemistry between them. And surely "between them" was right, because how could something that felt so strong possibly be one-sided?

It couldn't. He was almost certain of that. And assuming he was right, then if there was just some way to convince her that leaving Guatemala wouldn't mean the end of the world...

Taking a long, slow breath, he silently admitted that, somewhere along the line, he'd gone beyond merely thinking about her moving back to the U.S. and living *nearby*. Having her here in the house had started him wondering if...

But when it came to the idea of her living anywhere other than in Villa Rosa, she'd made her feelings only too clear.

"You know what scares the hell out of *me?*" she said, finally looking at him once more.

"No. What?"

"Your job."

"What?" This was the first time she'd said a word about that and it took him completely by surprise.

"My father had a younger brother who was a police officer," she said quietly.

Hank felt a cold chill when she used the past tense. It warned him this might well be a story he'd heard a hundred times before.

"My uncle Ted," she continued. "He wasn't married, and while I was a kid he was always dropping by the house.

"Sometimes, when he did, he'd take me on a 'date' and we'd go to a movie. I absolutely adored him.

"At any rate, he wanted to treat me to lunch for my sixteenth birthday. He made reservations at a really good restaurant, and was supposed to pick me up at noon.

"But he didn't."

Here it comes, Hank thought.

"It turned out he'd walked into a bank that morning, off duty, and discovered some guy in the process of robbing it. He intervened and...ended up dead."

Images of the cops *he'd* known who'd ended up dead formed in his head. Most of them had had families. Wives and children. Parents. Brothers and sisters. Nieces and nephews.

"I'm sorry," he murmured.

Natalie merely nodded. "After I'd read Rodger

Spicer's report and knew you were a homicide detective, I couldn't stop thinking—what if I hadn't found Robbie and you'd been killed? With your wife out of the picture, what would have happened to him?"

"I have no intention of getting killed."

"Neither did my uncle," she said softly.

"Maybe, because of him," she continued, "I have the sense that police work is even more dangerous than it actually is. But when you were late coming home this morning I couldn't help worrying. Imagining all sorts of awful things that might have happened.

"And after I leave, whenever Robbie's here, in the back of my mind I'll be afraid that one day you won't come home. That he'll have to go through the pain of losing you."

She gave a little shrug, then added, "You can't really know what it's like to lose a parent. Yours are both still alive. Living in Chicago. It's mentioned in the report."

"Uh-huh. But my father had a heart attack last year and at first we were afraid..."

"Well, that would have given you some idea. It's just awful at any age. And when you're only a child..."

"Natalie, there are a thousand different ways a child can lose a parent. But...what can I say? Being a detective is what I do."

"I know. And being a doctor in Guatemala is what I do."

"No." He shook his head. "That just isn't a valid

comparison. The risk here, what little risk there is, is to me. Not to Robbie. While he's there, though—''

''While he's *here*,'' she interrupted, ''he could go to school one day and be shot by a kid in his class. Hank, there are never any guarantees in life. You know that. And I'm not prepared to settle for any less than six months. Not right now.

''When he's older, after he's lived in both places...well, if he isn't happy with the arrangement, then we'll have to reconsider it. But right now, unless you have a better suggestion...''

''I don't,'' he admitted.

''Then where do we go from here?'' she said quietly.

''I guess we have to explain things to him. Tell him you're his mother and give him a while to get used to that before we do anything else.

''And when we reach the point of him going down there...well, I don't think you should just take him away with you. Because no matter how hard we try to make him understand everything, he won't. Not really.

''So I'll arrange for some time off, and either go down with the two of you or bring him on my own. Either way, I'll stay a week or so until he gets used to a routine there.''

''That would be very good of you,'' she murmured.

''Okay, then,'' he made himself say. ''We'll talk to him after I get up tomorrow.''

Natalie began gnawing on her lower lip.

''What?'' he said.

"Could we leave it until the evening? Or maybe give it one more day?"

"Sure. But why?"

"I have an appointment with someone tomorrow. At eleven. I can take Robbie with me and we'll be back before you get up, but it might not be the best time for me to talk to him about this."

"Oh?"

She clearly didn't want to give him any more details. He outwaited her.

"I'm going to St. Aidan's Hospital," she said at last. "That's where Emma's mother is."

"Oh?" he repeated.

Then he let the silence grow once more, until she added, "There's a baby-sitting service for visitors. A supervised playroom. So, as I said, taking Robbie won't be any problem."

"And you're going because...?"

She hesitated again. "Because," she finally said, "Emma asked me why her mother can't phone her. And...I promised I'd find out and tell her tomorrow.

"But hospitals have to be careful about the kind of patient information they give out over the phone. I mean, anyone could call claiming to be a doctor and...

"The point is, I want to be sure I know *exactly* where things stand before I try to..."

She shrugged, then added, "I don't expect the news will be good. And if I have to tell Emma... Well, I'm probably only up to one emotion-laden explanation a day."

TONIGHT, THEY'D WAITED until almost closing time to check out the Blue Cat.

Once again, Travis had suggested they wear their vests, which was fine with Hank—although it made him decide his partner seriously figured Joey Nogood would try something stupid when they finally caught up with him.

It turned out they'd have to wait a little longer to know for sure, though. There wasn't any sign of the guy.

"I'm already getting tired of this place," Hank said when the door closed behind them.

"Yeah. Me, too," Travis agreed.

But unless one of their informants came through and they learned where Joey was living, all they could do was keep trying the club.

As they walked back to where Travis had parked, he made a comment that Hank didn't catch. Then he said, "You still conscious in there?"

"Uh-huh. Just thinking about something."

"Robbie?"

"Yeah."

After he'd told Travis that he and Natalie had agreed to six months each, they'd let the subject drop. Travis had had the brains to realize Hank didn't really feel like an in-depth discussion.

But even though they hadn't been talking, he'd been unable to stop himself from thinking. And that had left him on autopilot, which was a good way for a cop to land in trouble.

Despite knowing that, though, when he wasn't

wondering how he could make Robbie understand why he'd be living with Natalie half the time, he'd been contemplating the situation she was involved with at the hospital.

It was hard to fathom why she'd let herself get in so deep, emotionally speaking, with the Perez family.

Yet she had—and he wished that wasn't the case. He didn't like to see people he cared about making mistakes.

He mentally shook his head as that thought formed.

At the start of this, if anyone had tried to tell him he'd end up caring for her he'd have laughed out loud. But, like it or not, that was how things had turned out.

And like it or not, she'd soon have Robbie in Guatemala with her.

He and Travis reached the car, then headed for Manhattan North. A ton of paperwork was waiting there for them, easily enough to take them through the rest of the shift.

Once they reached the squad room, he did his best to concentrate on what he was doing. It was tough, though, because he was back to feeling the same way he had the other day. As if he'd been driving nails into his own damn coffin.

He'd told Natalie they had to continue taking things one step at a time. Let Robbie get used to the idea that she was his mother before they said anything about his living with her part-time.

But all the while they were going slowly, she'd be right there under his roof with him—undoubtedly driving him crazier and crazier with her oh-so-kissable-looking lips and the cute little dimple that appeared beside her mouth when she smiled.

And then there was his offer to fly down to Guatemala with Robbie.

He had to do it, of course. Had to make sure Robbie was convinced that his staying there was okay with his dad.

It didn't take a child psychologist to know that sending a three-year-old off to spend six months in a strange country, with nothing more than a goodbye kiss at the airport, would simply be too much emotional upheaval.

Still, realizing it was the only way to go and being happy about it were two different things. He'd feel as if he were hand-delivering Robbie to the enemy.

Not that Natalie was *actually* the enemy.

He closed his eyes, and before he realized what was happening he'd started to wonder just *exactly* how she felt about him. Because there was *something* on her side of the equation. He was virtually certain of it.

She'd told him that when he'd been late getting home yesterday she'd been worried. Imagining all sorts of awful things had happened to him.

Of course, given the story about her uncle Ted, she *would* think the worst. But she'd definitely used the word *worried*. And why would she worry unless she cared? At least a bit.

So if they just gave their "relationship"—for lack of a better word—enough time to see how it developed…

But in his mind's eye he was picturing grains of sand spilling through an hourglass. And there were already far more of them in the lower half than in the top.

ROBBIE SENT yet another toy truck rolling down the ramp of his miniature parking garage, then looked over to where Natalie was sitting on the couch and said, "Can we go there again?"

"You mean to the hospital?"

He nodded.

"No, I don't think we will, honey."

"How come?"

"Oh...because I only had to go once."

That had been enough to learn what she'd needed to know. At this point, there wasn't even the slightest doubt that Emma's mother was going to die. And it would happen soon.

She swallowed hard. Robbie had enjoyed their outing, had made instant friends with another little boy in the playroom. But she'd come home feeling as if someone had put a rope around her neck and was gradually tightening it.

She could almost hear Emma asking whether her mother would be phoning—and she'd do it the minute Natalie walked into her room.

But how should she answer?

If she told the little girl that her mother was too sick to call right now, the next question would be about how soon she'd be well enough. Lord, Emma might even come right out and ask if she was going to die.

As Cynthia had said that very first day, seven-year-olds are worriers at the best of times.

"Let's go out," Robbie suggested. "For a walk in the woods."

"Out back, you mean?"

When he nodded, she made a mental note to ask Hank if that was allowed. Whoever owned the land might not like trespassers.

"Can we, Natalie?"

Glancing at her watch, she said, "It's almost time for your dad to get up. And if we're not here when he does, he'll wonder where we are."

"Write it down. Like Mrs. Chevy does."

"Well…I have to leave as soon as he's awake. And if we were outside I wouldn't know when that is. But I'm sure *he'll* take you out."

After giving her a frown, Robbie wandered across the living room and began taking things off his shelves and spreading them around the floor.

She watched him, her thoughts drifting back to Emma. How did you tell a seven-year-old child she'd never see her mother again? What could you say to make it hurt less?

And what about Señora Perez? What would become of her?

As she was thinking that she had far too many questions and not nearly enough answers, she heard Hank's footsteps in the hall.

He walked into the room still buttoning his shirt—

a green plaid flannel one, the sort that feels wonderfully soft to the touch.

She did her best to ignore the way her fingers began itching to touch it. To touch *him*.

"Hi, Daddy." Robbie gave him a grin.

"Hi, buddy.

"So?" he added, turning to her. "Are things as bad as you expected?"

She nodded. "It's only a matter of time."

"Can we go out, Daddy? For a walk? Natalie said you'd take me."

"Well, then I guess I'd better. Where are your shoes?"

Robbie scrunched up his nose and gave an elaborate shrug.

"Go find them, okay?"

When he started off, Hank sat down beside her. "What will you say to Emma?"

"I don't know," she murmured. "I should try talking to her grandmother again before I say *anything* to her. Maybe, if I do, Señora Perez will offer to explain what's happening."

"You think there's much chance?"

"No. And if she's still sick, she won't even be there to talk to."

"Why don't you phone the unit and check on that. Then at least you'll know what you're facing."

Natalie gazed at him for a moment, wondering why *she* hadn't thought of that.

Because she'd been too busy worrying, she silently answered herself.

"Good idea?" Hank said.

"Yes. I want to know how Cynthia figures I should handle things, anyway."

She picked up the cordless, got Cynthia on the line and quickly explained the situation.

"Señora Perez came in today," Cynthia told her. "She doesn't look very well, but she's here."

"Then do you think I should talk to her first? Have another shot at making her understand her daughter's condition?"

"I'd say it's definitely worth a try."

"All right, then that's what I'll do. But I've got a horrible feeling it won't get me anywhere. The odds are she'll fall apart."

"I've got a horrible feeling you're right," Cynthia agreed. "And…look, Natalie, I'm awfully sorry you're stuck with this."

"Well, there's no one else who speaks Spanish. I mean, it's hardly the sort of thing you can ask someone from another department to take care of for you."

"I know. But I still feel… Are you sure you don't mind too much?"

"No, I'll manage."

"Then…wait, can you hold on a sec? My secretary's saying I have to take a call on the other line."

"Sure.

"I'm on hold," she told Hank, who'd been listening to her side of the conversation with undisguised interest.

He nodded, hesitated a moment, then said, "I wish you didn't have to do this."

She forced a smile. "Me, too. But thanks for not saying you told me so."

"Yeah, well…"

He held her gaze, and even though she knew she'd be smart to look away, she didn't. He seemed so genuinely concerned about her that it made her warm inside.

"Natalie?" Cynthia said, coming back on the line.

"I'm still here."

"I…that call was from St. Aidan's. Emma's mother died half an hour ago."

She could feel a dull ache of sadness seeping through her. "I'll be there soon," she said.

"What?" Hank asked as she clicked off.

"She died."

"Oh, Natalie."

He hesitated for a moment, then wrapped his arm around her and pulled her close.

"You knew it was going to happen," he murmured into her hair.

"I know. But Emma didn't."

Pressing her face against the soft flannel of his shirt, against the hardness of his chest beneath it, she took a deep breath.

Instead of making her feel better, all it did was fill her nose with Hank's scent—and make her *very* aware of being in his arms.

He was warm and solid and smelled the way she liked a man to smell. Not of cologne but of himself. Fresh outdoors tinged with a smoky, big-city edge.

She took another breath, trying, just for a moment,

not to think about how badly she felt for Emma and her grandmother.

Then Hank tentatively began to stroke her hair and her sadness for them became tinged with a sense of her own losses. Losses of people and of time.

It had been forever since a man had tried to comfort her like this. And she hadn't realized just how very much she'd missed the sense of being...

Cared for. Those were the words she chose to finish the thought, rejecting the first one that came to mind.

Loved. It forced its way back into her head, but only as a quiet echo. So quiet she could scarcely hear it.

Still, she wished she couldn't hear it at all.

If she ever fell in love again, it would be with someone who lived in Guatemala. Not with a New York City homicide detective. Not in a million years.

At Uncle Ted's funeral, she'd sworn that she'd *never* let herself fall in love with a cop. As she'd told Hank last night, she'd absolutely adored her uncle, so his death had hit her hard.

He'd been the first person she'd loved who'd died, and the fact that he was killed because...

If he hadn't been a police officer, hadn't intervened in that robbery... But he had. And his death had convinced her that she should *never* become romantically involved with any man who routinely danced with danger.

Never ever.

Those words kept repeating themselves in her mind until Hank said, "You okay?"

"I think so," she whispered.

She forced herself to ease out of his embrace—which left her feeling strangely empty.

"Daddy?"

Her gaze flashed to the doorway, where Robbie stood with his shoes in his hands and a puzzled expression on his face.

CHAPTER TEN

HANK DIDN'T HAVE A CLUE how long Robbie had been standing watching. Or how he'd have read what he'd just seen. It was the first time he'd ever discovered his father holding a woman.

Oh, not that Hank had turned into a complete monk after Jane left. But dating hadn't been a priority. When you had a high-pressure job, plus a young child, there wasn't much time for other things. And he'd never brought anyone he *had* gone out with to the house.

"Natalie was feeling sad," he said by way of explanation.

Robbie eyed the two of them for another moment. "How come?"

"Oh, just something to do with a patient at the hospital."

"Where she took me?"

"No, the one I've been working at in the afternoons," Natalie told him.

Hank looked at her as she spoke. Her face was flushed, which made him wonder if she felt guilty. Or embarrassed.

"I found my shoes."

"Right, I can see that," he said. "But how about

if we go for a ride instead of a walk? We'll drive Natalie to work.''

"Thanks, but you don't need to," she said quickly. "I'll be fine."

He shrugged. "It's no big deal. And you might not be feeling too great by the time you're finished. You can call me when you are and we'll come get you."

"Hank, really, I—"

"Let's just do it that way, all right?"

"Well...all right."

She gave him a mere ghost of a smile; it made him glad he'd insisted.

"I'll be ready in a couple of minutes," she said.

While she headed out of the room, Robbie brought his shoes over for help with putting them on.

Hank knelt beside him, trying to convince himself that the sultry scent of Natalie's perfume couldn't *really* have left him light-headed. No more than the lingering trace of her body heat could be making his blood run hot.

There'd been nothing remotely sexual about what he'd done. He'd merely tried to comfort her. Yet the moment he'd taken her in his arms he'd felt desire...arousal...longing.

"Oh, man," he whispered to himself. "Man, oh, man, are you in trouble."

Having her living with him while they followed the rest of their "taking things slowly" plan would be even tougher than he'd realized.

But he'd be damned if he'd make the slightest

move that *was* sexual. Because he was absolutely certain there'd be nothing casual about sex with Natalie.

It would only turn the heat up. Turn it *way* up. Which would add another complication to what he was feeling for her—and that was already more than complicated enough.

Hell, if he wasn't careful he might even find himself...

Uh-uh. No way. He'd do whatever was necessary to keep from falling in love with a woman who lived as far away as Guatemala.

WHEN HANK STOPPED outside the front entrance of Madison Plains, Natalie had to fight the temptation to ask if he'd drive her straight back to the house.

A sense of dread had her tightly in its grasp—and she wasn't even on the unit yet, let alone doing what she had to do.

"Is this the hospital?" Robbie asked from his booster seat in the back.

"Yes," she said, turning and giving him the best smile she could muster. Then she looked at Hank and said, "Thanks for the ride. I'll call you later."

As she started to unfasten her seat belt, he reached across and covered her hand with his.

"Take it easy, huh?" he said quietly.

"I'll do my best."

She tried to smile again, but had the distinct feeling it must look more like a grimace.

He let his hand linger for another few seconds, then took it away.

Hers felt suddenly cold.

"Bye, Natalie," Robbie said as she opened her door.

"Bye, honey. You have some fun with your dad while I'm gone, okay?"

"'Kay."

She made herself get out of the Blazer and close the door. Then she gave them a wave and began forcing one foot in front of the other.

This time, she didn't stop by to see Betty before going to Pediatrics. Making cheery chitchat would just take too much out of her.

On her way up the stairs, she reminded herself that delivering bad news was simply something that went with being a doctor. But it was one of the tasks she'd always found very difficult. And when it came to Emma...

First things first, though, which in this case meant breaking the news to Señora Perez. And if she really lucked out, the woman wouldn't be too upset to tell Emma herself.

But as she'd said to Hank, she doubted there was any real chance of that. She was undoubtedly on the hook for both of them.

When she stuck her head into Cynthia's office, Cynthia gave her a sympathetic glance, then said, "You've got yourself psyched up?"

"I've been trying."

"Well...good luck. Oh, and last I saw, Señora Perez was having coffee in the visitors' lounge."

Hoping she'd still be there, which would avoid

having to fetch her from Emma's room, Natalie hurried down the hall—and there she was.

"Doctora Lawson," she said, smiling wanly.

"Señora Perez. Just who I was looking for," she continued in Spanish. "I wonder if we could talk in my office for a few minutes."

As soon as she said that, the older woman's expression turned anxious. But she didn't utter another word. She merely followed Natalie back along the hallway.

She closed her office door behind them, gestured that Señora Perez should sit in one of the visitors' chairs and sat down on the one beside it.

After taking a deep breath, she said, "Señora Perez, I'm afraid I have some bad news."

The woman waited, not taking her gaze from Natalie's face.

She ordered herself to go on. "I'm sorry, but your daughter has died. It happened about an hour ago."

Señora Perez's bottom lip began to tremble, she crossed herself, then tears were streaming down her face.

Natalie scootched her chair closer and wrapped her arm around the woman's shoulder.

She buried her face in her hands and sobbed so hard and for so long that Natalie started thinking they'd have to give her something to calm her down.

Finally, though, she regained a modicum of control and reached for the box of tissues Natalie offered.

After blowing her nose, she said, "*¿Que va pasarnos a nosotros?*"

Her voice was quavering so badly that her words were hard to make out. Not impossible, though. She'd asked, *What will become of us?*

The question made Natalie wish she were better prepared to answer it.

Both Señora Perez and Emma must qualify for some sort of social assistance, but she knew nothing about the New Jersey system. And as Cynthia had said the first day, there'd been no point in even beginning to try making any long-term arrangements until they knew for certain whether Emma's mother would live or die. Now, though—

"There isn't any money," Señora Perez continued. "Only my daughter had a job. And… How will I look after Emma?"

"There'll be help available," Natalie said as evenly as she could. "I'm not sure exactly what kind, but I'll find out for you."

But when it came to how Señora Perez would look after Emma…

She gazed at the floor, recalling once again what Cynthia had said. Since her grandmother was in no position to care for Emma, she'd become a ward of the state.

However, this was *not* the time to get into that.

"Señora Perez," she said softly. "What about Emma right now? She'll already be wondering why you haven't come back to her room. And she'll see that you've been crying. Do you feel up to talking to her?"

Fresh tears appeared. *"No puedo. No ahorita."*

"I understand," Natalie murmured.

It was hardly surprising that the woman needed time to pull herself together, but Emma *would* be wondering what was going on. And with her grand-mother so very upset... As much as Natalie didn't want to be the one to tell her...

She was in the process of convincing herself that she had to at least offer to do it when Señora Perez focused on her again.

"Would *you* talk to her?" she asked between sobs. "Explain? And I'll come as soon as I can stop crying. And I'll stay the night with her. If that's okay."

"Yes, of course it is. I'll arrange to have a cot brought into her room."

A HEAVY HEART.

The phrase might be a cliché, but it perfectly de-scribed the way Natalie's heart felt as she paused out-side the doorway to Emma's room.

Since the little girl was in traction, there was no way of handling this with much privacy. So thank heavens they could converse in Spanish.

She forced herself to walk into the room and say hello to the other patients before heading over to Emma's bed.

The smile Emma flashed made her wish she could turn around and walk right back out. And for some reason, it made her feel even worse that the little girl had Teddy tucked so carefully under the sheet beside her.

Lord, she already knew she wasn't going to get

through this anywhere nearly as professionally as she should.

When she pulled the curtain around the bed, Emma said, "Why are you doing that?"

"Oh...just because."

"You're not gonna give me a needle, are you?"

"No," she said, wishing with all her might she'd come for something so trivial.

"Do you know my grandma's better, Dr. Lawson? Well, mostly better?"

"Uh-huh. I was just talking to her," she said, switching into Spanish and pulling a chair up as close as she could get it.

"*¿Y has recordado a averiguar sí mi mama puede llamarme?*"

And had she remembered to find out if Emma's mother could phone her? Natalie swallowed hard. There was no delaying any longer.

She rested her hand on Emma's arm and collected her courage. Then, sticking with Spanish, she said, "Emma, I have to tell you something that will make you very sad. Your mother died a little while ago."

For a few seconds Emma merely stared at her, as if she didn't understand, then her face crumpled and she dissolved into tears.

"I'm so, so sorry," Natalie murmured, moving onto the edge of the bed and putting her arms around the little girl.

Emma wrapped hers around Natalie's neck and clung to her as she cried.

Stroking Emma's hair, Natalie held her close, aware there were tears trickling down her own face.

While Emma sobbed and sobbed, Natalie murmured every consoling thing she could think of—knowing that nothing would really help.

Finally, Emma's crying grew less tortured and the shudders racking her little body became weaker. Eventually she let go of Natalie and wiped her face.

She was such a picture of misery that merely looking at her brought fresh tears to Natalie's eyes.

"Here," she said, digging some tissues from her pocket. "Blow."

Emma blew her nose about a dozen times, then said, "Why did she have to die?"

Natalie took the girl's little hands in hers and quietly said, "She got too badly hurt in the fire, Emma. The doctors did everything they could, but she was just too badly hurt."

When more tears spilled down Emma's cheeks, she eased one of her hands from Natalie's to wipe them away—but continued to hold on tightly with the other.

"Did you tell my grandma?"

"Yes."

"Where is she?"

"In my office. She feels terribly sad, just like you, but she'll be here soon."

"Did she cry?"

"Yes."

Emma was silent for a long minute. "Now I don't

have a father *or* a mother,'' she whispered at last. *"Solo mi abuelita."* Only my grandma.

"Oh, darling," Natalie murmured, brushing a strand of hair back from Emma's face. "Oh, darling, I know how awful this is."

"But my grandma will take care of me. Won't she?" Emma gazed straight into Natalie's eyes, as if she was certain she'd find the truth there.

Natalie cringed inside. "Emma, you're going to be just fine. By the time you get out of the hospital there'll be a place for you to live and—"

"Will it be our old apartment?"

"I don't know, darling. But I *do* know there'll be a place."

"Are you *sure?*"

"Yes."

"You promise?"

Just as she said "I promise" the privacy curtain opened partway.

"Abuelita!" Emma cried.

"Nietecita!" Señora Perez stepped forward, her arms outstretched.

Natalie moved away from the bed and for a moment simply stood watching them embrace—both of them in tears.

She'd have to talk to the head nurse about keeping a special eye on Emma tonight. And on Señora Perez, for that matter.

After a few more seconds, she quietly pulled the curtain fully closed again and walked across the room, managing to make it into the hall before her own tears began to flow once more.

"SECOND OFFICE on the left," the nurse told Hank.

"Thanks."

He strode the few yards down the hall and stopped outside the open door.

Natalie was sitting at her desk, looking desperately unhappy and totally drained.

It wasn't tough to imagine how she felt. One of the worst parts of *his* job was having to tell people that a person they'd loved was dead.

Dammit, he'd *known* this would be rough on her. But there hadn't been a thing he could do about it.

Except what he'd done. Come straight back so she wouldn't have to wait around for him.

Just as he was about to say something, she noticed him standing there.

Looking puzzled, she said, "Wasn't I supposed to call you?"

He shrugged. "How bad was it?"

"Pretty bad."

When she left it at that, he said, "After we dropped you off, I started thinking you might end up wanting some quiet time. Without Robbie jabbering away, I mean. So while I was driving home I phoned Mary Gerard—the mother of his friend Gary.

"They live just down the road, and she's forever dropping Gary off to play at the house, so I figured she owes me. Well, actually, it's Audrey she owes, but…

"At any rate, I left Robbie at her place and came back here. I've been visiting Betty for the past half hour."

"They let you into ICU?"

"Uh-uh. She's doing so well they've moved her out of Intensive Care. And her daughter was there, so I got a full update. The daughter's arranging for twenty-four-hour private nursing, and barring the unexpected she'll be able to go home in only a day or two."

"That's great," Natalie said with a small smile.

He nodded. "But getting back to Robbie, Mary's keeping him until after dinner. So if you feel like going someplace for coffee we've got lots of time.

"You *are* finished here, aren't you?" he asked, suddenly wondering if this had been a bad idea.

Maybe she'd intended to leave calling him for a while. Maybe she'd have preferred to be alone right now.

"Yes, I'm finished," she said.

Good. Then he *hadn't* made a mistake.

"It's just that Cynthia's in a meeting, and I was thinking I should let her know how things went before I left. But that can wait till tomorrow."

She locked her office and they headed out of the hospital. Hank waited until they'd reached the Blazer before suggesting coffee again.

"If it doesn't matter to you," she said as he started the engine, "I'd just as soon go home and have some there. I think sitting out back and staring at the trees is about all I'm good for."

He nodded, the phrase "go home" lodging in his mind.

Oh, he knew she didn't actually consider his house her home, yet the words had started him thinking, once more, that if she'd only...

But he knew her feelings about where "home" was, and there was no point in contemplating a possibility that would never develop into anything concrete.

Given that, and since she clearly didn't feel like talking, he spent the remainder of the drive with his thoughts focused on a case that was giving him and Travis headaches.

There were some loose ends they had to tie up before they could arrest their perp, and neither of them had any brilliant ideas about how they were going to do it.

"Hank?" Natalie said as he turned into the drive.

"Uh-huh?"

"Thanks for insisting on playing chauffeur. You were right about how I'd be feeling."

"Of course I was. I'm psychic. Haven't you realized that by now?"

He smiled; she sort of smiled back.

"If you want to change out of your dress," he said, cutting the engine, "I'll put the coffee on."

"Hey, you *are* psychic. It's much better to sit and stare at the trees in jeans."

This time, she managed a smile so much closer to normal that the cute little dimple appeared beside her **mouth.**

He eyed it for a second, thinking thoughts he knew he should *not* be thinking. Then he forced his gaze from her and opened the truck's door.

NATALIE SIPPED a little more of her coffee, still wondering if she should have stayed at the hospital longer.

When she'd told Hank that she'd been waiting to talk to Cynthia, that had been only half the truth. She'd also been trying to decide whether to go back to Emma's room for a while.

On the one hand, she'd realized it was a bad idea from *her* perspective, knew she'd *already* let herself get too emotionally involved for her own good.

But on the other hand, she'd been worried that both Emma and Señora Perez were so upset it might be better if they had someone with them.

However, Hank's arrival had made her decision for her. If she'd told *him* she was considering spending the evening holding their hands...

She glanced at him, remembering how, in the very beginning, he'd warned her that agreeing to make the Perezes her special project was a mistake.

He'd been right, of course. The same as he'd been right about how badly she'd be feeling after telling them Emma's mother had died.

She simply hadn't managed to remain professionally detached, and now she felt utterly overwhelmed by their situation—just didn't know what she was going to do to help them. What she *could* do to help them.

Absently she pushed her hair back from her face,

telling herself that tomorrow she'd discuss it with Cynthia.

"Feeling restless?" Hank said.

She forced a smile. "Playing psychic again?"

He laughed a deep, quiet laugh that touched something inside her.

She wished with all her heart it hadn't, but wishing didn't make things so.

Somehow, her feelings for Hank had grown so strong that her heart beat faster every time she saw him. It was the last thing she'd wanted to happen, and probably the worst part was that there was far more to it than a mere physical attraction.

Oh, not that his dark good looks *didn't* affect her physically. When he was around, she could hardly keep her eyes off him.

But what had initially drawn her to him was his quiet manner, his sense of humor, the way he was with Robbie...the way he was with her.

When she'd shown up at his door he could have slammed it in her face. He hadn't, though. Instead, he was being as fair as he could be, as considerate as...

Lord, despite herself she'd fallen half in love with the man. And now...

Now it was going to hurt something fierce when she left.

But since sitting here contemplating that would do nothing to improve her mental state, she gestured toward the split-rail fence—with the woods stretching beyond it—and said, "Is that private property or could we take a walk?"

"It's a nature preserve. Robbie and I wander around in it all the time. I'm surprised he hasn't dragged you down there," he added, pushing himself out of his chair.

"Actually, he tried to this morning," she said, following Hank off the patio and letting her gaze drift from his broad shoulders to his jeans. There was something so very sexy about the way he moved that watching him was...

An incredibly unwise move, she told herself firmly.

They reached the fence, ducked between the two rails and started off into the trees. The woods quickly enveloped them, the air cooler here than by the house and heavy with the fresh smell of rich earth and spring growth.

After they'd walked a hundred yards or so, Hank said, "Do you feel up to talking to Robbie tonight, before he goes to bed? Or would you rather leave it till tomorrow?"

Her pulse skipped a beat. As much as she'd been wanting to tell him she was his mother, she wasn't sure she *did* feel up to it. Aside from everything else, the prospect made her very nervous.

What if he got upset? What if he didn't want her for a mother? What if...

Forcing away a dozen more "what ifs" she said, "It's going to be tricky, whenever we do it, isn't it. Considering you told him his mother was dead...

"I didn't intend that as a criticism," she added quickly, "but..."

Hank stopped walking and turned to face her. "I

explained why, didn't I? Because as far as I knew you *were* dead. And my ex-wife...well, when she left she said Robbie was all mine. That she wasn't interested in being part of his life.''

She nodded, wondering once again how a woman could adopt a baby, then just walk away from him. For that matter, how could a woman walk away from a man like Hank?

Before she'd even thought about whether she should just keep quiet or not, she was saying, ''Hank, can I ask what happened? I mean, I know what was in Rodger Spicer's report, but it really didn't tell me *why* your marriage broke up. Or is that totally none of my business?''

He eyed her for a few seconds, then shrugged and slowly said, ''My ex-wife, Jane, is the sort of person who's never entirely happy.

''I don't mean I figure it was all her fault that things didn't work out between us. Cops have a high divorce rate. The shift work and the stress of the job don't make for ideal husband material.

''But Jane...take the reason I live here, for example,'' he said, gesturing back in the direction of the now-invisible house.

''When we were first married we had an apartment in Brooklyn. She wanted a house, though. On a good-sized piece of property. So we bought here and I started commuting.

''Two months later, she was complaining about feeling isolated. And telling me she didn't like the fact that I was around even less than I'd been before.

Which, of course, was because I was spending so much time driving into the city and back.

"As for Robbie... She'd convinced herself that the problems in our marriage would be solved if we just had a baby. Then we got Robbie, and she discovered he was a lot of work and no solution at all."

Hank shrugged again. "End of story."

"I'm sorry," Natalie murmured.

"Don't be. By the time she left... Well, let's just say she didn't leave me brokenhearted."

"And you stayed here, commute and all."

"Uh-huh. Finding Audrey had a lot to do with that. Plus the house is comfortable. And having this practically outside the back door... It's like our own private forest."

They were silent for a moment, then Hank said, "We got off track."

"Yes, I guess we did."

"The question was, are we going to tell Robbie tonight?"

CHAPTER ELEVEN

STANDING ON THE PORCH beside Hank, Natalie uneasily watched a car turn into the driveway.

She knew it was Mary Gerard bringing Robbie home. And they'd decided that as soon as she left they'd sit down and explain things to him. However, the prospect of doing so had her anxiety level creeping higher by the minute.

She kept telling herself Hank was right. That they might as well get it over with. And that by the time he left for work Robbie would have asked his questions, gotten his answers and be fast asleep.

Still, she just couldn't shake the fear he'd wake up later, when only she was here, and...

But worrying about something that might not happen was a waste of energy. So she did her best to force her concerns away as Mary climbed out of the car—then opened the back door for Robbie and her own little boy.

Gary was a bit bigger and probably, Natalie guessed, the best part of a year older. But given the way they raced off together, as if only the two of them existed in the world, she'd also guess they got along just fine.

When she focused on Mary again, the woman was

heading toward the house, her expression a mixture of friendliness and curiosity.

After Hank introduced them, she said, "Robbie's been talking about you. He told us you're a doctor."

"Right, I am."

"Oh. I thought he must have been confused."

"Don't take that the wrong way," she added quickly. "I just meant it struck me as strange that a doctor would be baby-sitting him."

"It's a long, involved story," Hank said.

Mary glanced at him, then back at Natalie, clearly hoping one of them would elaborate. By then, though, Robbie and Gary were on the porch and Robbie was announcing they'd had hot dogs for dinner.

"And ice cream," Gary added.

"You did, huh? We had liver," Hank lied.

Robbie grimaced; Gary pretended he was throwing up.

The truth was, they'd had pizza, although it might as well have been cardboard for all Natalie had tasted.

"Did you remember to thank Mrs. Gerard?" Hank asked Robbie.

As he nodded emphatically, Hank focused on Mary. "I really appreciate your taking him."

"No problem. Anytime."

There were a few seconds of silence, then Hank said, "I'd ask you in for coffee, but I'm working nights."

"That's all right. I think these two have had enough of each other's company, anyhow. They were being really silly on the way here."

While Mary was speaking, Natalie wondered whether she realized that by "nights" Hank actually meant the shift starting at midnight. If she did, she'd wonder what that had to do with not asking her in for coffee when it was barely seven-thirty.

But she didn't say anything about it—just took her son's hand and said, "Well, we'd better be getting back home. We'll see you again, sweetie," she added to Robbie. "And nice meeting you, Natalie."

"Nice meeting you, too."

When she and Gary reached the bottom of the porch steps, she turned back. "Is Audrey still going to stay out west the full two weeks, Hank? Now that Betty's in the hospital?"

He nodded. "She offered to come back sooner, but I told her no way."

"Ah, well, in that case I might see you again, Natalie."

"I'd like that."

Mary smiled, then she and Gary headed for her car.

Robbie stood waving goodbye until she'd pulled out onto the road. As she began to pick up speed, he said, "Can I watch a video, Daddy?"

"Maybe later," Hank told him. "First, Natalie and I want to talk to you about something."

"What?"

Butterflies in her stomach. The tired phrase flitted through her mind, but it didn't precisely describe the sensation she was feeling. More accurately, there seemed to be gigantic moths beating their wings inside her.

Hank lifted Robbie up, then sat down with him on one of the two Adirondack chairs.

"Natalie?" he added, gesturing toward the other one while Robbie wiggled around, getting comfortable on his knee.

She made herself sit.

"What?" Robbie repeated.

"This is an *important* talk," Hank said. "So I need you to concentrate. And whenever you don't understand something, you stop me right away. Okay?"

He nodded solemnly.

"Good. Now, do you remember, a long time ago, you asked me why you don't have a mother?"

He shook his head.

"Well, you did. And I said it was because she died."

Robbie thought about that for a minute, then nodded.

"Well, I said that because I believed she had. Because that's what I'd been told. But the people who told me were wrong. She isn't dead. You *do* have a mother."

Robbie simply gazed at Hank, his expression uncertain.

"What happened," Hank continued, "was that when you were a tiny baby your mother got hurt. And she had to be in a hospital."

"Like where Natalie works?"

"Uh-huh. Like where Natalie works. And while she was getting better, some people she didn't know were taking care of you for her."

"How come *you* weren't taking care of me?"

"Because I hadn't adopted you yet. It was before you were my son."

"When I was just a *real* little baby."

"Yes. Now I need you to concentrate very hard on this next part, okay?"

"'Kay."

"All right. These people who were looking after you made a big mistake. They mixed you up with another baby—one who *didn't* have a mother. And that was when you came to live with me. So by the time your mother got out of the hospital, and went to get you from the people, you weren't there anymore."

"'Cuz I was here?"

"Exactly."

"But didn't they tell her I was here?"

"No. It was such a big mistake that they didn't know *where* you were. She started looking for you, though. And it took her a long, long time, but she finally found you."

"She did?" Robbie said, his eyes wide.

"Yes, she did," Hank said softly.

He glanced at Natalie then, and she could see what this was costing him emotionally.

She swallowed hard. For three years there'd been just the two of them. Then she'd come along and...

But she had every right. Robbie was her son. She only wished—

Before she could finish that thought, Hank was saying, "Robbie, Natalie is your mother. She came here because she finally learned where you were."

Robbie's glance flickered to her, then he focused on Hank again, his thumb sneaking into his mouth.

Natalie's heart began pounding, and the words she'd thought of to say at this point vanished from her mind.

"Robbie?" she finally said. "Robbie, I loved you so much that I spent three long years searching for you. Trying to find you every way I could."

When he merely buried his head against Hank's chest, her throat grew tight.

"Robbie, there's nothing to be afraid of," Hank murmured. "This is good. It's wonderful, in fact. Now you've got *both* a father and mother to love you."

"I don't *want* a mother," he whispered fiercely. "I want Mrs. Chevy to come home."

"She *will*," Hank said, resting his chin on Robbie's head and cuddling him. "We explained that before she left, remember? She's just going to help take care of her daughter's baby for a little while, then she'll be back with us again."

"Really?" Robbie shifted enough that he could look at Hank's face.

"Yes. Really."

"But where will she sleep?"

"In her room, like always."

"With Natalie?"

"No, Natalie's only using Mrs. Chevalier's room while she's gone."

"Then where will *she* sleep?"

"Natalie, you mean."

He nodded.

"Well, Natalie isn't going to be staying with us much longer. Remember I told you she lives a long, long way from here?"

"Uh-huh."

"Well, she'll be going back there soon."

"When Mrs. Chevy comes home?"

"We're not sure *exactly* when. But soon."

"Then she's not my mother."

"Why do you say that?"

He slowly shrugged.

"Robbie, she *is* your mother. And she loves you very much."

"No! If she loved me she'd live here. With me."

"Look, I realize this is tough to understand. But—"

Robbie pushed hard against Hank's chest and slid off his lap.

"Wait," Hank said, reaching for his arm.

He jerked it away and raced into the house.

"Oh, Lord," Natalie murmured.

"ARE YOU *SURE* YOU DON'T WANT your bedtime story?" Hank asked, tucking Robbie's sheet around him.

"No," he said, still refusing to meet Hank's gaze.

"You mean no, you're not sure, or no, you don't want it?"

Hank smiled; Robbie didn't.

"Don't want it," he said sullenly.

"Then do you want Natalie to come kiss you good-night?"

"No."

Hank rested his hand on the boy's shoulder. "Robbie, I'm really sorry you're so upset. But I think it's mostly because this came as such a big surprise. I was upset at first, too."

At last, Robbie looked at him. "Really?"

"Yes. But then, once I got to know Natalie... You like her, don't you?"

Robbie fiercely shook his head.

"Well, you liked her yesterday. And the day before. You even still liked her when we drove her to work this afternoon."

"I don't now!"

"Well...maybe you will again tomorrow."

"No."

Hank ruffled Robbie's hair, then kissed his forehead.

"You want me to check for monsters under the bed?"

"No."

"In the closet?"

"No."

"All right. But I'll leave the hall light on, okay?" he added, absolutely certain he wouldn't get a "no" to that.

What he got was silence.

"Well...good night, then. And if you wake up later, I'll be here. I'm not going to work."

He never called in sick unless he felt as though he

was dying. Still, he figured there should be exceptions to most rules. And he didn't know whether Robbie or Natalie was in worse shape, but he knew it would be a bad idea to leave them alone together tonight.

After walking out of Robbie's room, he simply stood in the hall, wondering what on earth he should say to Natalie.

Robbie hadn't *really* decided he hated her, of course. He was just confused as hell. And according to that well-worn copy of *Your-Three-Year-Old's-Behavior* confusion led to frustration—which, in turn, led to expressions of anger.

Man, oh, man, that book was sure bang-on in this instance. But how could a little kid be expected to understand a situation like this one? Or accept that his mother loved him, yet was still going back to Guatemala?

From Robbie's perspective, things were black and white. If Natalie intended to leave it meant she didn't even like him, let alone love him. So he sure wasn't going to admit he liked her.

Wearily shaking his head, Hank thought back to the beginning of all this. To when Natalie was "the enemy." To when his fantasy had been that Robbie would reject her and she'd go home.

Things had sure changed. Now he was trying to come up with a way of making her feel better because Robbie *had* rejected her. And when it came to the part about her going home...

Well, he'd done a full one-eighty on that. If there was any way of convincing her *not* to...

Telling himself only idiots kept banging their heads against brick walls, he looked back in at Robbie and discovered he was already asleep.

The emotional upheaval, following on the heels of a few hours hard play with Gary, must have really drained him.

Hank closed the bedroom door, then started for the living room. When he reached it, Natalie was sitting in the gathering darkness.

She glanced at him, so clearly morose that he could almost feel her distress, and said, "How is he?"

"Totally wiped and already dead to the world. I doubt he'll move a muscle until morning."

He realized that didn't answer the question she'd asked, but he needed a minute to ease into this.

"Bummer of a day, huh?" he said, sinking onto the couch beside her without bothering to turn on a light. The darkness seemed fitting, somehow.

"First Emma and her grandmother, then Robbie," he continued. "I guess we should have left telling him until tomorrow."

"Maybe we should have left it forever."

"What?"

"Maybe I should have simply waited until Audrey came back, then gone home. Should have been content with seeing that he's happy and healthy and..."

She paused, making him suspect her throat was too tight to go on, then said, "He hates me, Hank."

"No, he doesn't *hate* you. He—"

"Well, he doesn't want me for a mother. You heard him. He wants Audrey back."

"Natalie, he *didn't* say he doesn't want you for a mother. He just doesn't understand how you can be his mother if you don't live with him. *That's* what he said.

"As for Audrey, she's been around for longer than he can remember. She's like a grandmother to him. And...look, we knew this would take a while. But his reaction's only temporary. He needs time to get used to the idea, that's all."

Shaking her head, she said, "I didn't realize it would be so hard. That he'd feel so threatened. I just..."

"You've just had a hell of a day," he said quietly.

He hesitated for a long moment, telling himself not to do anything stupid. But she was so damned unhappy that he finally put his arm around her and drew her close, saying, "Everything's going to be okay."

"No, it's not," she murmured against his chest. "Robbie won't want to come to Guatemala. And if he does he'll be miserable there without you."

"Natalie..."

He tried to think of what else to say, but couldn't make his mind work right. He was too distracted by her soft warmth against him and the faint, sultry scent of her perfume.

It made him think of a garden filled with exotic flowers, their scent mingling with the scent of her. The scent of woman...of one specific woman whose nearness was filling him with desire.

"Natalie..." he said again.

This time, she eased away a little and gazed at him,

her eyes darker than the night, her lips so lush that just looking at her sent blood rushing to his groin.

"Hank," she whispered, "I don't know what I'm doing."

He wasn't the least bit sure what she meant. Was she talking about Robbie, or about what she was doing right this instant—with him?

But it didn't really matter, because he was beyond resisting any longer.

Assuring himself that one little kiss wouldn't be a major deal for either of them, he brushed her lips with his.

As Hank's kiss turned from tentative and gentle to deep and demanding, Natalie's entire body reacted to it—while her brain went on pause.

Suddenly she wasn't thinking about all the awful things she'd been through today. She was too caught up in the moment.

Her pulse was erratic and her heart had begun to race. Heat rushed through her, settling into a hot ache of longing between her legs.

From somewhere, a voice was warning her that this was anything but wise. She found ignoring it ludicrously easy.

She didn't care what was wise. She only cared about the way she felt in Hank's arms. And about him.

Oh, yes, definitely about him. As hard as she'd tried not to let herself feel *anything* for him, she'd failed miserably. And that was entirely *his* fault.

How could she not have fallen for him, when he was such a terrific man? When he was funny and gorgeous and right this minute was managing to drive her crazy with merely a kiss?

Not that his kiss qualified as "mere." Not by any stretch of the imagination.

Lord, it had been so, so long. And kissing him felt so, so good.

She slid her hand around the back of his neck and drew him closer. His arms felt deliciously strong around her, his chest was rock solid against her breasts and she could feel how fast *his* heart was beating.

"Natalie..." he whispered, his breath hot on her mouth.

She'd never heard him say her name like that before—in a ragged sort of way that made her want him even more.

"Natalie, listen, I know I started this, but you're in pretty rough shape and...I don't want us doing something you'll regret."

"Oh, Hank, after the day I've had, the way you're making me feel is exactly what I need."

He kissed her again, harder and possessively, then moved his hands to her breasts.

His touch sent a wave of desire crashing through her.

"Oh, jeez," he murmured. "If you're going to tell me to stop, tell me now."

"I'm not going to."

He cradled her face in his hands and gazed at her.

In the silence, she could hear the pounding of her heart, could feel it echoing in the throbbing lower down.

''Let's move this to a room with a door,'' he said at last.

His arm tightly around her, they made their way along the hall to his bedroom.

She stood in the darkness, watching him close the door and slide the bolt. Then he turned toward her and gazed at her once more, before finally reaching for her and giving her a lingering kiss that made her positively dizzy.

Or maybe it was the tantalizing way his hands were moving on her breasts that was making her dizzy. The way his thumbs were rhythmically brushing across her nipples—already hard and aching to have his mouth on them.

She slid her own hands down to his hips and pulled them more tightly to hers. His erection, pressing hard against her, took her breath away.

Then his hands were beneath her T-shirt, hot against her skin. Undoing her bra. Reaching down to the zipper of her jeans. Undressing her completely before he stripped off his own clothes and stood naked in the moonlight.

Gazing at him, she couldn't think of anything except that he truly *was* a gorgeous man. And that she wanted him desperately.

His body was all lean muscles and hard longing. Just watching him made the throbbing between her legs almost unbearable.

And when he moved nearer and draped his arms around her waist, pulling her so close their bodies were heat against heat, softness against hardness, desire against desire, she shivered with need.

He took a condom from the bedside table, then drew back the top sheet, eased her onto the bed and snuggled in beside her. Slowly he began caressing his way down her body, his mouth following his hands.

She wrapped her arms around him, a rush of need turning her liquid. She had to have him inside her, but as she tried to silently say that, he told her, ''Not yet,'' and went back to what he'd been doing—driving her to the brink of insanity.

She couldn't stop herself from moaning. Couldn't stop her hips from arching or keep from writhing on the bed like a woman possessed.

And when he slipped his hand between her legs and began caressing her even more intimately, the sweet relief of his touch sent her over the edge in a climax that racked her entire body.

He was inside her then, thrusting as fresh shudders seized her. They made breathing impossible, made her think they'd never end.

She didn't want them to, but if they went on much longer, she knew she'd die.

Hank came, whispering her name, and after that her tremors gradually began to grow weaker.

Eventually her brain began functioning once more—and she realized she was crying.

He lay pressed against her, stroking her hair and

wiping away her tears, finally saying, "Was it that bad?"

"Oh, Hank, no," she murmured. "It was that good."

THEY'D MADE LOVE, off and on, the whole night through. Wonderful, sensual love that had left Natalie more than a little achy—yet so warm and languid she was barely conscious of the fact.

Now, with the first faint light of dawn creeping into the bedroom, she lay in the sheltering circle of Hank's arms, her back snuggled to his chest as she listened to his even breathing.

She kept thinking he'd fallen asleep. But each time she tried to slip out of bed he'd tell her to stay, and she'd cuddle against him once more.

Not that she really *wanted* to go. Just the opposite. She could happily lie here with him forever, the sweet-salty scent of sex on their bodies and the warmth of his breath softly teasing her shoulder.

Sometime before Robbie was likely to wake up, though, she had to head for her own room. Or Audrey's room, as the case might be.

But it had been so long since Carlos had died, so long since she'd lain like this with a man in the afterglow of making love...

Carlos. As his name lingered in her mind, she realized that since she'd been here she hadn't thought about him nearly as often as she usually did.

Breathing slowly, she wondered how much she should read into that.

In the three years since the earthquake, she'd kept his memory locked tightly in her heart, rarely going more than a few hours at a stretch without something reminding her of him. Yet recently...

She closed her eyes, letting her thoughts drift back in time to the day she'd regained consciousness and learned she was in a hospital. To the day she'd been told her husband was dead.

For a while after that she'd almost wanted to die herself. She suspected she might have if it hadn't been for Robbie, if her love for him hadn't made her determined to recover.

Losing Carlos had been truly horrific, and part of her would never stop loving him. But maybe the fact that she was here like this with Hank meant she was finally ready to move on. If she was...

If she was, she wished with all her might that it could be with him. But that wouldn't happen. Even if she could come to terms with the idea of leaving Guatemala, she'd never let herself end up with Hank Ballantyne.

As wonderful as he might be, as strong as her feelings for him had grown, she hadn't forgotten the vow she'd made. She'd *never* let herself fall in love with a cop.

A little bit late on that one, an imaginary voice told her.

She silently admitted it was right. But whether she loved Hank or not, there wasn't a future with him. Not for her. There was just no way she'd marry a man knowing that she'd worry every time he was late getting home.

He nuzzled the back of her neck and kissed her shoulder; she began wishing he'd miraculously tell her that he'd decided to turn in his shield and become just about anything else he could possibly be.

Hank lay motionless beside Natalie for a minute, then kissed her shoulder a second time—still trying to decide whether he should speak up or not.

"Mmm," she murmured.

Smiling to himself, he trailed his hand down her naked body. Her skin was so soft that he absolutely *loved* touching her. And with each breath he took he could smell her exotic-flowers scent—mingled with the smell of sex.

Sex with him.

After deciding he was going to leave these sheets on his bed for eternity, he forced his mind back to where it had been.

Her being with him, like this, put their situation in an entirely different light. To his way of thinking, at least. Now that they'd fallen in love…

That *was* where they were at, wasn't it?

It was definitely where *he* was at. And he felt pretty damned sure that Natalie wasn't a casual-sex sort of woman, so the fact that she was lying here beside him…

Didn't that mean the most logical thing in the world would be for her to stay with him forever? For them to both be with Robbie all the time? For them to be a family?

He ordered his mind to slow down. His feelings for her had developed so fast—not to mention so unexpectedly—that he'd be a downright idiot to say too much too soon. His only sensible course of action was waiting to see if this truly was the real thing.

While he was doing that, though, surely it wouldn't hurt to ease into discussing the idea with her. Would it? If he made it clear he was only talking in terms of a speculative sort of possibility?

But what if he sent up a trial balloon and she shot it down with another of her "Guatemala is my home" responses?

Not a hard one to answer. It would just about kill him. She wouldn't, though. *Would* she?

He really didn't see how she could. Not if she had her priorities straight. And if she loved him even half as much as he loved her.

Of course, she hadn't actually said she loved him at all. Neither of them had come right out and used the *word*. So maybe he should do that right now. Maybe—

"Hank?" she whispered.

"Uh-huh?"

"I'd better go. In case Robbie wakes up early."

"Right," he forced himself to say.

What was wrong with his brain? This wasn't the time to initiate an important discussion.

She shifted around so she was facing him and gave him a kiss that aroused him yet again.

"Can I take a rain check on that?" she said with a sleepy smile.

"You bet."

He watched her scramble into her clothes, then cautiously open the door as if she half expected to find Robbie standing on the other side.

Once she'd disappeared, he drifted into a semi-sleep—vaguely aware of the shower running, followed by the faint sound of her footsteps as she went from the bathroom to Audrey's room.

A few minutes later, he could hear her in the kitchen, starting coffee. After that, she came back down the hall and quietly opened the door to Robbie's room.

And then she took such a sharp breath it was almost louder than a scream.

CHAPTER TWELVE

HANK LEAPED OUT OF BED, grabbed his robe and tugged it on as he raced into the hall.

Natalie was standing, tense and white faced, in Robbie's doorway.

"Hank," she said, her voice barely audible. "He's gone."

"Don't worry," he told her, trying to sound reassuring while his heart pounded in his ears. "He's got to be somewhere in the house."

"No, he doesn't. The back door was unlocked. I noticed when I went into the kitchen, but I thought you must have just forgotten about it last night."

Dread filled his chest. He *never* forgot to lock up. Although, given the events of last night, there was a remote chance he might have.

"Robbie?" he called loudly. "Son, where are you?"

Nothing.

He dropped to the floor and peered under the bed, then checked the closet.

When Robbie didn't burst out with a "Boo!" he said, "Okay, I'll search the basement. You start looking on this floor. Hopefully, he's just hiding."

"And if that's not it?" Natalie asked, her face still pale.

"We'll find him. If he went out he can't have gone far. He's too afraid of the dark to have left before daybreak."

Starting down the hall, he began praying that Robbie actually had just taken off on his own. There was no sign of a forced entry, but that didn't guarantee someone hadn't gotten in and kidnapped him.

Searching the house proved futile, and by the time they'd finished, Hank's expression was grim and Natalie felt utterly terrified.

Robbie was so upset about her being his mother that he'd run away. And if anything awful happened to him...

She'd lost him once. If she lost him again, after barely finding him...

Hank had decided Robbie must have gone into the woods, and she tried not to recall how thick they were. Or to imagine how easily a little boy would lose his bearings in them.

Bearings...bears... Oh, heavens, were there bears in that forest?

Telling herself to think about *anything* other than the fact there likely were, she forced her attention to Hank. He'd already called the Madison police and was now talking to someone with the state highway patrol.

"My property backs onto the Red Creek Nature Preserve," he was saying. "I think he'd have headed in there, but if you'll put out an APB for the whole area?

"Right, a little boy on his own. Or with an adult who might not be his parent.

"Someone could have already found him," he whispered to her.

Then, into the phone, he said, "Uh-huh. I think it's a possibility. But the preserve's got to be way more likely. His mother and I are going to head there now. If we don't find him fast, I'll call back about a full-scale search."

He rattled off his cell phone number so that if anyone else found Robbie they'd hear about it right away, then he grabbed Natalie's hand and they tore out the back door and down to the woods.

"Robbie!" he yelled as they reached the fence.

She held her breath and listened hard, but there was no reply.

"We can't split up," he muttered as they ducked between the rails. "If we did, you'd probably get lost. But you concentrate on the left and I'll concentrate on the right. That way, we can move faster."

They headed deep into the trees, taking turns calling Robbie's name.

After they'd gone a hundred yards or so, Hank stopped and said, "He and I usually come to about here, then turn either left or right."

"Left," she said without conscious thought.

"Mother's intuition?"

"Oh, Hank, I hope so."

They moved as rapidly as possible, their progress impeded by uneven ground and heavy vegetation.

"Robbie!" she shouted once more.

When there was still no response, she could feel panic threatening to overwhelm her.

"He's here someplace," Hank said, reaching for her hand and giving it a squeeze as they walked on. "I just know he is."

She nodded, almost asking about those bears but too frightened of what the answer would be.

"Robbie!" he hollered again.

Then again...and again...until he was sounding hoarse.

Every nerve ending in her body had begun feeling raw before they finally heard a response to Hank's shouts.

"Daddy?"

When she heard Robbie's voice in the distance, the relief that swept her was so strong it practically brought her to her knees.

"He's okay," Hank said, his voice breaking.

"Robbie! Call again so I know where you are."

"I'm here!" he cried.

They quickly made their way forward and found him sitting on a fallen log—a few scratches on his arms and his face stained with tears.

"Robbie," Hank said, sweeping him up. "Are you all right?"

"Uh-huh. But I can't walk anymore. My legs are too tired."

"Son, you *know* you're not allowed to come in here by yourself. Why on earth did you?"

He shrugged.

"You must have had a reason. What was it? Robbie, tell me."

"I was lookin' for Natalie," he said at last.

He'd been looking for *her?* A circle of warmth formed around her heart and began spreading through her entire body. Hank had been right. Her son *didn't* hate her. He'd just found things too confusing.

"Why were you looking for her out here?" Hank demanded.

"'Cuz she wasn't in the house."

"Oh, Lord," she whispered, catching Hank's gaze.

"You mean you looked for her in the house this morning?"

Robbie nodded against his shoulder. "But she wasn't in Mrs. Chevy's room. Or in the kitchen. Or anywhere. So I came to look here. In case she was lost."

"Son, you have to promise *never* to come in here on your own again. Not for *any* reason. If you think someone's lost, you tell *me* about it, okay?"

He nodded once more and said, "'Kay."

"I've got to call off the cavalry," Hank said, digging his cell phone from his pocket. "Would you take him for a minute?" he added, passing Robbie to her.

When he wrapped his arms around her neck, tears began to sting her eyes.

He was safe and sound. And he didn't hate her.

She wouldn't be surprised if she'd be able to float all the way back to the house.

AT FIVE MINUTES PAST NINE, Natalie and Hank were sitting in the kitchen, Natalie talking on the phone with Cynthia Koehler, explaining that she could be at the hospital *anytime* today and asking if they could get together to discuss the Perezes.

"Well, someone from Social Services is coming to see me about them at ten-thirty," Cynthia said. "Apparently, I've ended up as liaison—thanks to Emma's being my patient.

"At any rate, the immediate issue is a service for her mother. Señora Perez is going to need help arranging that. But I'm sure we'll be discussing the long-term picture, as well, so if you'd like to sit in..."

"Definitely. I'll see you in a little while. Bye.

"Cynthia's seeing someone from Social Services at ten-thirty," she explained to Hank as she clicked off. "And I told her—"

"I heard."

He waited a beat, then said, "I'm surprised you're going to let Robbie out of your sight."

She glanced toward the hall, where he was noisily racing two of his trucks.

Thinking it hadn't taken long for his tired legs to recover, she looked at Hank again. "I don't *want* to let him out of my sight. I want to hover over him like the proverbial mother hen.

"But as you said last night, he needs a while to get

used to the idea that I'm his mother. Have you noticed he hasn't said a word about it this morning?"

"Uh-huh."

"He's acting exactly the way he was before. As if we'd never told him."

Hank nodded. "He'll say something sooner or later. It's still not clear in his head yet, so he'll have more questions. But we should let him get around to asking them in his own time."

"Yes. Right. And since his own time could be days, then my going out—"

"Or it could be an hour," Hank interrupted. "And he might have things he'd like to ask you, too."

"I won't be gone that long, and..." Pausing, she shook her head, then added, "Hank, I've got to see this through. I can't simply desert Emma and her grandmother."

He took another sip of his coffee, not saying what she knew was on his mind. That despite his advice and despite her knowing it wasn't smart, she just kept getting in further and further with the two of them.

"Hank, I'm all they've got," she said.

"No, you're *not* all they've got. You're a volunteer. A *temporary* volunteer. And—"

"And they know me. And I speak Spanish. And I *care.* Who else is going to make sure that somebody does right by them?"

"Cynthia will, from the sound of it. Or someone from Social Services. Or from Child Welfare. Hell, I don't know exactly who does what in the system. But they're not going to end up on the street if you aren't involved.''

"I just want to be certain they get enough help. That there's a solid plan in place so neither of them will fall through a crack after Emma's discharged.''

Hank nodded once more, and even though she could tell there was a lot more he was dying to say, he didn't utter another word.

She searched her brain for a way of changing the subject before he decided to pursue it further.

Then he raised his mug to his lips again and she couldn't help thinking that a stranger wandering in would take them for a long-married couple—sitting together at the table over morning coffee, with nothing much to say to each other.

In reality, however, she wasn't feeling the slightest bit like half of a long-married couple. What she was suddenly feeling was absurdly conscious of Hank's maleness.

Yet how could she not be after last night? All she had to do was look at him to recall the pure bliss of their lovemaking.

She could practically feel his hot, hard body against hers. Could almost smell his scent. And if his four-o'clock shadow could talk, she knew it would be calling out for her to reach over and trail her fingers along his jaw.

Firmly she told herself she was not going to do anything remotely like that. She was thinking far straighter at the moment than she'd been last night.

Lord, then she hadn't been thinking at all. And even now, it was difficult to force her eyes from him.

It took a serious effort, but she finally succeeded. And as soon as she did, something reasonable to say popped into her head.

"I assume you're going to work tonight?" she asked, letting herself risk looking at him again.

He gazed at her for a long moment before giving her a slow, sexy smile that started her temperature rising.

"Maybe I should call in sick again," he said.

"I don't think that would be a good idea," she made herself say. "We can't have any repeats of last night."

"What?" His smile vanished. "You aren't serious."

"Trust me," she murmured. "I don't like the thought any more than you do. Last night was... incredible."

The smile reappeared. "Yeah, it was, wasn't it."

He reached across the table, but before he could take her hand in his, she tucked it into her lap and nodded in Robbie's direction.

"Hank, he's confused enough as it is. What if he'd walked in on us when we were...?"

"The bedroom door was locked."

"That *isn't* my point. He needs structure in his life right now. If he comes looking for me again, I have to be where he expects me to be, doing what he expects me to be doing. And so do you."

Hank sat eyeing her for another long moment, then

said, "Let's stop worrying about what Robbie needs for a minute and focus on us. What happened wasn't...it *meant* something to me. Meant a *lot* to me."

He took a deep breath, then added, "Because *you* mean a lot to me."

"Oh, Hank," she whispered.

His words sent a rush of emotion through her, yet she couldn't help wishing he hadn't said them, that he hadn't come right out and...

He had, though. And she just couldn't pretend she didn't feel the same way.

"Hank...you mean a lot to me, as well. If that wasn't true, I'd never have..."

Slowly shaking his head, he said, "Natalie...'mean a lot' wasn't exactly the right phrase. I...this is the last thing I'd ever have believed would happen, but...I've fallen in love with you."

She gazed at him, her heart racing and her thoughts tumbling all over one another. "I've fallen in love with you, too," she murmured.

She was going to regret telling him that. She knew she would before she'd even finished. Yet she doubted she could have stopped herself no matter how hard she'd tried.

A fresh smile appeared on his face. "You know, that's the greatest thing I've heard in my entire life."

But it wasn't! Because it didn't mean what he was reading into it. So she shouldn't have said it, shouldn't have given him the impression that...

She realized he was speaking again and made herself concentrate on his words.

"We're looking at an entirely different picture than we were in the beginning," he was saying. "And I can't help thinking that if we only had more time...

"What about the doctor who's filling in for you? How long is he expecting to be in Villa Rosa?"

"Well, we didn't agree to any specific date, because I couldn't say how much time I'd need here."

"Then you don't have to *rush* back."

"I...I guess not, but—"

"Natalie, just listen for a minute, okay? I realize this is too soon to talk seriously about anything long-term. But if you're down in Guatemala, and I'm up here, there won't be the slightest chance of our *having* a long term.

"If you stayed awhile longer, though, long enough for us to see whether..."

She slowly licked her lips, desperately wanting to say she'd consider the idea. Lord, she desperately wanted to just fall into his arms and hold him forever. But she couldn't.

"Hank...we need a lot more time to talk about this than we have at the moment. I told Cynthia I'd be there soon, so I've got to go and change."

"Right," he said, his tone suddenly uneasy. "Right. We'll pick it up again later."

Forcing a smile, she pushed herself away from the table and headed for Audrey's room, trying not to think about *later*. Because regardless of where she lived, there could never be a long term for them.

And given the way she felt about him, having to explain that was going to be excruciating.

JENNY RENZONI, the caseworker from Social Services, looked as if she should still be in high school. And she definitely needed a course in organizational skills.

That did *not* inspire confidence in Natalie, and she could tell that Cynthia wasn't impressed, either.

"So *you* will help me talk to Señora Perez after we're done here?" Jenny said to Natalie, even though that had already been established. "Make sure that cremation and a service in the chapel at St. Aidan's are acceptable to her?"

"Yes," she said, knowing they'd have to be.

Since Señora Perez had told her there was no money, even if she'd prefer a service in a funeral home and a burial plot, that was out of the question.

"Good," Jenny was saying. "If she agrees, we can probably have the service tomorrow or the day after. And once that's taken care of...

"Señora Perez will need to fill out a welfare application," she continued, shuffling through the papers in her briefcase.

"Hmm, I don't seem to have one with me, but that doesn't really matter. She'll have to go for an interview, anyway, so she can fill it out then."

"Will someone at Welfare speak Spanish?" Cynthia asked.

"Hmm, good question. Probably."

"Why don't you give me the address and phone

number and I'll check for her," Natalie said, knowing that she'd undoubtedly end up taking Señora Perez to the interview either way.

Jenny jotted down the information, then dug out a form and looked it over.

When she'd finished, she said to Cynthia, "According to the initial assessment, Señora Perez isn't capable of assuming responsibility for her granddaughter. Is that how things strike you?"

"From what I've seen and been told, yes. She's clearly not in the best of health, and I think she could have trouble coping day to day—even without a child to care for."

"In that case, there's a subsidized seniors' building that might work for her. Some of the residents speak Spanish, which would give her a support group. Or we have a list of people who rent rooms in their houses.

"As for the child, there aren't any other relatives willing to assume responsibility?"

"Not according to her grandmother."

"Okay, then as far as she goes..."

"Her name is Emma," Natalie said.

"Emma," Jenny repeated as if it was the first she'd heard of the little girl having a name.

"Well, if Emma won't be living with Señora Perez, I won't be her caseworker."

Natalie glanced at Cynthia, and the message "Thank heavens" passed between them.

"What will happen to her?" Natalie said.

"Well, she won't be part of my caseload, so—"

"Yes, but you must know the drill," she interrupted impatiently.

"Well, of course. She'll be assigned a caseworker from Child Welfare."

"And?"

"And she'll be temporarily placed while she's being assessed for adoption."

"Placed where?"

"That depends."

"On?"

Jenny gave Natalie a look that said she didn't have time for these questions.

"On?" she repeated, ignoring the look.

"On whether there's a suitable foster home available," Jenny told her stiffly. "If so, she'll go there. If not, she'll initially be placed in an institution."

"Just a sec," Natalie said as Jenny focused on Cynthia.

"What?" She glanced back at Natalie, not bothering to conceal her annoyance.

"I want to ask about the likelihood of adoption. What are her chances when she's seven?"

"The people at Child Welfare do their best."

"But what are her chances?"

"I really can't say. People generally prefer to adopt infants or toddlers. Still, you never know."

With that, she firmly turned toward to Cynthia. "You said that Señora Perez is just down the hall?"

"Yes. She's in Emma's room."

Jenny glanced at Natalie once more. "Then I guess we'd better go talk to her."

"Not in front of Emma."

"Natalie, why don't you and Jenny take Señora Perez to your office," Cynthia suggested.

"And while you do that, I'll explain to Emma that she won't be living with her grandmother. I don't think Señora Perez should be the one to tell her."

Natalie hesitated, really, really not wanting to offer, but finally saying, "Would you like me to do it?"

She began to breathe a little more easily when Cynthia shook her head and said, "No, you've had to do enough of the dirty work."

WHEN ROBBIE CLIMBED off the couch, Hank breathed a sigh of relief that he'd finally had enough. But it turned out he was only changing positions.

Plopping down onto the floor he said, "Again, Daddy."

Hank reminded himself that according to the book, wanting a lot of repetition was normal. At this point, though, they were already so far beyond "a lot" they were into excessive.

Of course, this was an awfully important subject, so that probably explained why he was still going strong.

"Natalie got hurt and had to be in a hospital," he began once more.

"And some people she didn't know were taking care of me."

"That's right."

By now, Robbie had the story memorized and Hank's throat was sore.

He wished Natalie was here to do some of the retelling, yet he suspected that Robbie had only felt comfortable enough to start in on the topic again because she was gone.

"But if she's my mommy, *why* doesn't she live with me?"

He'd stopped counting the number of times Robbie had asked that one. He'd bet they were past twenty, though.

"She couldn't find you, remember?"

"But now she did."

"Yes, now she's found you. Only…Robbie, I've explained that she lives far away." They were past twenty on that one, too.

"She could move," he muttered.

"Son, this part is really complicated." Hell, the entire thing was really complicated.

He hesitated before going on. He'd like to say there was a chance Natalie *would* move. He couldn't, though.

For a brief moment, when she'd said she loved him, he'd been the happiest man on earth. But then she'd told him that the idea of her staying here longer than she'd been intending needed a lot more discussion—and he'd known they were far from a done deal.

Still, if he loved her and she loved him…and she'd said that last night had been incredible.

Thinking about that again made him smile to himself, because people didn't just walk away from incredible. So, surely, the only problem was that he'd taken her by surprise, and she simply did want to talk some more. Simply needed to convince herself that staying on awhile wouldn't be a mistake.

"Daddy?"

"Uh-huh?"

"If she doesn't live here, then she isn't my mommy."

"No, Robbie, not *all* mommies live with their children," he said, telling himself that since he and Natalie had already agreed to the details of a sharing arrangement, he'd better take that route for the time being. Just in case she *wasn't* thinking the way he figured she should be.

"But maybe after she leaves we could go and visit her," he continued. "Maybe you could even stay with her for a while."

"No. I hafta stay here. With you. And Mrs. Chevy. So Natalie should move."

"Well...that would be really hard for her."

"Why?"

"Because, first of all, she likes living where she is. It's where her friends are, and where she works."

Robbie shook his head. "She works at the hospital. Where we drove her."

"Right now, she does. But that's only temporary. It's not her *real* job. And it would be hard for her to leave her real job and come all the way here to live. And even if she did...

"See...I know you think she could just move in with us, but it's not that easy. When a man and a woman live together, in the same house, they're usually married.''

"You and Mrs. Chevy aren't."

"No. That's different, though."

"Why?"

"Because it is," he said, trying to think of a simple explanation. "Because I pay Mrs. Chevalier to look after you," he settled on.

"You could pay Natalie."

"No, I couldn't."

"Why?"

"Because she's your mother."

"Then she should live with me."

His head was starting to hurt.

"You know what?" he said.

"What?"

"I think we need an ice cream break."

Robbie grinned.

"So let's hit the kitchen."

As they started off, he told himself this wasn't a cop-out. It was merely a delaying tactic.

CHAPTER THIRTEEN

NATALIE PAUSED outside the door of Emma's room, *really* not wanting to face her. Especially not when she was still torn up inside from telling Señora Perez that the authorities weren't going to let her grand-daughter live with her.

Not surprisingly, the woman had found the news awfully hard to take. But, at least, by the time they'd finished talking she'd acknowledged that—as tough as being separated was going to be for both of them—coping with Emma on her own probably *would* be too much for her.

And Jenny's assurance that she'd find Señora Perez a place to live and that there'd be money for her to live on had clearly made her feel a lot less fearful about the future.

But now there was Emma to face. And regardless of how good a job Cynthia had done of explaining, it would be a while before the reality of what was happening sank in.

Until it did, Emma would have a million questions. So instead of standing there, anticipating how difficult this was going to be…

Taking a deep breath, she forced herself to breeze into the room and say hello to the other patients.

The privacy curtain was drawn around Emma's bed, and when Natalie pulled it back a lump formed in her throat.

Emma's face was pinched, her dark eyes were filled with fear and uncertainty, and she had Teddy clutched to her chest.

"Hi," Natalie said softly, sitting down on the edge of the bed and taking Emma's hand in hers.

"Hi," Emma murmured.

"I hear Dr. Koehler's been in to see you."

The girl nodded, catching her lower lip between her teeth.

"Do you want to talk about what she had to say?"

"No."

Natalie brushed a strand of hair back from Emma's face, her heart aching for the child.

"She said I can't live with my *abuelita*," Emma whispered at last. "She said when my leg's better I've gotta go live with some other people. But she didn't know who. And I don't want to."

"I know. It's scary to even think about, isn't it."

Emma nodded.

"But we'll make sure you can still *see* your grandma. That you can visit with her. And the people you go to live with will be nice," she continued, praying that would prove true—then praying there actually *would* be people, that Emma wouldn't end up in some institution.

"And they'll *want* you to live with them," she added.

"But I don't want to live with *them!* Dr. Lawson, doesn't my *abuelita* want me to live with her?"

"Oh, yes. Yes, of course she does. But...do you understand why you can't?"

"No."

"Do you want me to try to explain?"

"Yes."

Natalie tried to come up with the right words. They were hard to find.

"You might not remember this," she finally began, "but the very first time I came to visit you, your grandma wasn't here in the room. And you told me she'd gone for a walk, because her ankles puff up if she sits too long."

"Did I?"

"Uh-huh. Then she couldn't come see you at all for a couple of days, because she was sick, right?"

Emma nodded again.

"Well, as people get older, they sometimes do get sick. And even when they're feeling just fine, they don't have as much energy as they used to. Not always enough energy to look after a little girl."

"I can look after myself."

"I know you can, in lots of ways. But you still need someone to make your meals and buy your clothes and take you places and talk to your teacher and help with your homework...all kinds of things like that."

"My grandma can do those things."

"Well, I'm sure she can do some of them. But I

don't think she can help with your homework, can she? Not when she doesn't read English.''

Emma simply stared at the doodles on her cast.

''And she wouldn't be able to talk to your teachers unless they spoke Spanish.''

''Yes, she would. I can translate.''

''That's true, but—''

''Dr. Lawson,'' Emma said, her eyes glistening with tears. ''I don't *want* to live with anyone else. I want to live with my mom and my grandma.''

''Oh, darling.'' Natalie edged closer and wrapped her arms around the girl's thin shoulders. ''Darling, you can't live with your mom anymore. She's gone to heaven, remember?''

''But I don't want her to be in heaven! I need her to still be here! So I can live with her and my grandma again!''

''Oh, darling,'' Natalie said once more, hugging Emma even harder as she began to sob.

NATALIE HAD SAID she wouldn't be gone long, but it was late in the afternoon before she arrived back from Madison Plains—late enough that all kinds of worries had begun snaking around in Hank's mind.

Maybe she'd stayed away because she didn't want to face him. Because she'd decided that, regardless of how they felt about each other, she still wasn't about to even consider the possibility of leaving Guatemala.

Standing on the porch next to Robbie, he watched her climb out of her rental. Whether she looked more tired or more unhappy was a toss-up, but she certainly bore little resemblance to the woman who'd been in his bed mere hours ago.

An image of her lying amongst the tangled sheets formed in his mind—her skin so creamy smooth he'd never get enough of touching her, her dark hair tousled and sexy against the white pillowcase.

"Hi!" Robbie called as she headed across the lawn.

"Hi."

The forced smile she gave them started Robbie scuffing the toe of his sneaker back and forth against a board. He might not know what was wrong, but he could tell something was.

"Daddy, I'm gonna go color, 'kay?"

"Sure."

Without another word, he scurried into the house.

Gonna go color was his way of saying he wanted to be left on his own for a while, and when he needed "alone" time Hank always tried to let him have it.

"I made lemonade," he said as Natalie reached the porch. "Feel like sitting out here with some?"

"Sounds perfect."

He went inside, unobtrusively checked that Robbie was settling in with his crayons, then poured a couple of glasses of lemonade. When he got back to the porch with them, Natalie was staring into space.

"So," he said, handing her a glass and sinking into the chair beside hers. "Want to talk about how things went?"

"I'm not sure I'm up to it."

"Ah." That bad.

The silence grew for a minute or two, then she said, "I had time to stop by and see Betty before the meeting with the caseworker."

"Oh?"

"Her daughter has the home care completely arranged now, so the plan's to discharge her tomorrow."

"Great. I'll call Audrey and let her know. And send some flowers to the house."

Natalie nodded. "That would be nice."

He waited to see if she was going to say anything else. When she didn't, he decided he might as well fill her in on *his* day.

"While you were gone," he said, "Robbie started in about your being his mother."

She looked at him. "And?"

"And I must have repeated the story of the mix-up a hundred times, so I think he's pretty clear on that now. But he's still convinced that if you're really his mother you should be living with him."

Stopping right there, he told himself this was *not* the time to press her about anything.

"Well, as we've been saying all along," she murmured, "it'll take him a while to understand things."

To understand *what* things? he wanted to ask. That she'd thought about the idea of staying on longer but had rejected it? That her plan was still to return to Villa Rosa once Audrey got home? And that she still wanted to go ahead with the sharing plan? Because she wasn't prepared to even give them the chance for a future together?

No, that just couldn't be it. Yet the uneasiness in his heart warned him it could.

Reminding himself, once again, that this was *not* a good time to press her, he simply took a sip of lemonade and waited.

"Maybe I *should* tell you about our meeting with the caseworker," she said at last. "Talking about it might help."

When she glanced at him, he nodded, then she went back to staring out across the lawn and said, "The woman hardly exuded competence, but at least I've got a clearer picture of how things stand.

"They'll help Señora Perez find a place to live and give her enough money to get by. That didn't seem to be much of a problem.

"And...I guess, up until today, I've been seeing her at her most stressed. But once we assured her she wouldn't have to cope entirely on her own, she really seemed a lot more...together.

"Oh, and the service is going to be the day after tomorrow. I think that being set helped her, too. I mean, knowing there would definitely *be* one, and that at least a few people..."

"I assume you'll go."

"Yes, of course. In fact, I told Señora Perez I'd drive her. She has no idea how to get to St. Aidan's."

"What time of day is it?"

"Three."

"Then why don't I drive both of you."

"Hank, you don't have to do that."

"I want to. I'll call Mary Gerard and see if we can leave Robbie with her."

"But..."

"It's not a big deal," he said. And he figured that with both Emma and Señora Perez leaning on her the way they'd been, she could do with someone to lean on herself.

"Well...then, thanks."

She lapsed into silence. After it had stretched for a while he said, "What about Emma?"

"In a way I wish she could be there with us. I think that might have helped her accept her mother's death. But since she's stuck in her bed, Cynthia and her grandmother and I decided that the best thing to do is just not mention it for the time being.

"At some point, whenever it seems right, Señora Perez can tell her there *was* a service. Right now, though, it might only upset her more."

Hank nodded. "It probably would. But I was actually asking what will happen to her in the long run."

"Oh," Natalie murmured, slowly shaking her head. "Well, I didn't figure the odds on her being adopted would be high. And, unfortunately, I was right. They're going to stick her in a foster home. Or, worse yet, an institution.

"Ostensibly, that will only be while they're assessing her, but I've got a horrible feeling that once they've placed her *temporarily* they'll forget all about her and...oh, Hank, it just breaks my heart."

Taking her hand in his, he gave it a squeeze.

"She's terrified about what will happen to her," she continued, "and..."

"And?" he said quietly when she paused again.

She was silent for a moment, then said, "If I tell you what I'm thinking you'll say I'm crazy."

"Uh-uh, I won't. I promise."

She hesitated, then shrugged. "All right. I'm thinking about trying to adopt Emma."

He breathed slowly, not uttering a word in case it was the wrong one.

"You're not *saying* I'm crazy, but you're thinking it," she said at last.

"No," he replied slowly. "I'm just wondering, with everything else..."

"I know." She shook her head. "Even I can see that in a way it *is* crazy. I came here to get my own child, and now I'm considering adopting someone else's. Which...well, in the first place, I don't even know if it's a viable option.

"I'm an unmarried woman who lives in a foreign country. Maybe that would completely rule me out as a suitable candidate. And you're right about the *everything else.*

"Until after I got here, I didn't realize how much work it will be to reestablish a close relationship with Robbie. So even the idea of... But she's such a sweet little girl. She deserves someone to love her, and..."

"Take it easy," he murmured, afraid she was on the verge of tears. "Let's think this through."

She eyed him, as if waiting for him to tell how to

make everything perfect in her little corner of the world.

He wished he could. But, of course, he couldn't. And *whatever* he said, he had to choose his words carefully.

The worst thing he could do was say something he'd regret later. And he honestly didn't know how many major life changes he was up to contemplating at once.

Yet if Natalie... But he was getting *miles* ahead of himself.

He took a few more seconds to think, then said, "Doesn't Emma's situation kind of fall into place with what we were talking about this morning? About the possibility of your staying here awhile longer?

"If you had a few more weeks, it would give you enough time to explore the possibility of adopting her. And it would give us a chance to see...

"I mean... Look, I know the only way we could end up together is if you uprooted your entire life. And I realize how much that would be asking.

"But it would be the only option, because there just can't be any demand for English-speaking homicide detectives in Villa Rosa."

The way she *almost* smiled at that made it a little easier to press on.

"Natalie, even though this has happened so fast, the way I feel about you... What I'm trying to say is that if you gave us a chance and we got to the point of considering marriage, I don't think I'd have a problem with adopting another child."

"Oh, Lord," she whispered. "Hank, please don't make it so tempting. Because...our getting married just isn't something I...I could never marry a cop."

WITH ROBBIE IN BED, Natalie and Hank found themselves discussing their situation yet again—even though they'd long ago reached the point of talking in circles.

Hank must have told her a hundred times why his job wasn't really as dangerous as most people assumed. He'd even gotten on his computer and tracked down statistics to back up the claim.

And she must have admitted a hundred times that she *knew* her fear wasn't entirely rational. Unfortunately, that didn't make it even slightly less real.

There was one potential compromise she still hadn't mentioned, though. And neither had he.

That made her almost certain she knew what he'd say if she suggested it. But since she didn't figure there was much to lose, she finally said, "Could you see yourself doing anything else? Not being a police detective?"

He gazed at her for a moment, then silently pushed himself up off the couch and paced across the room. When he turned and looked at her again, she held her breath until he quietly said, "Could you see yourself not being a doctor?"

She was tempted to lie. Instead, she shook her head.

"You understand, then," he said when she did. "I...I've been on the job my entire adult life. It's a major part of who I am. I'm good at it and…I don't know, it seems to somehow be in my blood. When I solve a case, take some scum-bag off the street so he can't kill again…

"It's a tough job with a lot of negatives. I'd never tell anyone otherwise. But the rewards, when they come…I'm not explaining it very well, but…"

He paused, then said, "I could think about it. If you and I decided…if that ended up being the only stumbling block…then I could think about it."

She stared at the floor, aware she'd been right. Neither of them had raised the possibility earlier because, deep down, they both knew it wasn't actually a possibility at all.

Hank *might* think about it. He might even make himself leave the force. And that told her an awful lot about how deeply his feelings ran for her.

But if he did leave and wasn't happy about the way his world unfolded afterward, how could he help but blame her? And then where would they be?

"WHY NOT?" Travis demanded, glancing across the Mustang as he drove.

It was almost 8:00 a.m., practically the end of the shift, so if Hank had managed to hold out just a little longer they wouldn't be having this conversation.

He really hadn't felt like discussing the latest developments between him and Natalie. But his partner had sensed that something was bothering him and had kept at him until he'd caved.

"She must have a reason," Travis added now.

"Yeah, she does."

He proceeded to fill Travis in on the story of her uncle being killed.

"She told me about that days ago," he continued. "She'd said that my being on the job made her uneasy and was explaining why.

"But it turns out *uneasy* was a major understatement. That she's always sworn she'd never let herself fall in love with a cop, let alone marry one."

"And you said?"

"Everything I could think of that might reassure her, but none of it helped."

He didn't go into anything more. Didn't mention her idea of adopting Emma. Or the fact that Natalie had asked him about leaving the force. He figured he'd already given his partner more than enough to chew on.

They drove a block or so in silence, then Travis said, "Remember how Celeste was into serious worrying for a while?"

He nodded. Not long after Travis had given her a ring, she'd gone through a period of thinking that by marrying a cop she'd be making a big mistake.

"We worked our way past it."

"Yeah, I know. But Natalie… We talked about it all evening without really… Hell, just when I figured I was making progress, convincing her to stay on, she hit me with that."

They'd reached Manhattan North and Travis pulled into the parking garage. After he found a spot, he cut the engine and said, "Let's not forget that a couple of weeks ago she was a total stranger."

"And?"

"And don't you think you could be giving this more weight than it deserves? I mean, in such a short time you can hardly have—"

Hank stopped him with a sharp look. "How long did it take you to fall in love with Celeste?"

Travis shrugged.

"As I recall, it happened practically the instant you met her. Didn't it?"

"Maybe. But...look, I'm no psychiatrist, but one day you open your door and Robbie's dead mother is standing on your porch—very much alive. Which means you've suddenly got a huge problem.

"Then it occurs to you that if you happened to fall in love and marry her your problem would be gone."

"You're saying I haven't actually fallen in love with her at all? That I've only convinced myself I have? Because it would be the ideal solution?"

When Travis merely shrugged again, he muttered, "Ideal solution. Yeah, right. All falling for her has done is create a whole, new, additional problem. I'm in love with a woman who can't even make herself consider the possibility of..."

"Give her time," Travis said.

"How can I give her time? She's determined to head back to Guatemala as soon as Audrey gets home."

"Well, maybe she'll be seeing things differently by then.

"It could happen," he added when Hank said nothing. "You know how women can be. Just because she tells you her mind's made up doesn't mean she won't change it."

"You don't know *this* woman," he said. Then, seriously not wanting to discuss the subject any further, he opened the car door and climbed out.

But he couldn't cut off his thoughts as abruptly as he had the conversation. Couldn't stop himself from recalling that, by the time he'd left the house last night, he'd been getting very bad vibes from Natalie.

He'd been sensing that she simply didn't believe there was much chance they'd end up together. Hell, maybe she wasn't even sure that was what she wanted.

He was sure about what *he* wanted, though. Regardless of what his partner figured, he *hadn't* simply convinced himself he was in love.

For the past while, his feelings for her seemed to have been growing deeper with each passing hour. And at this point they were so strong that...

Hell, no wonder those bad vibes had bothered him so much. They'd left him completely uncertain of exactly how she felt. Except that she was bound and determined not to marry a cop.

NATALIE POURED some cereal and milk into a bowl for Robbie, then stifled a yawn. She'd lain awake virtually the entire night, her mind refusing to shut down, her thoughts alternating between Hank and Emma.

She wasn't sure why she felt such a sense of urgency about the little girl, but if it was at all possible she wanted to talk to somebody about her today. So first thing after breakfast, she was going to call Cynthia.

Surely, as chief of Pediatrics, she had to know someone high up in Child Welfare. And maybe she could pull some strings that would get Natalie an appointment fast.

Then she'd at least be aware of how she stood with respect to their rules.

As for Hank... Thinking about where she stood with respect to him made her heart ache. Because no matter how much she wanted to, she just didn't see their sharing the rest of their lives together.

Even though she *knew* her fear about cops and danger went well beyond the rational, she couldn't simply wrap it up in a neat little parcel and stick it into some dark recess of her brain—never to be thought of again.

If that were possible, if people could dispense with their hang-ups so easily, there'd be a whole lot of therapists out of work.

But the idea of Hank's leaving the force...

In her mind's eye, she pictured the way he'd looked last night, when he'd said it wasn't *entirely* out of the question. His expression had belied his words, telling her that quitting was the last thing in the world he'd *want* to do.

She let his image linger for a few seconds, then forced it away and turned her attention to her son. He was playing with his cereal, and just watching him filled her heart with love.

Given that, how she could back away from the resolution that seemed so right for all three of them?

It wasn't her first choice. Not by a million miles. So didn't there have to be an angle they hadn't thought of? Some way of working things out that would let them...?

If there wasn't, though, how could she even consider marrying Hank? Consider living—day after day—with the fear her life might suddenly be shattered?

That had already happened to her once. She couldn't bear the thought of it happening again.

CHAPTER FOURTEEN

HANK READ ROBBIE his bedtime story, went through the checking-for-monsters routine, then kissed him good-night and wandered along to the living room.

He stood gazing through the window into the twilight, remembering how Natalie had taken off like the proverbial bat out of hell this afternoon—practically the moment he'd gotten up. And she'd said she might be later than usual getting home.

If she was late *enough,* he thought unhappily, she'd barely get here before he had to leave for work. And he had a depressing suspicion that was her plot.

It seemed obvious that those bad vibes last night had been every bit as significant as he'd feared. She must have decided that the two of them had reached a dead end, and that the best thing to do, from here on in, was spend as little time as possible together.

But that was only *her* take. *He* hadn't written them off yet. Not by any means.

No more than he'd begun hating her just because she had an irrational fear. Or an exaggerated one, as she preferred to call it.

Whichever word they used, though, unless she got over the fear...

Right, that was exactly where they were at. *She* had

to get over it. He couldn't do it for her. Couldn't *make* her come to terms with reality, couldn't *force* her to stop believing he was a walking bull's-eye. Yet if she didn't...

If she didn't, there'd be only two alternatives. Either they'd go their separate ways or he'd have to choose between her and his career. Assuming she'd have him if he chose her, of course.

But she'd *asked* if he'd consider leaving the job. So wasn't it obvious what she'd been thinking?

Mentally shaking his head, he told himself he'd just have to hope Travis was right. That once she'd had more time, she'd see her way clear to at least stay on for a while. And if she did, that would be a big step in the right direction.

On the other hand, if she didn't...

Headlights appeared down the road, distracting him from his thoughts. When the car pulled into the driveway, he saw it was Natalie's rental.

The interior light flashed on, illuminating her as she climbed out. He tried not to think that she seemed more beautiful with each passing day. Because if things didn't change, she wouldn't be here much longer. And all he'd be left with was memories of her.

As she walked across the lawn, he headed to the front door and opened it.

She smiled at him, making his heart skip a beat. Maybe things weren't as bad as he'd been assuming.

"Long day," he said, closing the door behind her.

She nodded. "Is Robbie asleep yet or can I say good-night?"

"He's probably still awake."

Without another word, she started toward his bedroom.

Hank returned to the living room and sat down, not at all sure that after she kissed Robbie good-night she wouldn't go and hide out in Audrey's room for a while.

But a couple of minutes later she was back.

"He was *just* dozing off," she said, sinking into one of the wing chairs facing the couch rather than sitting on it—beside him.

A bad sign, he couldn't help thinking.

"A lot of the patients' parents had questions for me tonight," she told him.

"Oh?"

He'd practically forgotten that she didn't spend *all* her time at Madison Plains with Emma and her grandmother. They were the only ones she generally talked much about.

"Way more of them than usual," she added. "And then I stayed for quite a while with Emma."

He waited, almost certain that she was working her way toward something important.

"I didn't go straight to the hospital today," she eventually said. "First, I had an appointment with a woman in a senior position at Child Welfare. A Willa Radaway. Cynthia set it up for me."

"To talk about adopting Emma?"

She nodded; he decided the meeting was another

bad sign. She hadn't even told him about it before she'd left, let alone asked him to go with her. So she sure hadn't been discussing the possibility of their adopting Emma together.

"And what's the story?" he said.

"Well...I only asked about adopting her on my own," she said as if she'd read his mind.

"Oh?"

"Hank, don't take that wrong," she said quickly. "It's not that I've given up on us. Really, I haven't."

Maybe not *entirely,* he thought, but close.

"It simply made sense, because I didn't want this Willa Radaway to think I wasn't serious—that I was just kind of considering various possibilities. And we already know there wouldn't be any problem at all if you and I, together, wanted to...Cynthia even said something about that."

"Oh?" he said again.

"I haven't told her what's happened between us, so she was only talking hypothetically. But when I explained why I wanted to talk to Social Services, asked if she could do anything to smooth the way, she said wouldn't it be ideal if you and I...so Robbie would be with both of us...and then adopting Emma would be a piece of cake."

He didn't say a word, although he badly wanted to. If even someone who had no idea they'd fallen in love could see their getting married would be the perfect solution, how could Natalie not—

"Since we aren't sure where things are going with us, though..."

When she stopped speaking and slowly brushed her hair back from her face, he wanted to say he had no doubts about where they *should* be going.

But as he'd been telling himself, not fifteen minutes ago, *she* had to come to terms with this in her own way. All he could do was hope to hell she would.

"My not being married wouldn't pose an obstacle," she finally continued.

"Single-parent adoptions are far more common than they used to be, especially with older children. But if I intended to take her back to Guatemala, it would give the authorities pause.

"On the plus side, though, Willa said that a positive reference from Cynthia would be a big help. And since I'd have no trouble arranging for child care while I was working...

"The biggest thing, of course, is that Emma and I have already developed a relationship. Plus the fact that, as Willa said, there are never a whole lot of families lined up to adopt a seven-year-old."

"At any rate, she couldn't *promise* I'd be approved, but I left with the feeling that it would probably be doable."

"Good. That's really good," he made himself say—trying to ignore the voice in his head that was whispering *Do-able without you.*

He resisted the temptation to ask whether she didn't think single-parenting both Emma *and* Robbie, in a country that was foreign to them, might be taking on an awful lot.

It would be pointless, because he had absolutely no

doubt that if the two of them didn't end up together she was still going to want Robbie half the time. Emma or no Emma.

THE FOLLOWING AFTERNOON, Hank was surprised to see Natalie emerge from the old apartment building accompanied by not one but *two* elderly women dressed in black. The second one proved to be the neighbor Señora Perez was staying with, Señora Barreda, who would be attending the service, as well.

During the drive to St. Aidan's, while the three women conversed quietly in Spanish he tried to focus on the most recent homicide he and Travis had been handed. But he no sooner began going over the facts than his thoughts returned to the way Natalie was acting.

Last night, she'd told him she hadn't given up on them. Yet when he'd rolled out of bed early today to get ready, she'd seemed surprised he was still intending to go with her. And that had only added to his sense that, deep down, she was convinced there just wasn't going to be any "they."

And if he couldn't *unconvince* her...

He unhappily ruminated on that for several blocks, then glanced across at her—and immediately wished he hadn't.

Merely looking at her was enough to make him want her. To make him start wishing, all over again, that there was some way he could magically banish her fear.

But there wasn't, he reminded himself as he pulled

into the St. Aidan's parking lot. So there was no point
in driving himself crazy trying to think of one.

The service was scheduled for three o'clock, and
by the time they located the chapel it was about a
quarter to. Initially, they were the only ones there.
Then other people gradually began arriving.

A few of them Señora Perez recognized. They'd
been friends of her daughter. The rest, if Natalie's
whispered guess was right, had either worked with
the woman or were staff members from the burn unit.

The service was brief and in Spanish. Natalie and
Señora Barreda cried a little; Señora Perez wept quietly through most of it. Afterward, though, she pulled
herself together and accepted condolences from those
who'd come. By the time the other mourners had left,
she seemed pretty much in control of her emotions.

As they headed for the elevators, she spoke rapidly
to Natalie for a minute.

When she was finished, Natalie said, "Hank?"

"Uh-huh?"

"She and Señora Barreda are going to see Emma
now, and she asked if we'd go up with them. Just to
say hi. We wouldn't have to stay long."

"Sure," he said. "We're in no hurry."

Natalie translated that for Señora Perez, who gave
him a wan smile, and barely fifteen minutes later the
four of them were on the pediatrics unit at Madison
Plains.

"I'm certain this will be the most visitors Emma's
ever had at once," Natalie murmured as they headed
down the corridor.

Hank nodded, the unsettled feeling in his chest growing stronger with each step he took.

The other day, when he'd said he didn't have a problem with the idea of adopting another child... Well, he hadn't *exactly* said it without thinking, but he sure hadn't given it much thought. And now, if he and Natalie *did* manage to end up together...

That, however, was looking about as likely as a night with a full moon over Manhattan and not a single homicide, which meant he didn't really have too much to worry about.

But at the time he'd spoken up he hadn't realized their relationship was probably doomed. So what had possessed him to say anything at all about Emma?

Not only had it been far too soon, but maybe he wouldn't even like her. Or she might not like him. And what did he know about seven-year-old girls, anyway?

Absolutely nothing. Besides, how would Robbie react if...

He told himself to just calm down. In the improbable event that he and Natalie worked things out, he'd simply take the rest as it came.

But telling himself that and believing it would be easy were two very different things. Of course, *nothing* had been easy lately. Not since Natalie had entered his life.

"It's this room," she said, leading the way in and saying hello to the four pint-size patients inside.

"Dr. Lawson! *Abuelita!* Señora Barreda!"

Hank's gaze came to rest on the child who'd called the greetings. *Emma.*

She was a tiny little thing, half lying, half sitting in the bed by the window—her leg in traction, as he'd known it would be, and a fat bear that had to be the infamous Teddy propped up against her.

As her grandmother kissed her hello, Natalie said, "We've brought someone new to visit you." Linking her arm with Hank's, she guided him closer to the bed.

Emma looked at him shyly.

"This is Mr. Ballantyne," Natalie told her.

"Hank," he said. "You can call me Hank."

She gave him a smile.

"And can I call you Emma?"

She giggled and nodded.

"And who's this furry guy with the red sweater?"

"Teddy."

"Ah. Is he good company?"

When she nodded again, Hank smiled. He was rapidly exhausting his supply of small talk for small people, but at least she hadn't taken an instant dislike to him. Or he to her.

And that was a damned good thing. Just in case the highly unlikely came to pass.

"WHAT DID YOU THINK OF HER?" Natalie asked as they headed out of the hospital.

"I can see how she stole your heart," Hank said truthfully. "She's really sweet. It's hard to believe…after all that's happened, I was expecting her to seem depressed.''

''Sometimes she is, but I think that when she gets distracted she forgets about the bad stuff for a while.''

Hank waited, half expecting Natalie to start talking about the adoption idea again. She didn't, though. In fact, she lapsed into silence.

''I guess the next stop is the Gerards',''' he said as they reached the Blazer.

She simply nodded, climbed in and sat staring out the window as he drove. Then, after they'd gone a mile or so, she murmured, ''Hank?''

He glanced at her.

''I wonder…before we get Robbie…could we go back to the house and talk for a bit?''

His pulse rate accelerated, even though he realized there were 101 different things she might be wanting to discuss.

''Sure,'' he said as casually as he could. ''You heard what Mary said. She doesn't care when we pick him up.''

The rest of the way home, he had to concentrate on staying within the speed limit. Because despite knowing the police around there had zero tolerance for speeders, he really, really wanted to find out what Natalie had on her mind.

If it *wasn't* any of those 101 different things, if it was about *them*, and she'd decided…

But he shouldn't get his hopes up. That would only be asking to have them dashed. Still, he couldn't *en-*

tirely keep from thinking that she might have convinced herself...

By the time he pulled into the driveway his mouth was dry and his palms were wet. Trying to appear nonchalant, he got out of the car and started toward the house with her.

"Coffee?" she said once they were inside.

"Sounds good," he made himself say, even though the last thing he wanted was a delay while she made it.

Once she'd headed for the kitchen, he removed his suit jacket, tossed it onto one of the wing chairs and stood staring out the window—until he couldn't stand the suspense anymore and followed along after her.

Natalie was putting the coffee into the maker when she heard Hank's footsteps...heard him stop in the kitchen doorway.

Knowing he was watching her made her even more anxious than she'd already been, but she managed to get the last spoonful in without spilling it.

She swung the basket shut, pressed the On switch and made herself turn to face him.

"Someone called," she said, nodding toward the answering machine's little flashing light.

He glanced at it with such a distinct lack of interest she thought he was going to leave it for the moment.

Then he said, "I guess I'd better check it," and stepped over to rewind the tape.

"Hank, this is Betty," the message began. "I'm just phoning to thank you for the flowers. I got some at the hospital, but it was such a nice surprise when these arrived at the house.

"I'm feeling a lot better, and I hope everything's fine there. I'm sure it is, though, with Natalie stepping in to help.

"So...well, thanks again. They're really beautiful. Bye."

"She sounds tired," Natalie murmured. "But that's to be expected."

As she started to turn back toward the coffeemaker, Hank said, "Natalie? What is it you want to talk about?"

She simply looked at him, her eyes drinking in his rugged masculinity. Detailing his firm jawline. Lingering on his sensual lips.

Gazing at his mouth made it impossible not to think about how delicious his kisses were. About the way they sent rushes of heat through her body and how his merest touch could melt her insides.

She loved him. She didn't have the slightest lingering doubt about it. But that didn't make her any less frightened. It only made her more desperately want what she was afraid to reach out and take.

"Aren't you going to tell me?" he said at last, giving her a smile that went straight to her heart.

"I..."

She paused, assuring herself this wasn't a major, irreversible step, then said, "I didn't get much sleep last night, because I couldn't stop thinking about everything you'd said. About how I should at least give us a chance to see... Not only for you and me, but for Robbie, as well.

"And I would. I mean, I've told you how hard it would be for me to leave Villa Rosa. But I'd consider it if only...Hank, no matter how many times I tell myself I'm not being entirely rational, I simply can't get past..."

He looked steadily at her, his dark eyes willing her to continue.

"I'm so scared," she whispered.

"I know."

"It's...losing Carlos was harder than I can say. If I let myself...and then I lost you..."

"And if you don't let yourself?" he said quietly. "Then you'd lose me for sure."

"I know. But it wouldn't hurt as much as..."

He took a slow step toward her, reaching for her hands. His grip was so firm, so strong, it made her wish that some of his strength could flow into her. Make her brave enough to—

"Natalie, just don't decide too fast that there's no possible future for us. Take long enough to... "

He gave her another smile. "Hey, if we give it a few more weeks, we might decide we don't even really like each other."

She managed a smile of her own. "Fat chance."

He gazed at her for a second longer, then drew her to him and wrapped his arms around her.

"I've been on the job for almost fifteen years," he said into her hair. "And nothing awful's ever happened to me."

Then maybe he's overdue, an imaginary voice warned her.

Pressing her cheek against his chest, she listened to the solid beating of his heart and tried to ignore the voice.

"You know," Hank said quietly, "since you didn't get much sleep last night, maybe we should have a little nap before we pick up Robbie."

She told herself that would be extremely unwise, that it would only make her want him more.

But maybe that would be a *good* thing.

"You think?" she murmured, smiling against his chest.

"Yeah, I think."

NATALIE LAY in Hank's arms, in the warm aftermath of making love, her fingers lazily playing with his chest hair, her mind musing that if they could stay right here in his bed forever she'd be perfectly content. And he'd be perfectly safe.

But that wasn't an option. Aside from anything else, they had Robbie to think about.

And she *had* been thinking about him. An awful lot. Because he had so much to gain if she and Hank...

Marriage. Ever since he'd raised that as a possibility, the word had been whispering in her mind. And if they *did* get married, instead of shuffling Robbie back and forth between them, the three of them would be a real family.

Or the four of them, she corrected herself, thinking again of what Hank had said about adopting Emma.

The way he'd barely had to consider before saying it wouldn't be a problem spoke volumes about the kind of man he was.

So how could she conceivably let her hang-up... And that *was* what it amounted to.

Maybe a police officer's odds on being killed or wounded was higher than the norm, but they weren't *that* much higher. Which meant, *logically*—

"What are you thinking about?" Hank asked, nuzzling her throat.

"Us," she admitted.

"Good." He eased down and kissed the swell of her breast.

"Nice word, *us*," he added, his breath hot against her skin and his hands moving to her hips.

"Are you completely insatiable?" she said, unable to keep from smiling.

"Never have been before. So it must be all your fault."

"Is that how it would be with us?" she teased. "You laying the blame on me for things?"

"No. How it would be with us...it would be wonderful."

She closed her eyes, certain he was right.

He kissed her breast again, his mouth finding her nipple this time.

"Oh, Hank," she murmured, the heat of longing beginning to seep through her once more. "As much as I hate to say this, shouldn't we be going to get Robbie?''

''Who?'' he said.

''Very funny.''

''Oh, you mean that little kid who lives here?''

With obvious reluctance, he gave her breast a final kiss, then propped himself up on his elbow.

Now, she told herself. Before you chicken out.

''Hank?''

''Uh-huh?''

''I was wondering…the police department has psychologists on staff? Stress counselors? People like that?''

''Sure. Why?''

She nervously licked her lips, telling herself it was too late to stop now. But she was afraid to go on.

''Why?'' Hank repeated.

''Well…I was thinking,'' she forced herself to say. ''If it's not against the rules for an outsider…it might help me to talk to one of them about…or to someone else.

''You know. Maybe a specialist on phobias. Or a behavior mod type.''

As a smile spread across his face, she quickly said, ''I can't make any promises. I can only try it and see if it helps. Then, if we decide this thing between us is definitely real, if—''

He stopped her from saying more with a kiss so real it warmed her all the way down to her toes.

''YOU KNOW, I've got a good feeling about tonight,''

Hank said, glancing across the dark interior of the Mustang at Travis. "I think we're finally going to catch up with Joey."

"You don't figure your good feeling's just fallout from Natalie's coming around?" Travis said wryly. "Which, in case you've forgotten, is exactly what I predicted would happen."

"Yeah, well, having a partner who's psychic can't be a bad thing. But we're still only talking. She said no promises. She's just willing to give it a try."

"It'll work out. So when do I meet her? Or I should probably say when does Celeste meet her? She's dying of curiosity."

"Why don't the four of us go out to dinner after we're finished midnights? Is any night I can line up a sitter okay with you?"

"As far as I know. I'll check with Celeste."

That said, Travis turned his attention back to his driving. They were getting close enough to the Blue Cat that they should be watching for a space.

After stopping next to one that Hank couldn't have parked the Blazer in for all the *quetzals* in Guatemala, he maneuvered the Mustang into it.

"Okay," he said, cutting the engine. "Let's go see if your hunch is right."

They silently strode down the street to the club, past the lineup of hopefuls waiting for admittance. When they reached the entrance, the bouncer gestured them inside before they could badge him. They'd wasted so much time here on previous nights that he recognized them.

Once again, the place was crowded and smoky.

"No seats," Travis said as they surveyed it.

"Well, how about if you keep a general eye on things and I'll have a look around."

"Just don't forget to stay sharp, Mr. Feel Good."

Hank laughed. Then, leaving Travis standing at the end of the bar, he began to casually wander toward the back of the room, pretending he was looking for someone he was supposed to meet.

He'd made it past at least half the tables when he spotted a guy who was either Joey Noguchi or a dead ringer for him—sitting with his arm around a busty blonde.

As he eyed the man, mentally comparing him with the mug shots they'd studied, his hand involuntarily brushed the jacket pocket his gun was in.

He doubted he'd need it. Even though Joey was probably carrying, he wouldn't likely try anything in a place full of witnesses. Not as long as they didn't unduly alarm him, and they sure as hell weren't going to do that.

Deciding it was definitely Joey Nogood, he glanced back at Travis.

When his partner nodded and started forward, Hank dug his shield from the other pocket of his jacket, palmed it, then wandered over to Joey.

"Mr. Noguchi?" he said, reaching the table.

Both Joey and the blonde looked up. She smiled; he didn't.

"Yeah?" he said.

Hank surreptitiously showed him the badge. "Detective Hank Ballantyne, NYPD," he said quietly. "If you wouldn't mind stepping outside for a minute, I'd like to talk to you in private."

"Joey?" the blonde murmured.

"It's nothing," he told her. "Wait here. I won't be gone long."

Hank resisted the temptation to say he'd likely be gone for life, and waited in silence as Joey pushed his chair away from the table.

"Lead the way," he said, then fell into step behind Joey. Halfway to the door, Travis joined them.

As they walked out into the night, the bouncer and the people waiting on line eyed them with bored expressions.

"So what's this about?" Joey demanded once they were a few yards down the street.

"We need you to come to the precinct with us," Hank told him.

Joey looked from him to Travis, then back, his anxiety level clearly rising.

"Why?"

"Just want to ask you some questions. About a killing in a liquor store."

"You mean you just want to see if you can frame me," Joey snapped, perspiration on his upper lip now. "Send me back to Sing Sing. Well, it ain't gonna happen. I done my time there. I'm never setting foot in that rathole again."

Hank shrugged. "Let's go."

He didn't see the gun in the man's hand—only heard its roar and felt the force of the shots that sent him reeling backward.

CHAPTER FIFTEEN

"NATALIE!" ROBBIE SHOUTED from the living room.

His next words came out garbled, but he sounded as if he were saying *Uncle* Somebody was here.

Natalie turned away from the toaster thinking that couldn't be it. Hank was originally from Chicago, and he'd told her that both his brother and sister still lived there.

She glanced down at the T-shirt and rumpled shorts she hadn't bothered ironing, telling herself that anyone paying a surprise visit at seven-thirty in the morning would just have to take what they got.

Then Robbie called, "Aunt Celeste, too," and she realized he'd said, "Uncle Travis."

The instant she did, hot, hard pain sliced through her—so sharp it almost doubled her over.

Hank and Travis shouldn't be finished their shift yet. So Travis's being here could only mean that something awful had happened to Hank.

She headed out of the kitchen, barely able to breathe, her lungs burning as she told herself that maybe Hank wasn't dead. Maybe he'd only been injured.

But even if that was it, he was hurt badly enough that Travis hadn't wanted to tell her about it over the phone. And badly enough that he'd brought his fiancée along.

Because, Natalie rapidly concluded, he'd figured another woman would be a comfort to her. And to Robbie. Oh, Lord, this was going to be so awful for Robbie.

She reached the living room, desperately clinging to the hope that things weren't as bad as she was imagining, and gathered him up into her arms.

"Whatsa matter?" he demanded as she gazed out at the black Mustang parked in the driveway and the somber-faced couple walking across the yard.

"I just need a hug," she told him.

He gave her a halfhearted one, then struggled to get down.

When she set him free, he raced for the door—and opened it as Travis and Celeste reached the porch.

"Uncle Travis!" he yelled, launching himself at the man.

"Hey, sport!"

She watched Travis swing him up, the tears stinging her eyes on the verge of spilling over.

"You come to the car with me for a minute," Travis said, settling Robbie on his shoulder. "I've got a surprise for you."

As Robbie asked "What?" Celeste stepped inside, closed the door and quickly said, "Hank's all right. Injured but nothing serious."

Relief sent the tears streaming down Natalie's face. She wiped at them, trying to say something but unable to make her voice work.

Hank was injured, and with half her brain all she could think was she'd *known* this would happen. This or worse. It had only been a matter of time.

But even though the incident validated her fear, gave her here-and-now proof that his life was at risk every time he walked out the door, the other half of her brain had latched onto Celeste's "nothing serious" phrase. And that had her feeling positively euphoric.

Later, she'd have to try to figure out what her double-edged reaction meant. Right now, she needed more details about what had happened.

When she looked at Celeste, silently asking for them, Celeste said, "They caught up with a murder suspect who pulled a gun. Fortunately, Hank was wearing his vest, which saved him. But he was shot at close range, so the bullets knocked him off his feet and broke a couple of ribs."

As Celeste spoke, Natalie visualized the scene— Hank's body no match for the impact of the bullets, only the vest saving him from certain death.

Only the vest and *extremely* good luck. If the shots had hit higher, they'd have blown his head off.

She swallowed hard, every trace of euphoria gone and her entire body trembling.

"He's going to be fine," Celeste said quietly. "Really he is. Travis talked to the doctor."

"Yes. I believe you. It's just such a shock."

"I know." Celeste steered her to the couch, murmuring, "This is a terrible way to meet you. I know how you must be feeling."

She nodded, collecting her thoughts as best she could.

"Where is he?" she asked at last.

"St. Vincent's Hospital. It's in the Village."

"He's still in the hospital?" she said, suddenly afraid Celeste hadn't told her everything. A couple of broken ribs shouldn't warrant a hospital stay.

"Well, when he went down he smacked his head," Celeste explained.

"A concussion?"

"Yes, so they want to keep him under observation for twenty-four hours. Just to be on the safe side is what they said."

Of course. With a concussion there was always the risk of a subdural hematoma. And if there was slow bleeding in your brain and nobody realized it, you died.

"Travis thought you might want to go into the city," Celeste was saying. "See how he is for yourself."

"Yes. Yes, of course."

"Then he'll drive you."

"Oh, thanks, but I have a car and—"

"Natalie, the traffic's awful when you're not used to it. And I can stay here to look after Robbie while you're gone.

"That's why I came. He'll be fine with me. And we figured you wouldn't want to take him to the hospital, that it would frighten him to see Hank there."

She tried to decide whether leaving Robbie with Celeste was the best thing to do, then realized it must be. Both Celeste and Travis were undoubtedly thinking a whole lot straighter than she was at the moment. Only…

"You don't have to get to work?" she asked.

"No, I work at home."

"Ah." Right. She recalled Hank mentioning that. Celeste was…a freelance editor, that was it.

She looked out the window—over to where Travis was opening his car trunk and Robbie was dancing excitedly beside him.

"I shouldn't tell Robbie what's happened just yet, should I," she said as much to herself as Celeste. "If I did… He'd pick up on how upset I am and assume things are worse than they are."

"I think you're right. Waiting till later makes sense."

"Yes, then that's what I'll do."

"Oh, and Hank asked Travis if he'd bring a shirt for when he gets discharged. The shirt and jacket he was wearing…"

Have bullet holes in them.

Natalie knew that was what Celeste had stopped short of saying. But even unsaid, the words sent a shiver through her.

They were both silent for a minute, until Celeste murmured, "It's terrifying, isn't it."

Natalie nodded. "I don't know how…"

She quit speaking before the words escaped, but Celeste finished the sentence. "…how anyone can marry a cop?"

Natalie felt her face growing warm. She hadn't quit speaking fast enough.

"I'm not a mind reader," Celeste said softly. "Hank's been talking to Travis about you. He told him about your uncle, and how you..."

"Sorry," she said, shaking her head. "That's not a good topic at the moment. But I can understand how it would have affected you.

"Even without anything like that, I went through a bad patch myself—thinking that if I married Travis I'd end up a young widow."

Natalie eyed her, wondering for a second whether she was only saying that. But it was probably the truth. It was hard to imagine anyone *not* worrying.

"How did you convince yourself that... Do you mind my asking?"

"No. It was... Well, I have to back up a bit and explain that Travis and I fell in love under pretty intense circumstances. He learned there was a contract on my life and decided to play bodyguard.

"And I was so glad I had him to lean on that I barely thought about his job until after everything was over and I was safe.

"I mean...I knew all along it could be dangerous. But somehow it was just kind of a vague awareness in the beginning.

"I guess I was worrying so much about the hit man that I couldn't worry about Travis's job at the same time. But once the killer was behind bars, I started thinking that one day Travis would head off to work and I'd never see him alive again. And the more I thought about it, the more certain I was it would happen.''

"But you got over that?"

Celeste gave her a slow shrug. "Not entirely. And something like what just happened to Hank sure doesn't help. I'm a lot better than I was, though. Back before Christmas I was almost at the stage of asking Travis to leave the force.

"Then I thought about it and realized that if he did he'd only be doing it for me. Not because he actually wanted to. And if he came to resent me for making him..."

"I *did* ask Hank," Natalie admitted. "At least, I asked if he could see himself doing anything else with his life. And just the look on his face when I did...I came to the same realization as you.

"But how did you even get to the worrying-*less* stage?" she asked.

Maybe Celeste had come up with something that would work for *her,* too. That possibility gave her hope and at the same time frightened the devil out of her.

She didn't *want* to marry a cop. She wanted to play things safe. Yet Hank wasn't just any old abstract fantasy cop. He was the man she'd fallen in love with.

She forced her attention back to Celeste, who was saying, "Travis and I talked about my fear. A lot. And...several things helped. His promising to wear his vest more was one of them.

"Detectives don't like to bother with them, but he

said he'd start using his whenever there was even the hint of a potential problem.''

''If Hank hadn't been wearing one...''

''Exactly. At any rate, that helped. And I tried something I used to do when I was a teenager and had to make a decision. I wrote down two lists—pros and cons.''

''And the pros won.''

''Not entirely. Being afraid the man you love might get killed is an awfully big con.''

The word *insurmountable* formed in Natalie's mind.

''But...I guess, in the end, it boiled down to how *much* I love Travis. Despite worrying, I just can't imagine living without him.''

Natalie stared at her bare feet. She loved Hank. Very, very much. But even if she told herself a zillion times that a life with him would be worth the risk it entailed, telling herself wasn't the same as waving a magic wand and making a deep-seated fear vanish.

Emotional baggage. She didn't like psychobabble, yet that was a good description of what she was carrying. And if she couldn't get rid of it...

She'd been trying to do that, though. Trying as hard as she could. And if...Lord when she hadn't been able to succeed *before* Hank had almost gotten killed...

''Want to hear a theory I came up with?'' Celeste asked.

She nodded.

''Well, back when I was still feeling *really* scared,

I told a couple of friends about it. And one of them, whose husband is away on business a lot, said that every time he travels, she worries about his plane crashing.

"Then the other one, who's married to a long-haul trucker, said that whenever he's on the road she's afraid to watch the news—in case there's footage of a fiery crash and it turns out he was in it.

"So I started thinking that maybe worrying about people just goes hand in hand with loving them. And when you love a cop, the obvious thing to fixate on is the danger of the job."

"That makes sense," Natalie said. For her, however, if simply making sense was *enough* she wouldn't be in such emotional turmoil.

"Did Hank tell you I've been married before?" Celeste asked.

"Yes, but he didn't elaborate."

"Well, my first marriage was a mistake. Which I guess is always far easier to see in hindsight.

"But the point is that my first husband and I just kind of drifted into it, without any really intense feelings and... In the three years I was married to Bryce, I don't recall ever once worrying about his safety.

"So my theory is that maybe the more you love someone, the more you worry. Or that's how it works with some of us, at least."

Before Natalie could reply, the front door opened and Travis and Robbie came in.

"Look, Natalie!" Robbie said, his eyes shining. "Uncle Travis gave me a Jeep!"

She eyed the bright-yellow Jeep clutched to his chest, absently wondering how many more cars and trucks the house could hold. Then she looked at Travis, in time to see him shoot Celeste a questioning glance.

When she nodded, he said to Robbie, "You know what?"

"What?"

"I need Natalie to come into the city with me for a while. So Aunt Celeste is going to stay here with you, okay?"

Robbie focused on Celeste. "Can we play trucks?"

"Sure."

"And do puzzles?"

"We can do whatever you want."

"I'll just go put on some decent clothes," Natalie said.

"And shoes," Robbie told her, looking at her bare feet.

She almost managed a smile. They were *constantly* reminding him about shoes.

"Right," she said. "I can't go walking around in New York without shoes."

"I know. 'Cuz there's junk. And glass. And dog *stuff*," he added with a grin.

ON THE WAY to Manhattan, Natalie asked Travis to tell her *exactly* what had happened outside the Blue Cat Club.

She'd had some vague notion that hearing the details might help her, but it didn't. It only gave her a more realistic scenario than the one her imagination had conjured up.

By the time she'd finished asking him questions, they'd driven through the Holland Tunnel and were heading north.

St. Vincent's Hospital, he'd said, was at 7th Avenue and 11th Street.

She gazed out at the pulsating city as he drove, thinking it could easily be on a different planet from Villa Rosa. Could be an entire galaxy away from *her* world. From where she belonged.

Or, at this point, did she belong back in the U.S.A., with Hank?

Even as the question formed in her mind, she was rephrasing it. Did she belong with a man who could as easily be lying in a morgue as in a hospital bed?

Her throat began to ache. This time, he'd been lucky. But no matter how much she loved him, she just didn't see how she could go through life terrified that there'd be a next time.

"You okay?" Travis said.

She glanced at him and nodded a lie.

He drove on until they stopped for a red light, then looked over and said, "Our backup got to the scene before the ambulance did. So I let them take charge of the perp and rode to the hospital with Hank. And the whole way there he talked about you."

"Oh?"

"Yeah, he was less upset about what had happened than about how you were going to react to it."

"You're exaggerating," she said quietly.

"Uh-uh. I'm not. Well, all right, maybe just a little. But I don't know if you realize how totally crazy he is about you, and he…

"Look, maybe you're thinking this is none of my business, but Hank isn't only my partner. He's the best friend I've got. And he's a great guy."

"Travis, I know he is."

When he eyed her for a second, as if trying to figure out exactly how much he should take from her words, she added, "That *isn't* the problem."

"No. No, of course it's not," he said wearily. "But Hank…"

"Natalie, I understand how you feel. And why. And I realize this *thing* will have made it even worse.

"But I know how Hank feels, too. And…I've never seen him like this about a woman before. Not even remotely *close* to like this. Since his marriage broke up he's hardly dated, let alone…"

The light turned green and they started forward again.

"When we came on shift last night," Travis continued, "the first thing he told me was that you'd decided you were going to see someone. Try to work through your fear.

"He said that was real progress, and he was just so damned happy…"

She wasn't at all sure she wanted to hear what Travis was saying. Last night *she'd* been happy, too. Then this morning, reality had come crashing down around her.

But whether she wanted to hear it or not, he wasn't

finished. "On the way to the hospital, he must have said a dozen times that now you'd never see your way clear to…"

"It would have been hard enough before," she murmured.

Now…well, as limited as her "progress" had been, at this point she was back to where she'd started—if not miles *farther* back.

Travis was silent for a few beats, then said, "Nothing worthwhile is easy. But the way he feels about you…

"Natalie, as the saying goes, people get killed crossing the street."

"I know."

"And nothing like this has ever happened to either Hank or me before. It'll probably never happen again."

"No guarantees, though."

"I only wish there were. But we all know life doesn't come with guarantees."

She nodded slowly, vaguely aware she'd said almost that exact same thing to Hank—when he'd been upset about the idea of her taking Robbie to a country prone to earthquakes.

"Even so," Travis was saying, "if you love Hank, doesn't it make sense to at least still talk to someone?"

She stared at her hands, thinking that loving someone wasn't supposed to be so hard.

"Doesn't it?" he repeated.

"I'm not sure," she said truthfully.

They made the rest of the trip in silence, but Travis might as well have still been in there pitching on Hank's behalf, because she couldn't stop thinking about what he'd said. And about what Celeste had said.

Hank couldn't ask for better friends.

Finally Travis said, "That's St. Vincent's up ahead."

She wasn't surprised to see it was the sort of ancient, sprawling hospital that stood near the center of most large American cities. And the instant they walked through the front entrance, a familiar, faintly stale and antiseptic smell enveloped them, reminding her of the hospital where she'd worked, a lifetime ago, in Detroit.

Travis led the way to the elevators and they rode up to the sixth floor.

As they got off, he said, "It's Room 6112 and Hank has it to himself. At least, there was nobody in the other bed earlier.

"I'll wait here for you," he added, gesturing toward a worn couch sitting off to one side.

"Oh, but you might as well take this." He held out the shirt on a hanger, which they'd brought from the house.

She took it, then started down the old corridor—awash with anxiety and wondering why she felt so anxious when everything was basically okay.

Because, thanks to his partner, she knew exactly how Hank was feeling, and she didn't want to make him feel even worse?

Yes, that was undoubtedly it. But she didn't want to give him false hopes, either.

Pausing outside his room, she took a deep breath before she walked in.

He was gazing at the doorway, so he spotted her the instant she did. And for a split second, until he masked it, she saw fear in his eyes. Fear of what the shooting meant to *them*.

It made her want to cry.

CHAPTER SIXTEEN

"IT LOOKS WORSE than it is," Hank said.

Natalie forced a smile. "If that wasn't true you'd be dead."

He was wearing a pair of pajama bottoms but no top, and his chest was a massive bruise from the shoulders on down. Portions of it were black, others purple, still others a dark shade of blue.

She crossed to the bed. Then, being careful not to brush against his chest, she leaned close and kissed him.

"Hurts to breathe, doesn't it," she said as she drew back and draped the shirt they'd brought him over a chair.

"A little."

"You're lying. Anything more than a shallow breath hurts like hell."

"Anyone ever told you your bedside manner needs work?"

She managed another smile and perched on the edge of the bed, taking one of his hands in both of hers. "What about your head? How does it feel?"

"Not as bad as it did earlier. You think the gazillion pain pills they gave me had something to do with that?"

"I think it's a pretty good guess."

"Did Travis bring you?"

"Yes."

"I asked him to go to the house rather than phone."

"He did. And Celeste came along to look after Robbie."

"Ah. That was good thinking. I was hoping you wouldn't bring him... Well, first of all, I was just hoping you'd come."

"You thought I might not?"

"I wasn't sure."

"Oh, Hank, this scared me half to death, but..."

"But what?"

"It...didn't change the way I feel about you."

He gazed at her uneasily for a moment, then said. "Did it change your decision to see someone? To try to..."

"I'll still have a go at it," she made herself say.

His relief was so obvious she had to resist the urge to warn him that "having a go" was a long, long way from succeeding.

"You know how that makes me feel?" he murmured.

She kissed him again, partly because she wanted to, partly because she didn't want him to tell her.

Last night, she'd promised she'd try counseling. And she wouldn't go back on her word.

But she'd given it before he'd almost gotten killed. And at this point, she suspected the odds that talking to someone would help her face down her fear were somewhere between low and zero.

When she ended the kiss and eased away, he said, "I've been doing a lot of thinking these past few hours."

Her heart began to thud. Maybe, even if counseling *didn't* help...? Had he been thinking about quitting the force? Had this incident woken him up to the reality of the danger?

"And I keep coming back to the fact that I've been asking you to do all the compromising," he continued.

She held her breath, waiting.

"I just didn't see how I could realistically do any of it. But it's occurred to me that we might be able to work things out so you wouldn't have to *entirely* give up your life in Villa Rosa."

"Meaning?"

"Meaning would American Physicians Abroad go for your spending only a couple of months a year working there? If they would, you could take Robbie down for the summers. And Emma, if we went ahead with..."

"Even though there's a risk of earthquakes?"

"I'm still not comfortable with that, but if I'm going to do some of the compromising..."

He started to shrug, then stopped himself—which told her that even a little upper body movement caused him pain.

"You said you wanted Robbie to learn what life is like in Guatemala. That way he would.

"And I could spend my vacation time with you. So we'd only really be apart for one month, yet you could still...

"What do you think, Natalie?"

She gazed at him, thinking he was trying so damned hard it hurt. And that it would break both their hearts if they didn't end up together.

As the silence stretched between them, Hank could feel himself growing more and more uneasy.

But at last Natalie said, "I think they *might* go for it. If the alternatives were two months or nothing."

He felt his heartbeat accelerating and warned himself not to let his hopes get too high. Her response hardly qualified as unbridled enthusiasm.

Still, before she'd walked in here, he hadn't dared dream he'd even be *this* lucky, had been virtually certain she'd tell him they were through, that there was simply no chance for them.

Now, knowing she hadn't entirely written them off made him feel like wrapping his arms around her and holding her forever.

However, since merely the wrapping-around part would likely start him screaming in agony, he just let her go on.

"A lot of doctors only sign up for brief stints," she said. "As breaks from their regular practices.

"And it's one of those organizations that's *always* short of qualified people. So if they knew they could count on me for a couple of months every summer...

"Well, I'd have to talk to them about it, of course, but if you and I *did* get to the stage of..."

If. He'd really begun to hate that word, would give anything to have her say she'd marry him and they'd deal with all the rest as it came.

She wasn't there yet, though. And for all he knew...

He gazed at her, wondering where she'd be after she'd had more time to consider things.

He'd come close enough to death in the Blue Cat that he'd smelled the stench of its breath in his face. But maybe that fact hadn't really hit her full force yet.

When she was sitting in the house tonight, though, thinking about how narrowly he'd escaped...

Well, he just couldn't let her be alone with her thoughts. Because if he did, she might decide...

"Why don't we get out of here," he said.

"Pardon?"

"There's no real reason I can't go home, is there?"

She gave him a skeptical look. "Celeste told me they want to keep you for observation."

"That's just routine, isn't it?"

"Uh-uh. You sustained a concussion, which means someone has to keep an eye on you for the first twenty-four hours. Wake you up regularly if you fall asleep to make sure you haven't lapsed into a coma."

"What's wrong with your doing it?"

"Hank, I—"

"You're a doctor."

"Yes, but—"

"And you can't go to Madison Plains this afternoon anyhow. Even if I discharge myself, I'm not in good enough shape to chase around after Robbie.''

"Oh, Lord, I hadn't given the hospital a second's thought.''

As she glanced at her watch, he said, ''Travis is here someplace?''

"He's waiting down the hall.''

"Then you can use his cell phone to call Cynthia. Mine's with my wallet and other stuff. Wherever they stashed it.''

She nodded. "Good idea. And I'll have to ask her to explain to Emma that I can't visit today.''

He gave her his best smile—at least smiling didn't hurt—then said, ''Since you'll be stuck at the house anyway…Natalie, it's not as if I'm hooked up to a monitor or something. All that's happening is a nurse sticks her head in now and then to ask how I feel. So as long as you're with me…and how about Robbie? Have you told him what happened?''

"No, not yet.''

"Even more reason, then. If I don't go home you'll have to explain that I got hurt. And if he can't see for himself it's not serious he'll be really scared.''

Natalie eyed him for a minute, then wordlessly walked over to the door and took his chart from its holder.

"I'd be okay at home, right?'' he said as she read it.

"Your lungs checked out fine, no heart damage, no ruptured arteries. Nothing but the ribs and the concussion. Dammit, Hank, we were just *so* lucky.''

We.

He exhaled slowly. He might have started to hate *if,* but *we* had to be the most beautiful word in the English language.

NATALIE HAD half expected Robbie to be watching for them when Travis pulled into the driveway. Fortunately, he wasn't.

If he had been, he'd probably have come racing out. And their preferred plan involved her going in first to explain that he couldn't greet his father with a flying tackle.

She made it all the way to the house without his spotting her. Once inside, she discovered why. He and Celeste were in the kitchen, eating ice cream.

"Hi!" He greeted her with a grin.

"We've been having a great time," Celeste said. "No problems. No tough questions for me. Everything's cool."

As she rose from the table, Robbie looked past Natalie and asked, "Where's Uncle Travis?"

"He's still in the car, talking to your dad."

Celeste raised her eyebrows.

Natalie gave her a quick nod, then added, "He drove both of us home."

"Why? Where's my daddy's car?"

"He left it in the city. In the precinct parking garage."

Robbie stuffed another spoonful of ice cream into his mouth, then slid off his chair.

"Darling, wait a minute," she said. "You've got

that all over your chin. Let's get it off before you go anywhere.''

She wet a paper towel and knelt down to wipe his face, aware he was just itching to head out to see Hank. Before he could make good his escape, she took his hands in hers.

''Robbie, listen for a minute. No, look at me and *listen*,'' she added when he turned his head toward the hall. ''This is important,''

He reluctantly turned to her again.

''Your dad is okay, but he got banged on the chest and it's sore. So you have to be really careful around him, okay? No playing rough for a while. Not even any hugs. You understand?''

He nodded, but she had a feeling that he'd forget what she'd said in about five seconds.

''Come on.'' She lifted him up. ''Why don't we all go see if he's finished talking to Uncle Travis.''

When the three of them got outside, the men were standing next to the Mustang. Hank, she realized, had seized the opportunity to get out of the car without Robbie watching—a good idea, considering the obvious pain that folding himself into it had caused.

''Hey, big guy,'' he called as they started across the lawn. ''Did you and Celeste have fun?''

''Uh-huh,'' Robbie said, squirming to be put down.

''You just stay with me for a minute, okay?'' Natalie whispered, holding on to him.

''I didn't expect to see you quite this soon,'' Celeste told Hank.

''Yeah, well, you know how it is. St. Vincent's has

a certain charm. But as the saying goes, there's no place like home.''

"Well, we'd better hit the road," Travis said, opening the car door for Celeste.

"You take care of yourself," he added to Hank while she kissed Robbie goodbye and gave Natalie's hand a hard squeeze.

"Thanks for everything. Both of you," Natalie told them—Hank echoing her thanks as they climbed into the car.

The moment Travis began backing down the driveway, Robbie held out his arms to Hank.

He glanced at Natalie; she nodded that, yes, she'd told him.

"How about if you walk," he suggested, focusing on Robbie again. "I'm not supposed to lug big guys like you around for the next couple of weeks."

"Why?" he asked as Natalie set him down.

"Because my chest hurts."

"Why?"

"It's kind of a long story. Let's go inside and I'll explain."

In the house, Robbie eyed Hank uncertainly as he eased himself onto the couch.

"Come sit here beside me," he said, patting the cushion next to him while Natalie sank into one of the wing chairs. "But don't knock against me, okay?"

Robbie crawled up onto the couch and cautiously settled a few inches away.

"All right," Hank said. "What happened is I had a little accident at work."

"Did a bad guy hurt you?"

Hank looked at Natalie.

She quickly shook her head, murmuring, "Celeste said no questions. That everything was cool."

He turned toward Robbie once more, saying, "What gave you that idea?"

His only response was a shrug.

"Robbie? It's okay to tell us. What gave you that idea?"

"Gary says."

"Gary says what?"

"That bad guys are *always* hurting policemen. And sometimes they even *kill* them," he added, his voice a pitch higher. "With guns. It's on TV."

"Son, those are just make-believe programs Gary's talking about."

"But *did* a bad guy hurt you?"

"Well, yes. But it's *very, very* unusual for anything like that to happen in real life."

Robbie's eyes grew bigger and darker. "But it did!"

Natalie gazed at the two of them, the little dark-haired boy staring up at the large dark-haired man. Waiting for reassurance. Waiting for Hank to tell him that no bad guy could ever kill his dad.

Her heart ached for them both. A child shouldn't have to worry that his father might die. No more than a woman should have to worry that her husband might die. Not before his time.

Hank slowly raised his hand and ruffled Robbie's hair.

She knew that had to be causing him pain, but he didn't let it show.

"Robbie, I've been a policeman for fifteen years. Do you understand how long that is?"

He shook his head.

"Well, it's a really long time. Almost five times as long as you've been alive.

"And in all those years, no bad guy has ever hurt me before. So the next time Gary says anything about policemen getting hurt, you tell him that TV isn't like real life. And that in real life it hardly ever happens."

"But sometimes?"

"Yeah, sometimes. Not often, though."

"But...but I love you, Daddy."

"And I love you. And no bad guy's going to ever hurt me again. So don't worry, huh?"

Natalie swallowed hard. From the first moment she'd seen them together, it had been obvious how close Hank and Robbie were. And right this minute...

She couldn't force them to spend half of each year apart.

The realization hit her as hard and fast as a jolt from a stun gun.

After the three years she'd spent looking for Robbie, after all the nights she'd dreamed about having him back, now that she had a clear picture of his life with Hank, she simply couldn't destroy it.

Closing her eyes, she let the ramifications of that sink in.

She was left with two choices. She could either go back, full-time, to her work in Villa Rosa—and essentially give up her son. Or she could choose to spend the majority of her time with the two people she loved most in the world.

But she could only choose that if she were brave enough.

HANK WAS FEELING a sharp twinge with every breath he took, and since speaking meant extra breathing, he'd been only too happy when Natalie had offered to read Robbie's bedtime story.

He sat on the edge of the bed, hoping the Sparky book Robbie had chosen wouldn't lead to another discussion about getting a dog. Because until Natalie decided...

Maybe she already had, though.

He gazed surreptitiously across the bed at her, not paying any attention to the words she was reading—merely listening to the lulling tone of her voice.

It was a voice he wanted to continue hearing for the rest of his life. And she was the woman he wanted to spend the rest of his life with. But he had a horrible feeling...

Several times, since they'd gotten home, he'd caught her watching him. Each time, her expression had warned him that she was gearing up for a serious conversation. And he didn't have high hopes about what she was going to tell him.

Dammit, he seriously wished he could strangle Joey Nogood. Not only for trying to kill him, but for his terrible timing. Just when Natalie had seemed to be...

But now... Even though she'd said she'd still talk to someone, he had the sense that she simply hadn't wanted to make him feel any worse than he'd already been feeling. And that if she actually *did* see a counselor, at this stage she'd only be going through the motions.

The shooting had set them back a million years. And they didn't *have* a million years. They only had this one lifetime.

He tried to force his eyes from her but couldn't. She was just too darned gorgeous not to keep looking at.

The way she was staring down at the book made her lashes seem impossibly long. And so dark against the pale smoothness of her skin.

He could almost feel its softness, could almost taste its slight saltiness, could almost smell the sensuous scent of her naked body.

His gaze drifted to her lips, and the thought of being without her, of never tasting the sweetness of her kisses, started his chest hurting even more than it had already been.

"'So Sparky curled up at the bottom of Billy's bed, and they both fell fast asleep,'" she concluded.

"Another one?" Robbie asked.

"No," Hank said firmly. "It's time to go to sleep."

"You hafta check for the monsters first."

"Robbie, I—"

"I can do it," Natalie said. "Where do I check?"

"Under the bed," Robbie told her.

When she knelt down and looked under it, Hank decided she had the cutest little behind in the entire world.

"And in the closet," Robbie added as she pushed herself up.

"Nothing but clothes," she said, peering in.

"On the floor?"

"Nothing but shoes. Ah, and some dirty socks."

"Now just make sure the window's locked," Hank said.

She walked over and looked, then turned back toward the bed. "Absolutely safe. All you need is a good-night kiss."

When she bent down, Robbie wrapped his arms around her neck—and all Hank could think about was not having him here to kiss good-night for months on end.

He just didn't know how he'd cope with that.

The house would be so empty.

His *life* would be so empty.

"Daddy?"

He edged along the bed. "I can't hug you, okay. So just a kiss."

"'Kay."

Pain stabbed him as he leaned forward, but a good-night kiss was more important than a little pain.

"'Night, Son," he said, easing himself up and trying not to grimace.

"'Night, Daddy. 'Night, Natalie."

They walked out into the hall, and as he shut the

door partway, she said, "Would you like some lemonade?"

"Thanks, but I'd rather have a Scotch."

"Uh-uh." She shook her head. "Not with those pain pills you've taken."

He almost asked if being married to a doctor would mean having to adopt a healthier lifestyle—then stopped himself.

There probably wasn't a chance in a trillion he'd ever be married to a doctor. Not this one, at any rate.

"Do you want to sit out back?" she said. "We'd hear Robbie through the screen."

"Sure."

He trailed along to the patio and gingerly lowered himself into the chair next to hers.

The sun had set and dusk was closing in around them, but the air hadn't yet cooled enough to make it uncomfortable.

They sat in silence for a couple of minutes, gazing out at the darkening woods. Then she said, "It's funny, you know. When Robbie was lost and we were searching for him, I thought that forest was the scariest place I'd ever been. But sitting here looking at it…it's hard to even imagine being frightened of anything so peaceful."

"Just a question of perspective, I guess."

"I guess," she murmured. "I…Hank, I've been thinking a lot about what you suggested earlier."

When he turned to her, she was staring straight down the yard, as if she couldn't bear to meet his gaze when she said what she was going to say.

"About the possibility," she continued, "of spending a couple of months a year in Villa Rosa and the rest here."

He stopped breathing and began praying.

"And...I'm going to talk to the Physicians Abroad people about it. See if it's feasible. That's..."

She looked at him, then. "That's if you haven't changed your mind. If you still think it's a good compromise."

He cleared his throat. It hurt his chest. He didn't care in the least.

"Of *course* I still think it is. Natalie, I want you with me so badly... But what about the rest?" he made himself ask. "What about your fear?"

She slowly licked her lips, which made him desperately want to kiss her—no matter how painful leaning closer would be.

Yet he felt as if his entire future depended on what she said next, and if he was kissing her she wouldn't be able to say anything.

"I'm going to deal with it," she murmured at last. "If Celeste could do it, I can, too. I mean, I understand both *why* it's a problem and why it runs so deep."

"That sounds like a good start."

She nodded. "I've always lost the people I've really loved. My uncle Ted, my parents, Carlos. I was never even sure I hadn't lost Robbie forever.

"But that doesn't mean I'd lose you. Logically, I know it doesn't. It's just that somewhere in my subconscious..."

"Hank, I don't care if it takes psychotherapy or behavior modification or hypnosis or... Oh, hell, I don't care if they have to stick electrodes on my head and zap my brain. *Something* will work.

"And...I guess what it comes down to is that I want to be with you and Robbie more than anything else on earth. And I'm not going to let my fear keep me from being happy."

He could feel an incredibly goofy smile spreading across his face.

"Well...that's great. I mean, it's wonderful. I wish I could take you in my arms and show you *how* wonderful I think it is, but..."

"That's all right," Natalie said, trailing her fingers lightly down his arm. "You'll have the rest of our lives to show me."

EPILOGUE

Five Months Later

THE DAY WAS SUNNY and unseasonably warm, ideal for an outdoor party. But beyond the split-rail fence, autumn had painted the nature preserve with brilliant reds and yellows that hinted winter wasn't far off.

After so long in the land of eternal spring, Natalie absently mused, being back living in a place with such dramatic changes of season would take a while to get used to.

"What do you think?" Hank said, wrapping his arm around her waist and drawing her close. "Everyone enjoying themselves?"

"Looks like."

She let her gaze drift over their guests: Celeste and Travis, married now, chatting with some of Hank's other friends; Cynthia Koehler and a few more people from Madison Plains; Señora Perez and her friend Señora Barreda.

And over by the fence were Mary Gerard and her husband, talking with Audrey and Betty Harmand—who was feeling pretty much back to her old self.

Then, of course, there were Robbie and Gary, as

well as Emma and the three little girls she'd already made fast friends with at school.

"An adoption party was a good idea," Hank said.

"Only *good?*" she teased. "How about *inspired?*"

"Yeah, well, I guess I could give you inspired."

When she looked over at Emma again, the little girl was smiling so broadly it made *her* smile.

Robbie would be turning four in only a week, so they'd considered a combined party. But she was glad they'd decided against that, because Emma was absolutely thrilled that they'd wanted a party solely to celebrate the finalization of her adoption.

Of course, she'd been a full-time member of their family for quite a while now. Cynthia had pulled a few more strings with the Child Welfare people, and Emma had come here directly from the hospital.

That had been mere days after Natalie and Hank had gotten married, and the caseworker had said she'd never before dealt with adoptive parents who were newlyweds.

Natalie suspected she'd never run into a birth mother who'd married her son's adoptive father, either. Theirs was definitely not an ordinary set of circumstances.

Things would gradually normalize, though. Especially after they were finished living in a construction zone.

She glanced at the addition they were putting across the back of the house. Once it was done, they'd have twice as much space. And with two active children plus a live-in housekeeper, they really needed it.

But, all in all, everything was shaping up better than she and Hank could ever have realistically hoped.

She'd gotten her license to practice in New Jersey, and had begun working four days a week in a clinic that was loosely affiliated with the Madison Plains. And even though she still worried about Hank when he was at work, the counseling had helped her a lot.

As for Robbie and Emma, they'd been fine together from day one. Emma was even teaching him Spanish, which had prompted Hank to decide he'd better learn it, as well, so he wouldn't find himself not understanding what his own children were talking about.

And when it came to Audrey, she was delighted that the house plans included a self-contained little living area for her, not to mention being pleased about the prospect of having two months free each summer, while Natalie and the children were in Villa Rosa.

Villa Rosa. Natalie hadn't spent long there this summer, of course. With everything else that was happening, she'd only gone back briefly, to tie up a few loose ends and pack what she'd wanted to ship.

It had been a bittersweet visit, because there were things about her life in Guatemala that she knew she'd miss. But there were things here that she'd have missed far more. And one of them was streaking across the yard toward her and Hank this very minute.

"Mommy!" Robbie cried when he saw she'd spotted him.

Mommy. Once she and Hank had told him she'd be staying, that they were getting married, he'd been pretty quick about deciding that if she was going to live with them she really *must* be his mother. And now they were making up for those years apart.

He screeched to a stop in front of them and gave them a grin.

"What's up, big guy?" Hank said.

"Emma taught me some new words."

"She did, huh?"

"Well, kinda. Her friends wanted to know them. And I listened."

Hank smiled at Natalie and she felt warm inside.

"Wanna hear?"

"Sure."

Robbie screwed up his face, thinking hard, then said, *"Te quiero."*

"Oh, darling," she murmured. "We love you, too."

He gave them another grin, then turned on his heel and raced away.

"Hey," Hank whispered, his breath against her ear making her feel even warmer. "Know what?"

"What?" she whispered back.

"Te quiero, Natalie. And I'll be saying that forever."

HARLEQUIN *Super*ROMANCE

CREATURE COMFORT

A heartwarming new series by
Carolyn McSparren

Creature Comfort, the largest veterinary clinic in Tennessee, treats animals of all sizes—horses and cattle as well as family pets. Meet the patients—and their owners. And share the laughter and the tears with the men and women who love and care for all creatures great and small.

#996 THE MONEY MAN
(July 2001)

#1011 THE PAYBACK MAN
(September 2001)

Look for these Harlequin Superromance titles coming soon to your favorite retail outlet.

HARLEQUIN®
Makes any time special ®

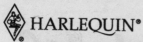

Harlequin truly does make any time special. . . . This year we are celebrating weddings in style!

A Walk Down the Aisle

WEDDING CELEBRATION

To help us celebrate, we want you to tell us how wearing the Harlequin wedding gown will make your wedding day special. As the grand prize, Harlequin will offer one lucky bride the chance to **"Walk Down the Aisle" in the Harlequin wedding gown!**

There's more...

For her honeymoon, she and her groom will spend five nights at the **Hyatt Regency Maui.** As part of this five-night honeymoon at the hotel renowned for its romantic attractions, the couple will enjoy a candlelit dinner for two in Swan Court, a sunset sail on the hotel's catamaran, and duet spa treatments.

A HYATT RESORT AND SPA

Maui • Molokai • Lanai

To enter, please write, in, 250 words or less, how wearing the Harlequin wedding gown will make your wedding day special. The entry will be judged based on its emotionally compelling nature, its originality and creativity, and its sincerity. This contest is open to Canadian and U.S. residents only and to those who are 18 years of age and older. There is no purchase necessary to enter. Void where prohibited. See further contest rules attached. Please send your entry to:

Walk Down the Aisle Contest

In Canada
P.O. Box 637
Fort Erie, Ontario
L2A 5X3

In U.S.A.
P.O. Box 9076
3010 Walden Ave.
Buffalo, NY 14269-9076

You can also enter by visiting www.eHarlequin.com
Win the Harlequin wedding gown and the vacation of a lifetime!
The deadline for entries is October 1, 2001.

HARLEQUIN®
Makes any time special ®

HARLEQUIN WALK DOWN THE AISLE TO MAUI CONTEST 1197
OFFICIAL RULES
NO PURCHASE NECESSARY TO ENTER

1. To enter, follow directions published in the offer to which you are responding. Contest begins April 2, 2001, and ends on October 1, 2001. Method of entry may vary. Mailed entries must be postmarked by October 1, 2001, and received by October 8, 2001.

2. Contest entry may be, at times, presented via the Internet, but will be restricted solely to residents of certain geographic areas that are disclosed on the Web site. To enter via the Internet, if permissible, access the Harlequin Web site (www.eHarlequin.com) and follow the directions displayed online. Online entries must be received by 11:59 p.m. E.S.T. on October 1, 2001.

   In lieu of submitting an entry online, enter by mail by hand-printing (or typing) on an 8½" x 11" plain piece of paper, your name, address (including zip code), Contest number/name and in 250 words or fewer, why winning a Harlequin wedding dress would make your wedding day special. Mail via first-class mail to: Harlequin Walk Down the Aisle Contest 1197, (in the U.S.) P.O. Box 9076, 3010 Walden Avenue, Buffalo, NY 14269-9076, (in Canada) P.O. Box 637, Fort Erie, Ontario L2A 5X3, Canada.

   Limit one entry per person, household address and e-mail address. Online and/or mailed entries received from persons residing in geographic areas in which Internet entry is not permissible will be disqualified.

3. Contests will be judged by a panel of members of the Harlequin editorial, marketing and public relations staff based on the following criteria:

   - Originality and Creativity—50%
   - Emotionally Compelling—25%
   - Sincerity—25%

   In the event of a tie, duplicate prizes will be awarded. Decisions of the judges are final.

4. All entries become the property of Torstar Corp. and will not be returned. No responsibility is assumed for lost, late, illegible, incomplete, inaccurate, nondelivered or misdirected mail or misdirected e-mail, for technical, hardware or software failures of any kind, lost or unavailable network connections, or failed, incomplete, garbled or delayed computer transmission or any human error which may occur in the receipt or processing of the entries in this Contest.

5. Contest open only to residents of the U.S. (except Puerto Rico) and Canada, who are 18 years of age or older, and is void wherever prohibited by law; all applicable laws and regulations apply. Any litigation within the Province of Quebec respecting the conduct or organization of a publicity contest may be submitted to the Régie des alcools, des courses et des jeux for a ruling. Any litigation respecting the awarding of a prize may be submitted to the Régie des alcools, des courses et des jeux only for the purpose of helping the parties reach a settlement. Employees and immediate family members of Torstar Corp. and D. L. Blair, Inc., their affiliates, subsidiaries and all other agencies, entities and persons connected with the use, marketing or conduct of this Contest are not eligible to enter. Taxes on prizes are the sole responsibility of winners. Acceptance of any prize offered constitutes permission to use winner's name, photograph or other likeness for the purposes of advertising, trade and promotion on behalf of Torstar Corp., its affiliates and subsidiaries without further compensation to the winner, unless prohibited by law.

6. Winners will be determined no later than November 15, 2001, and will be notified by mail. Winners will be required to sign and return an Affidavit of Eligibility form within 15 days after winner notification. Noncompliance within that time period may result in disqualification and an alternative winner may be selected. Winners of trip must execute a Release of Liability prior to ticketing and must possess required travel documents (e.g. passport, photo ID) where applicable. Trip must be completed by November 2002. No substitution of prize permitted by winner. Torstar Corp. and D. L. Blair, Inc., their parents, affiliates, and subsidiaries are not responsible for errors in printing or electronic presentation of Contest, entries and/or game pieces. In the event of printing or other errors which may result in unintended prize values or duplication of prizes, all affected game pieces or entries shall be null and void. If for any reason the Internet portion of the Contest is not capable of running as planned, including infection by computer virus, bugs, tampering, unauthorized intervention, fraud, technical failures, or any other causes beyond the control of Torstar Corp. which corrupt or affect the administration, secrecy, fairness, integrity or proper conduct of the Contest, Torstar Corp. reserves the right, at its sole discretion, to disqualify any individual who tampers with the entry process and to cancel, terminate, modify or suspend the Contest or the Internet portion thereof. In the event of a dispute regarding an online entry, the entry will be deemed submitted by the authorized holder of the e-mail account submitted at the time of entry. Authorized account holder is defined as the natural person who is assigned to an e-mail address by an Internet access provider, online service provider or other organization that is responsible for arranging e-mail address for the domain associated with the submitted e-mail address. **Purchase or acceptance of a product offer does not improve your chances of winning.**

7. Prizes: (1) Grand Prize—A Harlequin wedding dress (approximate retail value: $3,500) and a 5-night/6-day honeymoon trip to Maui, HI, including round-trip air transportation provided by Maui Visitors Bureau from Los Angeles International Airport (winner is responsible for transportation to and from Los Angeles International Airport) and a Harlequin Romance Package, including hotel accomodations (double occupancy) at the Hyatt Regency Maui Resort and Spa, dinner for (2) two at Swan Court, a sunset sail on Kiele V and a spa treatment for the winner (approximate retail value: $4,000); (5) Five runner-up prizes of a $1000 gift certificate to selected retail outlets to be determined by Sponsor (retail value $1000 ea.). Prizes consist of only those items listed as part of the prize. Limit one prize per person. All prizes are valued in U.S. currency.

8. For a list of winners (available after December 17, 2001) send a self-addressed, stamped envelope to: Harlequin Walk Down the Aisle Contest 1197 Winners, P.O. Box 4200 Blair, NE 68009-4200 or you may access the www.eHarlequin.com Web site through January 15, 2002.

Contest sponsored by Torstar Corp., P.O. Box 9042, Buffalo, NY 14269-9042, U.S.A.

Double your pleasure—
with this collection containing two full-length

Harlequin Romance®

novels

New York Times bestselling author

DEBBIE MACOMBER

delivers

RAINY DAY KISSES

While Susannah Simmons struggles up the corporate
ladder, her neighbor Nate Townsend stays home baking
cookies and flying kites. She resents the way he questions
her values—and the way he messes up her five-year plan
when she falls in love with him!

PLUS

THE BRIDE PRICE

a brand-new novel by reader favorite

DAY LECLAIRE

On sale July 2001

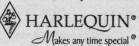

HARLEQUIN *Super*ROMANCE®

**To celebrate the
1000th Superromance book
We're presenting you with 3 books
from 3 of your favorite authors in**

All Summer Long

Home, Hearth and Haley
by **Muriel Jensen**

Meet the men and women of Muriel's
upcoming **Men of Maple Hill** trilogy

Daddy's Girl
by **Judith Arnold**

Another **Daddy School** story!

Temperature Rising
by **Bobby Hutchinson**

Life and love at St. Joe's Hospital are as feverish
as ever in this **Emergency!** story

On sale July 2001
Available wherever Harlequin books are sold.

HARLEQUIN®
Makes any time special ®